Leslie Charteris   ay
1907. In 1919 he   ....u..er
and brother and attended Rossall School in Lancashire
before moving on to Cambridge University. His studies
there came to a halt when a publisher accepted his first
novel. His third book, entitled *Meet – The Tiger!*, was
written when he was twenty years old and published in
1928. It introduced the world to Simon Templar, a.k.a.
the Saint.

He continued to write about the Saint up until 1983,
when the last book, *Salvage for the Saint*, was published
by Hodder & Stoughton. The books, which have been
translated into over twenty languages, have sold over 40
million copies around the world. They've inspired
fifteen feature films, three TV series, ten radio series
and a comic strip that was written by Charteris and
syndicated around the world for over a decade.

Leslie Charteris enjoyed travelling, but settled for
long periods in Hollywood, Florida, and finally in
Surrey, England. In 1992 he was awarded the Cartier
Diamond Dagger in recognition of a lifetime of achieve-
ment. He died the following year.

LESLIE CHARTERIS

Follow the Saint

Series Editor: Ian Dickerson

MULHOLLAND
BOOKS
HODDER

First published in Great Britain in 1939 by Hodder & Stoughton

This paperback edition first published in 2013 by Mulholland Books
An imprint of Hodder & Stoughton
An Hachette UK company

1

Copyright © Interfund (London) Ltd 2013
Originally registered in 1939 by Leslie Charteris
Introduction © Adrian Magson 2013

Cover artwork by Andrew Howard
www.andrewhoward.co.uk

A CIP catalogue record for this title is available from the British Library

Paperback ISBN 978 1 444 76624 0
eBook ISBN 978 1 444 76625 7

Printed and bound by Clays Ltd, St Ives plc

Hodder & Stoughton policy is to use papers that are natural, renewable
and recyclable products and made from wood grown in sustainable
forests. The logging and manufacturing processes are expected to
conform to the environmental regulations of the country of origin.

Hodder & Stoughton Ltd
338 Euston Road
London NW1 3BH

www.hodder.co.uk

To Hap and Bonnie with love

CONTENTS

INTRODUCTION

It might seem odd for a Saint fan to recall one particular
volume over another, and to be honest, it wasn't easy. But
Follow the Saint seems to resonate most for me because it
brings together various aspects about the series which go to
make Simon Templar what he is. (Indeed the front cover
blurb on my copy reads, 'Nothing Ordinary ever happens to
the SAINT' – a statement which, to me as a young boy, held
all the promise of a good read that I could possibly imagine,
and formulated my desire to write crime fiction.)

The book consists of three stories:

'The Miracle Tea Party' opens with an introduction (for
those who need it) to the Saint's main poking fun victim –
Chief Inspector Claud Eustace Teal. As the hapless representative of Scotland Yard, Teal's shoulders had to cope with
all the criticism that Templar loved heaping on the police. As
the author states, '. . . Teal was allergic to the Saint.' And like
most allergies, it follows him around. Yet Teal was not merely
a whipping post for the Saint's barbed wit; he was an important part of the Saint's story, an anchor point to the conventional world, and the exchanges between the two have a part
to play.

'The Invisible Millionaire' brings in another of the Saint's
happy band, Hoppy Uniatz. Hoppy is an American gangster,
short on brains (thinking causes him pain) and looks (face
like a gorilla), with a love of Vat 69 and hitting people – or
shooting them – either will do. He's a sharp contrast to the

urbane Templar, but he has his uses and introduces an element of humour and handy violence when needed. Indeed, I think it was meeting Uniatz that eventually drew me to reading American crime fiction.

'The Affair of Hogsbotham' displays the ability of the author to begin a story in an unremarkable way (Templar reading a newspaper and commenting on it to Patricia Holm, his paramour and elegant sidekick) . . . then to ramp it up by degrees into something less ordinary. It also allows him to comment on war (briefly), on his annoyance with society's insistence on interfering with public morals – something the Saint has no time for – and most of all, to turn a profit from adversity by relieving the villains of some cold, hard cash.

In all, *Follow the Saint* is a useful introduction to anyone new to this character, serving as a form of short-hand to Leslie Charteris' loveable rogue and the world he inhabits.

Adrian Magson

The Miracle Tea Party

I

This story starts with four wild coincidences; so we may as well admit them at once and get it over with, and then there will be no more argument. The chronicler makes no apologies for them. A lot of much more far-fetched coincidences have been allowed to happen without protest in the history of the world, and all that can be done about it is to relate them exactly as they took place. And if it should be objected that these particular coincidences led to the downfall of sundry criminals who might otherwise never have been detected, it must be pointed out that at least half the convicts at present taking a cure in the cooler were caught that way.

Chief Inspector Claud Eustace Teal sat in a tea shoppe that was not much more than a powerful stone's throw from Scotland Yard. Dispassionately considered, it was quite a suitable target for stone-throwing, being one of those dens of ghastly chintz-curtained cheerfulness which stand as grisly omens of what the English-speaking races can expect from a few more generations of purity and hygiene; but Mr Teal held it in a sort of affection born of habit.

He had finished his tea, and he sat glancing over a newspaper. And in order that there may be positively no deception about this, it must be admitted at once that not even the most enthusiastic advocate of temperance would have chosen him as an advertisement of the place that he was in. Mr Teal, in fact, who even at his best suffered from certain physical disadvantages which made it permanently impossible for

him to model for a statue of Dancing Spring, was at that
moment not even in the running for a picture of Mellow
Autumn. His round pink face had a distinctly muddy tinge
under its roseate bloom; the champing of his jaws on the
inevitable wodge of spearmint was visibly listless; and his
china-blue eyes contained an expression of joyless but stoical
endurance. He looked, to speak with complete candour,
rather like a discontented cow with a toothache.

After a while he put the newspaper aside and simply sat,
gazing mournfully into space. It was a Sunday afternoon, and
at that rather late hour he had the place to himself, except for
a vacant-faced waitress who sat in a corner knitting some
garment in a peculiarly dreadful shade of mustard yellow. A
small radio on the mantelpiece, strategically placed between a
vase of artificial flowers and a bowl of wax fruit, was emitting
strains of that singularly lugubrious and eviscerated music
which supplies the theme song of modern romance. Mr Teal
appeared to be enduring that infliction in the same spirit as Job
might have endured the development of his sixty-second boil.
He looked as if he was only waiting for someone to come along
and relieve him of the cares of the Universe.

Someone did come along, but not with that intention. The
crash of the door opening made Mr Teal's overwrought nerves
wince; and when he saw who it was he closed his eyes for a
moment in sheer agony. For although Mr William Kennedy
was easily the most popular of the Assistant Commissioners,
his vast and jovial personality was approximately the last thing
that a man in Mr Teal's condition is able to appreciate.

'Hullo, laddie!' he roared, in a voice that boomed through
the room like a gale. 'What's the matter? You look like a cold
poached egg left over from yesterday's breakfast. What are
you doing – thinking about the Saint?'

Mr Teal started as if an electric current had been applied
to his posterior. He had expected the worst, but this was

worse than that. If anything could have been said to fill his cup of suffering to the brim, that something had been said. Mr Teal now looked as if there was nothing left except for him to find some suitably awful spot in which to die.

Scientists, whose restless researches leave no phenomenon unprobed, have discovered that certain persons are subject to quite disproportionately grievous reactions from stimuli which to other persons are entirely innocuous. These inordinate sensitivities are known as allergies. Some people are allergic to oysters, others to onions; others need only eat a strawberry to be attacked by violent pains and break out in a rash.

Chief Inspector Teal was allergic to the Saint. But it must be admitted that this was an acquired rather than a congenital allergy. It is true that Mr Teal, on account of his profession, was theoretically required to be allergic to every kind of law breaker; but there was nothing in his implied contract with the State which required him to be pierced by such excruciating pains or to break out in such a vivid erythema as he was apt to do whenever he heard the name or nickname of that incorrigible outlaw who had been christened Simon Templar.

But the Saint was the kind of outlaw that no officer of the Law can ever have had to cope with since the Sheriff of Nottingham was pestered into apoplexy by the Robin Hood of those more limited days. There was no precedent in modern times for anything like him; and Mr Teal was convinced that it could only be taken as evidence of the deliberate maliciousness of Fate that out of all the other police officers who might have been chosen for the experiment the lot had fallen upon him. For there was no doubt at all in his mind that all the griefs and woes which had been visited upon him in recent years could be directly attributed to that amazing buccaneer whose unlawful excursions against evildoers had made criminal history, and yet whose legal conviction and punishment was beginning to seem as hopelessly improbable an event as the capture of a genuine and indisputable sea-serpent. Kennedy was not being deliberately cruel. It was simply his uninhibited proclamation of what was an almost automatic association of ideas to anyone who knew anything at all about Teal's professional life: that whenever Mr Teal looked as if he was in acute agony he was undergoing a spell of Saint trouble. The fact that Mr Teal, as it happened, had not been thinking about the Saint at all when Kennedy came in only gave the reminder a deeper power to wound.

'No, sir,' said Mr Teal, with the flimsiest quality of restraint. 'I was not thinking about the Saint. I haven't seen him for weeks; I don't know what he's doing; and what's more, I don't care.'

Kennedy raised his eyebrows.

'Sorry, laddie. I thought from your appearance—'

'What's wrong with my blasted appearance?' snarled the detective, with a reckless disregard for discipline of which in normal times he would never have been capable; but Kennedy had no great respect for trivial formalities.

'Blasted is right,' he agreed readily. 'You look like something the lightning had started out to strike and then given up as a work of supererogation. What is it, then? Have you been getting hell for falling down on that espionage business?'

Mr Teal was able to ignore that. It was true that he had made very little headway with the case referred to, but that was not worrying him unduly. When official secrets spring a leak, it is usually a slow job to trace the leakage to its source, and Teal was too old a hand to let himself be disturbed by the slowness of it.

His trouble was far more intimate and personal; and the time has now come when it must be revealed.

Mr Teal was suffering from indigestion.

It was a complaint that had first intruded itself on his consciousness some weeks ago; since when its symptoms had become steadily more severe and regular, until by this time he had come to regard a stomach-ache as the practically inevitable sequel to any meal he ate. Since Mr Teal's tummy constituted a very large proportion of Mr Teal, his sufferings were considerable. They made him pessimistic and depressed, and more than usually morose. His working days had become long hours of discomfort and misery, and it seemed an eternity since he had spent a really restful and dreamless night. Even now, after having forgone his Sunday dinner in penitence for the price he had had to pay for bacon and eggs at breakfast, the cream bun to whose succulent temptation he had not long ago succumbed was already beginning to give him the unhappily familiar sensation of having swallowed a live and singularly vicious crab. And this was the mortal dolour in addition to which he had had to receive a superfluous reminder of the Saint.

The waitress at last succeeded in gaining audience.

'Yes,' boomed Kennedy. 'Tea. Strong tea. And about half a ton of hot buttered crumpets.'

Mr Teal closed his eyes again as another excruciating cramp curled through him.

In his darkened loneliness he became aware that the music had been interrupted and the radio was talking.

'. . . *and this amazing tea is not only guaranteed to relieve indigestion immediately, but to effect a complete and permanent cure,*' said a clear young voice with a beautiful Oxford accent. '*Every day we are receiving fresh testimonials—*'

'My God,' said Teal with a shudder, 'where is that Eric-or-Little-by-Little drivelling from?'

'Radio Calvados,' answered Kennedy. 'One of the new continental stations. They go to work every Sunday. I suppose we shall have to put up with it as long as the BBC refuses to produce anything but string quartets and instructive talks on Sundays.'

'*Miracle Tea,*' said Eric, continuing little by little. '*Remember that name. Miracle Tea. Obtainable from all high-class chemists, or direct by post from the Miracle Tea Company,*

*909 Victoria Street, London. Buy some Miracle Tea tonight! ...
And now we shall conclude this programme with our signature
song – Tea for You.'*

Mr Teal held on to his stomach as the anguishing parody
proceeded to rend the air.

'Miracle Tea!' he rasped savagely. 'What'll they think of
next? As if tea could cure indigestion! Pah!'

The way he said '*Pah!*' almost blew his front teeth out; and
Kennedy glanced at him discerningly.

'Oh, so that's the trouble, is it? The mystery is solved.'

'I didn't say—'

Kennedy grinned at him.

The door of the tea shoppe opened again, to admit
Inspector Peters, Kennedy's chief assistant.

'Sorry I was so long, sir,' he apologized, taking the vacant
chair at their table. 'The man was out—'

'Never mind that,' said Kennedy. 'Teal's got indigestion.'

'You can fix that with a bit of bicarb,' said Peters
helpfully.

'So long as it isn't something more serious,' said Kennedy,
reaching for the freshly-arrived plate of hot buttered crumpets with a hand like a leg of mutton and the air of massive
confidence which can only be achieved by a man of herculean
physique who knows that his interior would never dare to
give him any backchat. 'I've been noticing his face lately. I
must say I've been worried about it, but I didn't like to
mention it before he brought it up.'

'You mean the twitching?' asked Peters.

'Not so much the twitching as the jaundiced colour. It
looks bad to me.'

'Damn it,' began Teal explosively.

'Acid,' pronounced Kennedy, engulfing crumpets. 'That's
generally the beginning of the trouble. Too much acid swilling
around the lining of your stomach, and where are you? In next

to no time you're a walking mass of gastric ulcers. You know what happens when a gastric ulcer eats into a blood vessel?'

'You bleed to death?' asked Peters interestedly.

'Like a shot,' said Kennedy, apparently unaware of the fact that Teal was starting to simmer and splutter like a pan full of hot grease. 'It's even worse when the ulcer makes a whacking great hole in the wall of the stomach and your dinner falls through into the abdominal cavity . . .'

Mr Teal clung to his chair and wished that he had been born deaf.

It was no consolation at all to him to recall that it had actually been the Saint himself who had started the fashion of making familiar and even disgusting comments on the shape and dimensions of the stomach under discussion, a fashion which Mr Teal's own colleagues, to their eternal disgrace, had been surprisingly quick to adopt. And now that it had been revealed that his recent irritability had been caused by acute indigestion, the joke would take a new lease of life. It is a curious but undeniable fact that a man may have a headache or a toothache or an earache and receive nothing but sympathy from those about him; but let his stomach ache and all he can expect is facetiousness of the most callous and offensive kind. Mr Teal's stomach was a magnificently well-developed organ, measuring more inches from east to west than he cared to calculate, and he was perhaps excessively sensitive about it; but in its present condition the most faintly flippant reference to it was exquisite torment.

He stood up.

'Will you excuse me, sir?' he said, with as much dignity as he could muster. 'I've got a job to do this evening.'

'Don't forget to buy some Miracle Tea on your way home,' was Kennedy's farewell.

Mr Teal walked up Victoria Street in the direction of his modest lodgings. He had no job to do at all; but it would have been physically impossible for him to have stomached another minute of the conversation he had left behind him. He walked, because he had not far to go, and the exercise helped to distract his thoughts from the feeling that his intestines were being gnawed by a colony of hungry rats. Not that the distraction was by any means complete: the rats continued their remorseless depredations. But he was able to give them only half his attention instead of the whole of it.

In the circumstances it was perhaps natural that the broadcast which had been added to his current griefs should remain vaguely present in the background of his mind. The address given had been in Victoria Street. And therefore it was perhaps not such a wild coincidence after all that he should presently have found himself gazing at a large showcard in the window of a chemist's shop which he must have been passing practically every day for the last two months.

INDIGESTION?
Try
MIRACLE TEA
2/6 a packet

Mr Teal was not even averagely gullible; but a man in his state of mind is not fully responsible for his actions. The tribulations of the last few weeks had reduced him to a state of desperation in which he would have tried a dose of prussic acid if it had been recommended with sufficient promises of alleviating his distress.

With a furtive glance around him, as if he was afraid of being caught in a disreputable act, he entered the shop and approached the counter, behind which stood a shifty-eyed young man in a soiled white coat.

'A packet of Miracle Tea,' said Mr Teal, lowering his voice to a mumble, although the shop was empty, as though he had been asking for some unmentionable merchandise.

He planked down a half-crown with unconvincing defiance.

The assistant hesitated for a moment, turned, and took an oblong yellow packet from a shelf behind him. He hesitated again, still holding it as if he was reluctant to part with it.

'Yes, sir?' he said suggestively.

'What d'you mean – "yes, sir?" ' blared Mr Teal with the belligerence of increasing embarrassment.

'Isn't there something else, sir?'

'No, there isn't anything else!' retorted the detective, whose sole remaining ambition was to get out of the place as quickly as possible with his guilty purchase. 'Give me that stuff and take your money.'

He reached over and fairly snatched the yellow packet out of the young man's hand, stuffed it into his pocket, and lumbered out as if he were trying to catch a train. He was in such a hurry that he almost bowled over another customer who was just entering the shop – and this customer, for some reason, quickly averted his face.

Mr Teal was too flustered even to notice him. He went plodding more rapidly than usual on his homeward way, feeling as if his face was a bright crimson which would announce his shame to any passerby, and never dreaming that Destiny had already grasped him firmly by the scruff of the neck.

Five minutes later he was trudging through a narrow side street within a couple of blocks of his apartment. The comatose dusk of Sunday evening lay over it like a shroud: not a single other human creature was in sight, and the only sound apart from the solid tread of his own regulation boots was a patter of hurried footsteps coming up behind him. There was nothing in that to make him turn his head . . . The footsteps caught up until they were almost on his heels; and then something hit him a terrific blow on the side of the head and everything dissolved into black darkness.

2

Simon Templar's views on the subject of Chief Inspector Teal, unlike Chief Inspector Teal's views on the subject of the Saint, were apt to fluctuate between very contradictory extremes. There were times when he felt that life would lose half its savour if he were deprived of the perpetual joy of dodging Teal's constant frantic efforts to put him behind bars; but there were other times when he felt that his life would be a lot less strenuous if Teal's cardinal ambition had been a little less tenacious. There had been times when he had felt sincere remorse for the more bitter humiliations which he had sometimes been compelled to inflict on Mr Teal, even though these times had been the only alternatives to his own defeat in their endless duel; there had been other times when he could have derived much satisfaction from beating Teal over the head with a heavy bar of iron with large knobs on the end.

One thing which the Saint was certain about, however, was that his own occasional urges to assault the detective's cranium with a blunt instrument did not mean that he was at any time prepared to permit any common or garden thug to take the same liberties with that long-suffering dome.

This was the last of the coincidences of which due warning has already been given – that Simon Templar's long sleek Hirondel chanced to be taking a short cut through the back streets of the district at that fateful hour, and whirled round a corner into the one street where it was most needed at the precise moment when Teal's ample body was spreading itself over the pavement as flat as a body of that architecture can conveniently be spread without the aid of a steam roller.

The Saint's foot on the accelerator gave the great car a last burst in the direction of the spot where these exciting things were happening, and then he stood on the brakes. The thug who had committed the assault was already bending over Teal's prostrate form when the screech of skidding tyres made him stop and look up in startled fear. For a split second he hesitated, as if considering whether to stand his ground and give battle; but something about the sinewy breadth of the Saint's shoulders and the athletic and purposeful speed with which the Saint's tall frame catapulted itself out of the still sliding car must have discouraged him. A profound antipathy to the whole scene and everyone in it appeared to overwhelm him; and he turned and began to depart from it like a stone out of a sling.

The Saint started after him. At that moment the Saint had no idea that the object of his timely rescue was Chief Inspector Teal in person: it was simply that the sight of one bloke hitting another bloke with a length of gaspipe was a spectacle which inevitably impelled him to join in the festivities with the least possible delay. But as he started in pursuit he caught his first glimpse of the fallen victim's face, and the surprise checked his stride as if he had run into a wall. He paused involuntarily to confirm the identification; and that brief delay lost him any chance he might have had of making a capture. The thug was already covering the ground with quite remarkable velocity, and the extra start he had gained from the Saint's hesitation had given him a lead which even Simon Templar's long legs doubted their ability to make up. Simon gave up the idea with a regretful sigh, and stooped to find out how much damage had been sustained by his favourite enemy.

It only took him a moment to assure himself that

his existence was unlikely to be rendered permanently uneventful by the premature removal of its most pungent spice; but nevertheless there was also no doubt that Teal was temporarily in the land of dreams, and that it would do the Saint himself no good to be found standing over his sleeping body. On the other hand, to leave Mr Teal to finish his sleep in peace on the sidewalk was something which no self-respecting buccaneer could do. The actual commotion from which the situation had evolved had been practically negligible. Not a window had been flung up; not a door had been opened. The street remained sunken in its twilight torpor, and once again there was no other living soul in sight.

The Saint shrugged. There seemed to be only one thing to do, so he did it. With a certain amount of effort, he picked up Mr Teal's weighty person and heaved it into the car, dumped Teal's macintosh and hat on top of him, picked up an oblong yellow package which had fallen out of his pocket and slung that in as well, got into the driving seat himself, and drove away.

That Simon's diagnosis had been accurate was proved by the fact that Teal was beginning to groan and blink his eyes when the Hirondel pulled up at his front door. The Saint lighted a cigarette and looked at him reproachfully.

'I'm ashamed of you,' he said. 'An old man of your age, letting yourself be picked up in the gutter like that. And not even during licensing hours, either. Where did you get the embalming fluid?'

'So it was you, was it?' Teal muttered thickly.

'I beg your pardon?'

'What the hell was the idea?' demanded Teal, with a growing indignation which left no doubt of his recovery.

'The idea of what?'

'Creeping up behind me and knocking me on the head! If you think I'm going to let you get away with that—'

'Claud,' said the Saint, 'do I understand that you're accusing me again?'

'Oh, no!' Teal had his eyes wide open now, and they were red with wrath. The edge of his sarcasm was as silky and delicate as the blade of a crosscut saw. 'It was two other people. They fell out of the sky with parachutes—'

The Saint sighed.

'I don't want to interrupt you. But can this great brain of yours see any particular reason why I should cosh you today? We haven't seen each other for ages, and so far as I know you haven't been doing anything to make me angry. And even if you had, and I thought it would be good for you to be bopped over the bean, do you think I'd take the trouble to bring you home afterwards? And even if I brought you home afterwards, do you think I'd let you wake up while I was still around, instead of bopping you again and leaving you to wake up without knowing I'd been anywhere near you? I am a very modest man, Claud,' said the Saint untruthfully, 'but there are some aspersions on my intelligence which cut me to the quick, and you always seem to be the guy who thinks of them.'

Mr Teal rubbed his head.

'Well, what did happen?' he demanded grudgingly.

'I don't really know. When I shot over the horizon, there was some guy in the act of belting you over the lid with a handy piece of lead pipe. I thought of asking him to stop and talk it over, but he ran too fast. So I just loaded you into the old jalopy and brought you home. Of course, if you really wanted to go on dozing in the gutter I can take you back.'

The detective looked about him. His aching skull was clearing a little, enough at least for him to be able to see that this latest misfortune was something which, for once, might not be chargeable to the Saint's account. The realization did not actually improve his temper.

'Have you any idea who it was?'

'That's a large order, isn't it? If you're as charming to all your other clients as you usually are to me, I should say that London must be crawling with birds who'd pay large sums of money for the fun of whacking you on the roof with a lump of iron.'

'Well, what did this one look like?' snarled Teal impatiently.

'I'm blowed if I could draw his picture, Claud. The light was pretty bad, and he didn't stay very long. Medium height, ordinary build, thin face – nothing definite enough to help you much, I'm afraid.'

Teal grunted.

Presently he said: 'Thanks, anyway.'

He said it as if he hated to say it, which he did. Being under any obligation to the Saint hurt him almost as much as his indigestion. Promptly he wished that he hadn't thought of that comparison. He stomach, reviving from a too fleeting anaesthesia, reminded him that it was still his most constant companion. And now he had a sore and splitting head as well. He realized that he felt about as unhappy as a man can feel.

He opened the door of the car, and took hold of his raincoat and bowler hat.

'G'night,' he said.

'Goodnight,' said the Saint cheerfully. 'You know where I live, any time you decide you want a bodyguard.'

Mr Teal did not deign to reply. He crossed the sidewalk rather unsteadily, mounted the steps of the house, and let himself in without looking back. The door closed again behind him.

Simon chuckled as he let in the clutch and drove on towards the appointment to which he had been on his way. The episode which had just taken place would make a mildly amusing story to tell: aside from that obvious face value, he didn't give it a second thought. There was no reason why he should. There must have been enough hood-lums in the metropolis with long-cherished dreams of vengeance against Mr Teal, aside from ordinary casual foot-pads, to account for the sprinting beater-up who had made such an agile getaway: the only entertaining angle was that Coincidence should have chosen the Saint himself, of all possible people, to be the rescuer.

That was as much as the Saint's powers of clairvoyance were worth on that occasion.

Two hours later, when he had parked the Hirondel in the garage at Cornwall House, his foot kicked something out of the door as he got out. It was the yellow packet that had slipped out of Teal's pocket, which had fallen on to the floor and been left there forgotten by both men.

Simon picked it up; and when he saw the label he sighed, and then grinned again. So that was a new depth to which Mr Teal had sunk; and the revelation of the detective's dyspepsia would provide a little extra piquancy to their next encounter in badinage . . .

He went on reading the exaggerated claims made for Miracle Tea on the wrapper as he rode up in the elevator to his apartment. And as he read on, a new idea came to him, an idea which could only have found a welcome in such a scape-grace sense of mischief as the Saint's. The product was called Miracle Tea, and there seemed to be no reason why it should not be endowed with miraculous properties before being returned to its owner. Chief Inspector Teal would surely be disappointed if it failed to perform miracles. And that could so easily be arranged. The admixture of a quantity of crushed senna pods, together with a certain amount of powdered calomel – the indicated specific in all cases of concussion . . .

In his own living-room, the Saint proceeded to open the packet with great care, in such a way that it could be sealed again and bear no trace of having been tampered with.

Inside, there seemed to be a second paper wrapping. He took hold of one corner of it and pulled experimentally. A complete crumpled piece of paper came out in his fingers. Below that, there was another crumpled white pad. And after that, another. It went on until the whole package was empty, and the table on which he was working was covered with those creased white scraps. But no tea came to light. He picked up one of the pieces of paper and cautiously unfolded it, in case it should be the container of an individual dose. And then suddenly he sat quite still, while his blue eyes froze into narrowed pools of electrified ice as he realized what he was looking at.

It was a Bank of England note for fifty pounds.

3

'Miracle Tea,' said the Saint reverently, 'is a good name for it.'

There were thirty of those notes – a total of fifteen hundred pounds in unquestionably genuine cash, legal tender and ripe for immediate circulation.

There was a light step behind him, and Patricia Holm's hand fell on his shoulder.

'I didn't know you'd come in, boy,' she said; and then she didn't go on. He felt her standing unnaturally still. After some seconds she said: 'What have you been doing – breaking into the baby's moneybox?'

'Getting ready to write some letters,' he said. 'How do you like the new notepaper?'

She pulled him round to face her.

'Come on,' she said. 'I like to know when you're going to be arrested. What's the charge going to be this time – burgling a bank?'

He smiled at her.

She was easy to smile at. Hair like ripe corn in the sun, a skin like rose petals, blue eyes that could be as wicked as his own, the figure of a young nymph, and something else that could not have been captured in any picture, something in her that laughed with him in all his misdeeds.

'Tea-drinking is the charge,' he said. 'I've signed the pledge, and henceforward this will be my only beverage.'

She raised her fist.

'I'll push your face in.'

'But it's true.'

He handed her the packet from which the money had come. She sat on the table and studied every side of it. And after that she was only more helplessly perplexed.

'Go on,' she said.

He told her the story exactly as it had happened.

'And now you know just as much as I do,' he concluded. 'I haven't even had time to do any thinking on it. Maybe we needn't bother. We shall wake up soon, and everything will be quite all right.'

She put the box down again and looked at one of the notes.

'Are they real?'

'There isn't a doubt of it.'

'Maybe you've got away with Teal's life savings.'

'Maybe. But he has got a bank account. And can you really see Claud Eustace hoarding his worldly wealth in packets of patent tea?'

'Then it must be evidence in some case he's working on.'

'It could be. But again, why keep it in this box?' Simon turned the yellow packet over in his supple hands. 'It was perfectly sealed before I opened it. It looked as if it had never been touched. Why should he go to all that trouble? And suppose it was evidence just as it stood, how did he know what the evidence was without opening it? If he didn't know, he'd surely have opened it on the spot, in front of witnesses. And if he did know, he had no business to take it home. Besides, if he did know that he was carrying danger-ous evidence, he wouldn't have had to think twice about what motive there might be for slugging him on his way home; but he didn't seem to have the slightest idea what it was all about.'

Patricia frowned.

'Could he be taking graft? This might be a way of slipping him the money.'

Simon thought that over for a while; but in the end he shook his head.

'We've said a lot of rude things about Claud Eustace in our time, but I don't think even we could ever have said that seriously. He may be a nuisance, but he's so honest that it runs out of his ears. And still again, he'd have known what he was carrying, and known what anybody who slugged him might have been after, and the first thing he did when he woke up would have been to see if he's still got the dough. But he didn't. He didn't even feel in his pockets.'

'But wasn't he knocked silly?'

'Not that silly.'

'Perhaps he was quite sure what had happened, and didn't want to give himself away.'

'With me sitting beside him? If he'd even thought he'd lost something valuable, it wouldn't have been quite so easy for me to convince him that I wasn't the warrior with the gaspipe. He could have arrested me himself and searched me on the spot without necessarily giving anything away.'

The girl shrugged despairingly.

'All right. So you think of something.'

The Saint lighted a cigarette.

'I suppose I'm barmy, but there's only one thing I can think of. Claud Eustace didn't have the foggiest idea what was in the packet. He had a pain in his tum-tum, and he just bought it for medicine on the way home. It was meant to be handed to someone else, and the fellow in the shop got mixed up. As soon as Teal's gone out with it, the right man comes in, and there is a good deal of commotion. Somebody realizes what's happened, and goes dashing after Teal to get the packet back. He bends his blunt instrument over Teal's head, and is just about to frisk him when I arrive and spoil everything, and he has to lam. I take Teal home, and Teal has something else to think about besides his tummy-ache, so he forgets all about his Miracle Tea, and I win it. And is it something to win!'

The Saint's eyes were kindling with an impish excitement that had no direct connection with the windfall that had just dropped into his lap. Patricia did not need him to say any more to tell her what was going on in his mind. To the Saint, any puzzle was a potential adventure; and the Saint on the trail of adventure was a man transformed, a dynamic focus of ageless and superhuman forces against which no ordinary mortal could argue. She had known him so well for so many years, had known so long that he was beyond her power to change, even if she had wished to change him.

She said slowly: 'But what is the racket?'

'That would be worth knowing,' he said; and he had no need to say that he intended to know. He leaned back ecstatically. 'But just think of it, darling! If we could only see the uproar and agitation that must be going on at this minute in the place where this tea came from . . .'

As a matter of record, the quality of the uproar and the agitation in the shop where Mr Teal had made his purchase would not have disappointed him at all; although in fact it had preceded this conversation by some time.

Mr Henry Osbett, registered proprietor of the drug store at 909 Victoria Street which was also the registered premises of the Miracle Tea Company, was normally a man of quite distinguished and even haughty aspect, being not only tall and erect, but also equipped with a pair of long and gracefully curved moustaches which stuck out on either side of his face like the wings of a soaring gull, which gave him a rather old-fashioned military air in spite of his horn-rimmed glasses. Under the stress of emotion, however, his dignity was visibly frayed. He listened to his shifty-eyed assistant's explanations with fuming impatience.

'How was I to know?' the young man was protesting. 'He

came at exactly the right time, and I've never seen Nancock before. I didn't mean to give him the packet without the password, but he snatched it right out of my hand and rushed off.'

'Excuses!' snarled the chemist, absent-mindedly grabbing handfuls of his whiskers and tying them in knots. 'Why if you'd even known who he was—'

'I didn't know – not until Nancock told me. How could I know?'

'At least you could have got the package back.'

The other swallowed.

'I'd only have got myself caught,' he said sullenly. 'That chap who jumped out of the car was twice my size. He'd've killed me!'

Mr Osbett stopped maltreating his moustache and looked at him for a long moment in curiously contrasting immobility.

'That might have saved someone else the trouble,' he said; and the tone in which he said it made the young man's face turn grey.

Osbett's cold stare lasted for a moment longer: and then he took a fresh grip on his whiskers and turned and scuttled through to the back of the shop. One might almost have thought that he had gone off in the full flush of enthusiasm to fetch an axe.

Beyond the dispensing room there was a dark staircase. As he mounted the stairs his gait and carriage changed in subtle ways until it was as if a different man had entered his clothes. On the upper landing his movements were measured and deliberate. He opened a door and went into a rather shabby and nondescript room which served as his private office. There were two or three old-fashioned filing cabinets, a littered desk with the polish worn off at the edges, a dingy carpet, and a couple of junkstore chairs. Mr Osbett sat down at the desk and opened a packet of cheap cigarettes.

He was a very worried man, and with good reason: but he no longer looked flustered. He had, at that moment, a very cold-blooded idea of his position. He was convinced that Teal's getaway with the packet of Miracle Tea had been neither premeditated nor intentional – otherwise there would have been further developments before this. It had simply been one of those fantastic accidents which lie in wait for the most careful conspiracies. That was a certain consolation; but not much. As soon as the contents of the packet were opened there would be questions to answer; and while it was quite certain that nothing criminal could be proved from any answers he cared to give, it would still make him the object of an amount of suspicious attention which might easily lead to disaster later. There remained the chance that Teal might not decide to actually take a dose of Miracle Tea for some hours yet, and it was a chance that had to be seized quickly.

After another moment's intensive consideration, Mr Osbett picked up the telephone.

4

Simon Templar had been out and come in again after a visit to the nearest chemist. Now he was industriously stirring an interesting mixture in a large basin borrowed from the kitchen. Patricia Holm sat in an armchair and watched him despairingly.

'Did you ever hear a proverb about little things pleasing little minds?' she said.

Unabashed, the Saint put down his spoon and admired his handiwork. To any but the most minute examination, it looked exactly like a high-grade small-leaf tea. And some of it was. The other ingredients were hardly less ordinary, except in that particular combination.

'Did you ever hear another proverb about a prophet in his own country?' he answered. 'If you had a little more reverence for my mind, you'd see that it was nearly double its normal size. Don't you get the idea?'

'Not yet.'

'This is what I originally meant to do. Maybe it wasn't such a huge idea then; although if I could get enough little ideas that handed me fifteen hundred quid a time I wouldn't worry so much about passing up the big stuff. But still that was just good clean fun. Now it's more than that. If I'm right, and Teal still doesn't know what he had in his pocket this afternoon, we don't want him to even start thinking about it. Therefore I just want to return him his Miracle Tea, and I'll be sure he won't give it another thought. But I never had any Miracle Tea. Therefore I've got to concoct a passable substitute. I don't know the original formula; but if this recipe doesn't live up to the name I'll drink a gallon of it.'

'Of course,' she said, 'you couldn't just go out and buy another packet to give him.'

Simon gazed at her in stunned admiration.

'Could you believe that I never thought of that?'

'No,' said Patricia.

'Maybe you're right,' said the Saint ruefully.

He gave the basin another stir, and shrugged.

'Anyway,' he said, 'it'd be a pity to waste all this work, and the chance of a lifetime as well.'

He sat down at the table and cheerfully proceeded to pack his own remarkable version of Miracle Tea into the original carton. Having stuffed it full, he replaced the seals and wrappings with as much care as he had removed them; and when he had finished there was not a trace to show that the package had ever been tampered with.

'What will you do if he dies?' asked the girl.

'Send a wreath of tea roses to his funeral,' said the Saint. He put down the completed packet after he had inspected it closely from every angle, and moved himself over to a more comfortable lounging site on the settee. His eyes were alert and hot with a gathering zest of devilment. 'Now we go into the second half of this brilliant conspiracy.'

'What does that mean?'

'Finding out where Claud Eustace buys fifteen hundred quid for half a dollar. Just think, sweetheart – we can go shopping once a week and keep ourselves in caviar without ever doing another stroke of work!'

He reached for the telephone and set it on his lap while he dialled Teal's private number with a swift and dancing forefinger. The telephone, he knew, was beside Teal's bed; and the promptness with which his ring was answered established the detective's location with quite miraculous certainty.

'I hope,' said the Saint, with instantaneous politeness, 'that I haven't interrupted you in the middle of any important business, Claud.'

The receiver did not actually explode in his ear. It was a soundly constructed instrument, designed to resist spontaneous detonation. It did, however, appear to feel some strain in reproducing the cracked-foghorn cadence in which the answering voice said: 'Who's that?'

'And how,' said the Saint, 'is the little tum-tum tonight?'

Mr Teal did not repeat his question. He had no need to. There was only one voice in the whole world which was capable of inquiring after his stomach with the exact inflection which was required to make that hypersensitive organ curl up into tight knots that sent red and yellow flashes squirting across his eyeballs.

Mr Teal did not groan aloud; but a minute organic groan swept through him like a cramp from his fingertips to his toes.

It is true that he was in bed, and it is also true that he had been interrupted in the middle of some important business; but that important business had been simply and exclusively concerned with trying to drown his multitudinous woes in sleep. For a man in the full bloom of health to be smitten over the knob with a blunt instrument is usually a somewhat trying experience; but for a man in Mr Teal's dyspeptic condition to be thus beaned is ultimate disaster. Mr Teal now had two fearful pains rivalling for his attention, which he had been trying to give to neither. The only way of evading this responsibility which he had been able to think of had been to go to bed and go to sleep, which is what he had set out to do as soon as the Saint had left him at his door; but sleep had steadfastly eluded him until barely five minutes before the telephone bell had blared its recall to conscious suffering into his anguished ear. And when he became aware that the emotions which he had been caused by that recall had been wrung out of him for no better object than to answer some Saintly badinage about his abdomen, his throat closed up so that it was an effort for him to breathe.

'Is that all you want to know?' he got out in a strangled squawk. 'Because if so—'

'But it bothers me, Claud. You know how I love your tummy. It would break my heart if anything went wrong with it.'

'Who told you anything was wrong with it?'

'Only my famous deductive genius. Or do you mean to tell me you drink Miracle Tea because you like it?'

There was a pause. With the aid of television, Mr Teal could have been seen to wriggle. The belligerent blare crumpled out of his voice.

'Oh,' he said weakly. 'What miracle tea?'

'The stuff you had in your pocket this afternoon. I threw it into the car with your other things when I picked you up, but we forgot it when you got out. I've just found it. Guaranteed to cure indigestion, colic, flatulence, constipation, venomous bile, spots before the eyes . . . I didn't know you had so many troubles, Claud.'

'I haven't!' Teal roared defiantly. His stomach promptly performed two complicated and unprecedented evolutions and made a liar of him. He winced, and floundered. 'I – I just happened to hear it advertised on the radio, and then I saw another advertisement in a shop window on the way home, so I thought I'd try some. I – I haven't been feeling very fit lately—'

'Then I certainly think you ought to try something,' said the Saint charitably. 'I'll beetle over with your poison right away; and if I can help out with a spot of massage, you only have to say the word.'

Mr Teal closed his eyes. Of all the things he could think of which might aggravate his miseries, a visit from the Saint at that time was the worst.

'Thanks,' he said with frantic earnestness, 'but all I want now is to get some sleep. Bring it over some other time, Saint.'

Simon reached thoughtfully for a cigarette.

'Just as you like, Claud. Shall we say the May Fair tomorrow, at four o'clock?'

'You could send it round,' Teal said desperately. 'Or just throw it away. I can get some more. If it's any bother—'

'No bother at all, dear old collywobble. Let's call it a date. Tomorrow at four – and we'll have a cup of tea together . . .'

The Saint laid the telephone gently back on its bracket and replaced it on the table beside him. His thumb flicked over the wheel of his lighter; and the tip of his cigarette kindled to a glow that matched the brightening gleam of certainty in his blue eyes.

He had obtained all the information he wanted without pressing a single conspicuous question. Mr Teal had bought his Miracle Tea on the way home – and Simon knew that Mr Teal's way home, across Parliament Square and up Victoria Street, was so rigidly established by years of unconscious habit that a blind man could almost have followed it by tracing the groove which the detective's regulation boots must by that time have worn along the pavement. Even if there were more than one chemist's along that short trail with a Miracle Tea advertisement in the window, the process of elimination could not take long . . .

Patricia was watching him.

She said: 'So what?'

'So we were right,' said the Saint; and his voice was lilting with incorrigible magic. 'Claud doesn't give a damn about his tea. It doesn't mean a thing in his young life. He doesn't care if he never sees it again. He just bought it by a fluke, and he doesn't even know what sort of a fluke it was.'

'Are you sure?' asked Patricia cautiously. 'If he just doesn't want you to suspect anything—'

The Saint shook his head.

'I know all Claud's voices much too well. If he'd tried to get away with anything like that, I should have heard it. And why should he try? I offered to bring it round at once, and he could have just said nothing and let me bring it. Why should he take any risk at all of something going wrong when he could have had the package back in half an hour. Teal may look dumb sometimes, but you can't see him being so dumb as that.' Simon stood up, and his smile was irresistibly expectant. 'Come out into the wide world with me, darling, and let's look for this shop where they sell miracles!'

His energy carried her off like a tide race; the deep purr of the Hirondel as he drove it at fantastic speed to Parliament Square was in tune with his mood. Why it should have happened again, like this, he didn't know; but it might as well have been this way as any other. Whatever the way, it had been bound to happen. Destiny could never leave him alone for long, and it must have been at least a week since anything exciting had happened to him. But now that would be all put right, and there would be trouble and adventure and mystery again, and with a little luck some boodle at the end; that was all that mattered. Somewhere in this delirious business of Miracle Tea and Bank of England notes there must be crime and dark conspiracies and all manner of mischief – he couldn't surmise yet what kind of racket could subsist on trading handfuls of bank notes for half-crowns, but it was even harder to imagine anything like that in a line of legitimate business, so some racket or other it must be, and new rackets could never be altogether dull. He parked the car illegally on the corner of Victoria Street, and got out.

'Let's walk,' he said.

He took Patricia's arm and strolled with her up the street; and as they went he burbled exuberantly.

'Maybe it's an eccentric millionaire who suffered from acute dyspepsia all his life, and in his will he directed that all his fortune was to be distributed among other sufferers, because he knew that there really wasn't any cure at all, but at least the money would be some consolation. So without any publicity his executors had the dough wrapped up in packets labelled as an indigestion cure, feeling pretty sure that nobody who didn't have indigestion would buy it, and thereby saving themselves the trouble of sorting through a lot of applicants with bogus belly-aches ... Or maybe it's some guy who has made all the money in the world out of defrauding the poor nitwitted public with various patent medicines, whose conscience has pricked him in his old age so that he is trying to fix himself up for the Hereafter by making restitution, and the most appropriate way he can think of to do that is to distribute the geetus in the shape of another patent medicine, figuring that that is the way it's most likely to fall into the same hands that it originally came from ... Or maybe—'

'Or maybe,' said Patricia, 'this is the place you're looking for.'

Simon stopped walking and looked at it.

There was a showcard in the centre of the window – the same card, as a matter of fact, which Mr Teal had seen. But the Saint was taking no chances.

'Let's make sure,' he said.

He led her the rest of the way up the street for a block beyond the turning where Mr Teal would have branched off on the most direct route to his lodgings, and back down the opposite side; but no other drug-store window revealed a similar sign.

Simon stood on the other side of the road again, and gazed

across at the brightly lighted window which they had first looked at. He read the name 'HENRY OSBETT & CO.' across the front of the shop.

He let go Patricia's arm.

'Toddle over, darling,' he said, 'and buy me a packet of Miracle Tea.'

'What happens if I get shot?' she asked suspiciously.

'I shall hear the bang,' he said, 'and phone for an ambulance.'

Two minutes later she rejoined him with a small neat parcel in her hand. He fell in beside her as she came across the road, and turned in the direction of the lower end of the street, where he had left the car.

'How was Comrade Osbett?' he murmured. 'Still keeping up with the world?'

'He looked all right, if he was the fellow who served me.' She passed him the packet she was carrying. 'Now do you mind telling me what good this is supposed to do?'

'We must listen to one of their broadcasts and find out. According to the wrapper, it disperses bile—'

She reached across to his hip pocket, and he laughed.

'Okay, darling. Don't waste any bullets – we may need them. I just wanted to find out if there were any curious features about buying Miracle Tea, and I didn't want to go in myself because I'm liable to want to go in again without being noticed too much.'

'I didn't see anything curious,' she said. 'I just asked for it, and he wrapped it up and gave it to me.'

'No questions or stalling?'

'No. It was just like buying a toothbrush or anything else.'

'Didn't he seem to be at all interested in who was buying it?'

'Not a bit.'

He held the package to his ear, shook it, and crunched it speculatively.

'We'll have a drink somewhere and see if we've won anything,' he said.

At a secluded corner table in the Florida, a while later, he opened the packet, with the same care to preserve the seals and wrappings as he had given to the first consignment, and tipped out the contents on to a plate. The contents, to any ordinary examination, consisted of nothing but tea – and, by the smell and feel of it, not very good tea either.

The Saint sighed, and called a waiter to remove the mess.

'It looks as if we were wrong about that eccentric million-aire,' he said. 'Or else the supply of doremi has run out . . . Well, I suppose we shall just have to go to work again.' He folded the container and stowed it carefully away in his pocket; and if he was disappointed he was able to conceal his grief. A glimmer of reckless optimism curled the corners of his mouth. 'You know, darling, I have a hunch that some interesting things are going to happen before this time tomor-row night.'

He was a better prophet than he knew, and it took only a few hours to prove it.

5

Simon Templar slept like a child. A thunderstorm bursting over his roof would not have woken him; a herd of wild elephants stampeding past his bed would scarcely have made him stir; but one kind of noise that other ears might not have heard at all even in full wakefulness brought him back instantaneously to life with every faculty sharpened and on tiptoe.

He awoke in a breathless flash, like a watchdog, without the slightest perceptible alteration in his rate of breathing or any sudden movement. Anyone standing over him would not have even sensed the change that had taken place. But his eyes were half open, and his wits were skidding back over the last split second of sleep like the recoil of taut elastic, searching for a definition of the sound that had aroused him.

The luminous face of a clock across the room told him that he had slept less than two hours. And the thinly phosphorescent hands hadn't moved on enough for the naked eye to see when he knew why he was awake.

In the adjoining living-room, something human had moved.

Simon drew down the automatic from under his pillow and slid out of bed like a phantom. He left the communicating door alone, and sidled noiselessly through the other door which led out into the hall. The front door was open just enough to split the darkness with a knife-edge of illumination from the lights on the landing outside: he eased over to it like a cat, slipped his fingers through the gap, and felt the burred edges of the hole which had been drilled through the outside of the frame so that the catch of the spring lock would be pushed back.

A light blinked beyond the open door of the living-room. The Saint came to the entrance and looked in. Silhouetted against the subdued glow of an electric torch he saw the shape of a man standing by the table with his back to the door, and his bare feet padded over the carpet without a breath of sound until they were almost under the intruder's heels. He leaned over until his lips were barely a couple of inches from the visitor's right ear.

'Boo,' said the Saint.

It was perhaps fortunate for the intruder that he had a strong heart, for if he had had the slightest cardiac weakness the nervous shock which spun him round would have probably popped it like a balloon. As it was, an involuntary yammer of sheer primitive fright dribbled out of his throat before he lashed out blindly in no less instinctive self-defence.

Simon had anticipated that. He was crouching almost to his knees by that time, and his left arm snaked around the lower part of the man's legs simultaneously with a quick thrust of his shoulder against the other's thighs.

The burglar went over backwards with a violent thud; and as most of his breath jolted out of him he freighted it with a selection of picturesque expletives which opened up new vistas of biologic theory. One hand, swinging up in a vicious arc, was caught clearly in the beam of the fallen flashlight, and it was not empty.

'I think,' said the Saint, 'we can do without the persuader.'

He jabbed the muzzle of his gun very hard into the place where his guest's ribs forked, and heard a satisfactory gasp of pain in response. His left hand caught the other's wrist as it descended, twisted with all the skill of a manipulative surgeon, and let go again to grab the life-preserver as it dropped out of the man's numbed fingers.

'You mustn't hit people with things like this,' he said reprovingly. 'It hurts . . . Doesn't it?'

The intruder, with jagged stars shooting through his head, did not offer an opinion; but his squirming lost nearly all of its early vigour. The Saint sat on him easily, and made sure that there were no other weapons on his person before he stood up again.

The main lights clicked on with a sudden dazzling brightness. Patricia Holm stood in the doorway, the lines of her figure draping exquisite contours into the folds of a filmy négligé, her fair hair tousled with sleep and hazy startlement in her blue eyes.

'I'm sorry,' she said. 'I didn't know you had company.'

'That's all right,' said the Saint. 'We're keeping open house.'

He lounged back to rest the base of his spine against the edge of the table and inspected the caller in more detail. He saw a short-legged barrel-chested individual with a thatch of carroty hair, a wide coarse-lipped mouth, and a livid scar running from one side of a flattened nose to near the lobe of a misshapen ear; and recognition dawned in his gaze.

He waved his gun in a genial gesture.

'You remember our old pal and playmate, Red McGuire?' he murmured. 'Just back from a holiday at Parkhurst after his last job of robbery with violence. Somebody told him about all those jewels we keep around, and he couldn't wait to drop in and see them. Why didn't you ring the bell, Red, and save yourself the trouble of carving up our door?'

McGuire sat on the floor and tenderly rubbed his head.

'Okay,' he growled. 'I can do without the funny stuff. Go on an' call the cops.'

Simon considered the suggestion. It seemed a very logical procedure. But it left an unfinished edge of puzzlement still in his mind.

There was something about finding himself the victim of an ordinary burglary that didn't quite ring bells. He knew well enough that his reputation was enough to make any ordinary burglar steer as far away from him as the landscape would allow. And serious burglars didn't break into any dwelling chosen at random and hope for the best, without even knowing the identity of the occupant – certainly not burglars with the professional status of Red McGuire. Therefore . . .

His eyes drained detail from the scene with fine drawn intentness. Nothing seemed to have been touched. Perhaps he had arrived too quickly for that. Everything was as he had left it when he went to bed. Except—

The emptied packet of Miracle Tea which Patricia had bought for him that evening was still in his coat pocket. The packet which he had refilled for Teal's personal consumption was still on the table . . . Or was it?

For on the floor, a yard from where Red McGuire had fallen, lay another identical packet of Miracle Tea.

Simon absorbed the jar of realization without batting an eyelid. But a slowly increasing joy crept into the casual radiance of his smile.

'Why ask me to be so unfriendly, Red?' he drawled. 'After all, what's a packet of tea between friends?'

If he needed any confirmation of his surmise, he had it in the way Red McGuire's small green eyes circled the room and froze on the yellow carton beside him before they switched furtively back to the Saint's face.

'Wot tea?' McGuire mumbled sullenly.

'Miracle Tea,' said the Saint gently. 'The juice that pours balm into the twinging tripes. That's what you came here for tonight, Red. You came here to swipe my beautiful packet of gut-grease and leave some phony imitation behind instead!'

McGuire glowered at him stubbornly.

'I dunno wot yer talkin' abaht.'

'Don't you?' said the Saint, and his smile had become almost affectionate. 'Then you're going to find the next half hour tremendously instructive.'

He straightened up and reached over for a steel chair that stood close to him, and slid it across in the direction of his guest.

'Don't you find the floor rather hard?' he said. 'Take a pew and make yourself happy, because it looks as if we may be in for a longish talk.'

A wave of his gun added a certain amount of emphasis to the invitation, and there was a crispness in his eyes that carried even more emphasis than the gun.

McGuire hauled himself up hesitantly and perched on the edge of the chair. And the Saint beamed at him.

'Now if you'll look in the top drawer of the desk, Pat – I think there's quite a collection of handcuffs there. About three pairs ought to be enough. One for each of his ankles, and one to fasten his hands behind him.'

McGuire shifted where he sat.

'Wot's the idea?' he demanded uneasily.

'Just doing everything we can to make you feel at home,' answered the Saint breezily. 'Would you mind putting your hands behind you so that the lady can fix you up? . . . Thanks ever so much . . . Now if you'll just move your feet back up against the legs of the chair—'

Rebellious rage boiled behind the other's sulky scowl, a rage that had its roots in a formless but intensifying fear. But the Saint's steady hand held the conclusive argument, and he kept that argument accurately aligned on McGuire's wishbone until the last cuff had been locked in place and the strong-arm expert was shackled to the steel chair-frame as solidly as if he had been riveted on to it.

Then Simon put down his automatic and languidly flipped open the cigarette box.

'I hate to do this to you,' he said conversationally, 'but we've really got to do something about that memory of yours. Or have you changed your mind about answering a few questions?'

McGuire glared at him without replying.

Simon touched a match to his cigarette and glanced at Patricia through a placid trail of smoke.

'Can I trouble you some more, darling? If you wouldn't mind plugging in that old electric curling-iron of yours—'

McGuire's eyes jerked and the handcuffs clinked as he strained against them.

'Go on, why don't yer call the cops?' he blurted hoarsely. 'You can't do anything to me!'

The Saint strolled over to him.

'Just who do you think is going to stop me?' he asked kindly.

He slipped his hands down inside McGuire's collar, one on each side of the neck, and ripped his shirt open clear to the waist with one swift wrench that sprung the buttons pinging across the room like bullets.

'Get it good and hot, darling,' he said over his shoulder, 'and we'll see how dear old Red likes the hair on his chest waved.'

6

Red McGuire stared up at the Saint's gentle smile and ice-cold eyes, and the breath stopped in his throat. He was by no means a timorous man, but he knew when to be afraid – or thought he did.

'You ain't given me a charnce, guv'nor,' he whined. 'Why don't yer arsk me somethink I can answer? I don't want to give no trouble.'

Simon turned away from him to flash a grin at Patricia – a grin that McGuire was never meant to see.

'Go ahead and get the iron, sweetheart,' he said, with bloodcurdling distinctness, and winked at her. 'Just in case old dear Red changes his mind.'

Then the wink and the grin vanished together as he whipped round on his prisoner.

'All right,' he snapped. 'Tell me all you know about Miracle Tea!'

'I dunno anythink about it, so help me, guv'nor. I never heard of it before tonight. All I know is I was told to come here wiv a packet, an' if I found another packet here I was to swop them over an' bring your packet back. That's all I know about it, strike me dead if it ain't.'

'I shall probably strike you dead if it is,' said the Saint coldly. 'D'you mean to tell me that Comrade Osbett didn't say any more than that?'

'Who's that?'

'I said Osbett. You know who I'm talking about.'

'I never heard of 'im.'

Simon moved towards him with one fist drawn back.

'That's Gawd's own truth!' shouted McGuire desperately. 'I said I'd tell yer anythink I could, didn't I? It ain't my fault if I don't know everything—'

'Then who was it told you to come here and play tea-parties?'

'I dunno . . . Listen!' begged McGuire frantically. 'This is a squeal, ain't it? Well, why won't yer believe me? I tell yer, I don't know. It was someone who met me when I come out of stir. I dunno wot is name is, an' in this business yer don't arsk questions. He ses to me, would I like fifty quid a week to do any dirty work there is going, more er less. I ses, for fifty quid a week I'll do anythink he can think of. So he gives me twenty quid on account, an' tells me to go anywhere where there's a telephone an' just sit there beside it until he calls me. So tonight he rings up—'

'And you never knew who he was?'

'Never in me life, strike me dead—'

'How do you get the rest of your money?'

'He just makes a date to meet me somewhere an' hands it over.'

'And you don't even know where he lives?'

'So help me, I don't. All I got is a phone number where I can ring him.'

'What is this number?'

'Berkeley 3100.'

Simon studied him calculatingly. The story had at least a possibility of truth, and the way McGuire told it it sounded convincing. But the Saint didn't let any premature camaraderie soften his implacably dissecting gaze.

He said: 'What sort of a guy is he?'

'A tall thin foreign-looking bloke wiv a black beard.'

It still sounded possible. Whatever Mr Osbett's normal

appearance might be, and whatever kind of racket he might be in, he might easily be anxious not to have his identity known by such dubiously efficient subordinates as Red McGuire.

'And exactly how,' said the Saint, 'did your foreign-looking bloke know that I had any miracles in the house?'

'I dunno—'

Patricia Holm came back into the room with a curling-iron that glowed dull red.

Simon turned and reached for it.

'You're just in time, darling,' he murmured. 'Comrade McGuire's memory is going back on him again.'

Comrade McGuire gaped at the hot iron, and licked his lips.

'I found that out meself, guv'nor,' he said hurriedly. 'I was goin' to tell yer—'

'How did you find out?'

'I heard somethink on the telephone.'

The Saint's eyes narrowed.

'Where?'

'In the fust house I went to – somewhere near Victoria Station. That was where I was told to go fust an' swop over the tea. I got in all right, but the bloke was there in the bedroom. I could hear 'im tossing about in bed. I was standin' outside the door, wondering if I should jump in an' cosh him, when the telephone rang. I listened to wot he said, an' all of a sudding I guessed it was about some tea, an' then once he called you "Saint", an' I knew who he must be talkin' to. So I got out again an' phoned the guvnor an' told him about it; an' he ses, go ahead an' do the same thing here.'

Simon thought back over his conversation with Mr Teal; and belief grew upon him. No liar could have invented that story, for it hung on the fact of a telephone call which nobody else besides Teal and Patricia and himself could have known about.

He could see how the mind of Mr Osbett would have

worked on it. Mr Osbett would already know that someone had interrupted the attempt to recover the package of tea from Chief Inspector Teal on his way home, that that some-one had arrived in a car, and that he had presumably driven Teal the rest of the way after the rescue. If someone was phoning Teal later about a packet of tea, the remainder of the sequence of accidents would only have taken a moment to reconstruct . . . And when the Saint thought about it, he would have given a fair percentage of his fifteen hundred pounds for a glimpse of Mr Osbett's face when he learned into what new hands the packet of tea had fallen.

He still looked at Red McGuire.

'How would you like to split this packet of tea with me?' he asked casually.

McGuire blinked at him.

'Blimey, guv'nor, wot would I do wiv arf a packet of tea?'

Simon did not try to enlighten him. The answer was enough to consolidate the conclusion he had already reached. Red McGuire really didn't know what it was all about – that was also becoming credible. After all, any intelligent employer would know that Red McGuire was not a man who could be safely led into temptation.

The Saint had something else to think about. His own brief introductory anonymity was over, and henceforward all the attentions of the ungodly would be lavished on himself – while he was still without one single solid target to shoot back at.

He sank into a chair and blew the rest of his cigarette into a meditative chain of smoke rings; and then he crushed the butt into an ashtray and looked at McGuire again.

'What happens to your fifty-quid-a-week job if you go back to stir, Red?' he inquired deliberately.

The thug chewed his teeth.

'I s'pose it's all over with, guv'nor.'

'How would you like to phone your boss now – for me?'

Fear swelled in McGuire's eyes again as the Saint's meaning wore its way relentlessly into his understanding. His mouth opened once or twice without producing any sound.

'Yer carn't arsk me to do that!' he got out at last. 'If he knew I'd double-crorst 'im – he said—'

Simon rose with a shrug.

'Just as you like,' he said carelessly. 'But one of us is going to use the telephone, and I don't care which it is. If I ring up Vine Street and tell 'em to come over and fetch you away, I should think you'd get about ten years, with a record like yours. Still, they say it's a healthy life, with no worries—'

'Wait a minute,' McGuire said chokily. 'What do you do if I make this call?'

'I'll give you a hundred quid in cash; and I'll guarantee that when I'm through with your boss he won't be able to do any of those things he promised.'

McGuire was no mathematician, but he could do simple arithmetic. He gulped something out of his throat.

'Okay,' he grunted. 'It's a bet.'

Simon summed him up for a moment longer, and then hauled his chair over to within reach of the table where the telephone stood. He picked up the microphone and prodded his forefinger into the first perforation of the dial.

'All you're going to do,' he said, as he went on spelling out BER 3100, 'is tell the big bearded chief that you've been through this place with a fine comb, and the only tea-leaf in it is yourself. Do you get it? No Saint, no tea – no soap . . . And I don't want to frighten you or anything like that, Red, but I just want you to remember that if you try to say any more than that, I've still got you here, and we can easily warm up the curling-tongs again.'

'Don't yer think I know wot's good for me?' retorted the other sourly.

The Saint nodded warily, and heard the ring of the call in the receiver. It was answered almost at once, in a sharp cultured voice with a slight foreign intonation.

'Yes? Who is that?'

Simon put the mouthpiece to McGuire's lips.

'McGuire calling,' said the burglar thickly.

'Well?'

'No luck, guv'nor. It ain't here. The Saint's out, so I had plenty of time. I couldn't 've helped findin' it if it'd been here.'

There was a long pause.

'All right,' said the voice curtly. 'Go home and wait for further orders. I'll call you tomorrow.'

The line went down with a click.

'And I wouldn't mind betting,' said the Saint, as he put the telephone back, 'that that's the easiest hundred quid you ever earned.'

'Well, yer got wot yer wanted, didn't yer?' he snarled. 'Come on an' take orf these ruddy bracelets an' let me go.'

The Saint shook his head.

'Not quite so fast, brother,' he said. 'You might think of calling up your boss again and having another chat with him before you went to bed, and I'd hate him to get worried at this hour of the night. You stay right where you are and get some of that beauty sleep which you need so badly, because after what I'm going to do tomorrow your boss may be looking for you with a gun!'

7

Early rising had never been one of the Saint's favourite virtues, but there were times when business looked more important than leisure. It was eleven o'clock the next morning – an hour at which he was usually beginning to think drowsily about breakfast – when he sauntered into the apothecarium of Mr Henry Osbett.

In honour of the occasion, he had put on his newest and most beautiful suit, a creation in pearl-grey fresco over which his tailor had shed tears of ecstasy in the fitting room; his piratically tilted hat was unbelievably spotless; his tie would have humbled the gaudiest hues of dawn. He had also put on, at less expense, a vacuous expression and an inanely chirpy grin that completed the job of typing him to the point where his uncle, the gouty duke, loomed almost visible in his background.

The shifty-eyed young assistant who came to the counter might have been pardoned for keeling over backwards at the spectacle; but he only recoiled half a step and uttered a perfunctory 'Yes, sir?'

He looked nervous and preoccupied. Simon wondered whether this nervousness and preoccupation might have had some connection with a stout and agitated-looking man who had entered the shop a few yards ahead of the Saint himself. Simon's brightly vacant eyes took in the essential items of the topography without appearing to notice anything – the counter with its showcases and displays of patent pills and liver salts, the glazed compartment at one end where presumably prescriptions were dispensed, the dark doorway at the other end which must have led to the intimate fastnesses of the establishment. Nowhere was the stout man visible; therefore, unless he had dissolved into thin air, or disguised himself as a bottle of bunion cure, he must have passed through that one doorway . . . The prospects began to look even more promising than the Saint had expected . . .

'This jolly old tea, old boy,' bleated the Saint, producing a package from his pocket. 'A friend of mine – chappie named Teal, y'know, great detective and all that sort of thing – bought it off you last night and then he wouldn't risk taking it. He was goin' to throw it down the drain; but I said to him "Why waste a perfectly good half-dollar, what?" I said. "I'll bet they'll change it for a cake of soap, or something," I said. "I'll take it in and change it myself," I told him. That's right, isn't it? You will change it, won't you?'

The shifty-eyed youth was a bad actor. His face had gone white, then red, and finally compromised by remaining blotchy. He gaped at the packet as if he was really starting to believe that there were miracles in Miracle Tea.

'We – we should be glad to change it for you, sir,' he gibbered.

'Fine!' chortled the Saint. 'That's just what I told jolly old Teal. You take the tea, and give me a nice box of soap. I expect Teal can use that, but I'm dashed if I know what he could do with tea—'

He was talking to a vanishing audience. The youth, with a spluttered 'Excuse me, sir,' had grabbed the package off the counter and was already making a dive for the doorway at the far end; and the imbecile grin melted out of the Saint's face like a wax mould from a casting of hot bronze.

One skeleton instant after the assistant had disappeared, he was over the counter with the swift silence of a cat.

But even if he had made any noise, it is doubtful whether

the other would have noticed it. The shifty-eyed youth was so drunk with excitement that his brain had for the time being practically ceased to function. If it hadn't he might have stopped to wonder why Mr Teal should have handed the tea to a third party; or why the third party, being so obviously a member of the idle rich, should have even bothered about exchanging it for a box of soap. He might have asked himself a great many inconvenient questions; but he didn't. Perhaps the peculiarly fatuous and guileless character which the Saint had adopted for the interview had something to do with that egregious oversight – at least, that was what Simon Templar had hoped for . . . And it is at least certain that the young man went blundering up the stairs without a backward glance, while the Saint glided like a ghost into the gloomy passage-way at the foot of the stairs . . .

In the dingy upper room which was the young man's destination, Mr Osbett was entertaining the stout and agitated man. That is to say, he was talking to him. The agitated man did not look very entertained.

'It's no good cursing me, Nancock,' Osbett was saying, in his flustered old-maidish way. 'If you'd been on time last night—'

'I was on time!' yelped the perspiring Mr Nancock. 'It was that young idiot's fault for handing the package over without the password – and to Teal, of all people. I tell you, I've been through hell! Waiting for something to happen every minute – waiting, waiting . . . It isn't even safe for me to be here now—'

'That's true,' said Osbett, with one of his curiously abrupt transformations to deadly coldness. 'Who told you to come here?'

'I came here because I want my money!' bawled the other hysterically. 'What do you think I've done your dirty work for? Do you think I'd have taken a risk like this if I didn't need the money? Is it my fault if your fool of an assistant gives the money to the wrong man? I don't care a damn for your pennydreadful precautions, and all this nonsense about signs and countersigns and keeping out of sight. What good has that done this time? I tell you, if I think you're trying to cheat me—'

'Cheat you?' repeated the chemist softly. The idea seemed to interest him. 'Now, I wonder why you should be the first to think of that?'

There was a quality of menace in his voice which the stout man did not seem to hear. His mouth opened for a fresh outburst; but the outburst never came. The first word was on his lips when the door opened and the shifty-eyed youth burst in without the formality of a knock.

'It's Teal's – packet!' he panted out. 'A man just came in and said he wanted to change it! He said – Teal gave it to him. It hasn't been opened!'

Nancock jumped up like a startled pig, with his mouth still open where the interruption had caught it. An inarticulate yelp was the only sound that came out of it.

Osbett got up more slowly.

'What sort of man?' he snapped, and his voice was hard and suspicious.

The youth wagged his hands vaguely.

'A silly-ass sort of fellow – Burlington Bertie kind of chap – I didn't notice him particularly—'

'Well, go back and notice him now!' Mr Osbett was flapping ditherily again. 'Keep him talking. Make some excuse, but keep him there till I can have a look at him.'

The assistant darted out again and went pelting down the stairs – so precipitately that he never noticed the shadow that faded beyond the doorway of the stockroom on the opposite side of the landing.

Osbett had seized the packet of tea and was feeling it eagerly. The suspicious look was still in his eyes, but his hands were shaking with excitement.

'It feels like it!' he muttered. 'There's something funny about this—'

'Funny!' squeaked Nancock shrilly. 'It's my money, isn't it? Give it to me and let me get out of here!'

'It will be lucky for you if it is your money,' Osbett said thinly. 'Better let me make sure.' He ripped open the package. There was no tea in it – only crumpled pieces of thin white paper. 'Yes, this is it. But why . . . My God!'

The oath crawled through his lips in a tremulous whisper. He looked as if he had opened the package and found a snake in his hands. Nancock, staring at him, saw that his face had turned into a blank grey mask in which the eyes bulged like marbles.

Osbett spread out the piece of paper which he had opened. It was not a banknote. It was simply a piece of perforated tissue on which had been stamped in red the drawing of a quaint little figure with straight lines for body and legs and arms and an elliptical halo slanted over his round featureless head . . . Osbett tore open the other papers with suddenly savage hands. Every one of them was the same, stamped with the same symbolic figure . . .

'The Saint!' he whispered.

Nancock goggled stupidly at the scattered drawings.

'I – I don't understand,' he faltered, and he was white at the lips.

Osbett looked up at him.

'Then you'd better start thinking!' he rasped, and his eyes had gone flat and emotionless again. 'The Saint sent this, and if he knows about the money—'

'Not "sent", dear old Whiskers, not "sent",' a coolly mocking voice corrected him from the doorway. 'I brought it along myself, just for the pleasure of seeing your happy faces.'

The Saint stood leaning against the jamb of the door smiling and debonair.

8

The two men stood and gawped at him as if he had been a visitor from Mars. A gamut of emotions that must have strained their endocrine glands to bursting point skittered over their faces like foam over a waterfall. They looked as if they had been simultaneously goosed with high-voltage wires and slugged in the solar plexus with invisible sledgehammers. Simon had to admit that there was some excuse for them. In fact, he had himself intentionally provided the excuse. There were certain reactions which only the ungodly could perform in their full richness that never failed to give him the same exquisite and fundamental joy that the flight and impact of a well-aimed custard pie gives to a movie audience; and for some seconds he was regaled with as ripe and rounded an exhibition of its kind as the hungriest heart could desire.

The Saint propped himself a little more comfortably against his backrest, and flicked a tiny bombshell of ash from his cigarette.

'I hope you don't mind my asking myself in like this,' he remarked engagingly. 'But I thought we ought to get together on this tea business. Maybe I could give you some new ideas. I was mixing a few odds and ends together myself yesterday—'

Credit must be given to Mr Osbett for making the first recovery. He was light-years ahead of Nancock, who stood as if his feet had sunk into the floor above the ankles, looking as though his lower jaw had dislocated itself at its fullest stretch. In one sheeting flash of dazzling clarity it dawned upon him that the man who stood there was unarmed – that the Saint's hands were empty except for a cigarette. His mouth shut tight under the spreading plumes of his moustache as he made a lightning grab towards the inside of his coat.

'Really!' protested the Saint. 'Weren't you ever taught not to scratch yourself in public?'

Osbett had just time to blink – once. And then he felt as if a cyclone had hit him. His fingers had not even closed on the butt of the automatic in his shoulder holster when he found himself full in the path of what seemed like a ton of incarnate dynamite moving with the speed of an express train. Something like a chunk of teak zoomed out of the cyclone and collided with his jaw: as if from a great distance, he heard it make a noise like a plank snapping in half. Then his head seemed to split open and let in a gash of light through which his brain sank down into cottony darkness.

The rest of him cannoned soggily into Nancock, bounded sideways, and cascaded over a chair. Osbett and the chair crashed to the floor together; and the stout man reeled drunkenly.

'Here,' he began.

Perhaps he did not mean the word as an invitation, but it appeared to have that effect. Something possessed of staggering velocity and hardness accepted the suggestion and moved into his stomach. The stout man said '*Oof!*' and folded over like a jack-knife. This put his chin in line with another projectile that seemed to be travelling up from the floor. His teeth clicked together and he lay down quite slowly, like a collapsing concertina.

Simon Templar straightened his tie and picked up the cigarette which he had dropped when the fun started. It had not even had time to scorch the carpet.

He surveyed the scene with a certain shadow of regret. That was the worst of having to work quickly – it merely whetted the appetite for exercise, and then left nothing for it to expend itself on. However, it was doubtful whether Osbett and Nancock could ever have provided a satisfactory workout, even with plenty of time to develop it . . . The Saint relieved Osbett of his gun, felt Nancock's pockets for a weapon and found nothing, and then rose quickly as a scutter of footsteps on the stairs reminded him that he still had one more chance to practise his favourite uppercut. He leaped behind the door as the shifty-eyed assistant tumbled in.

The assistant was blurting out his news as he came.

'Hey, the fellow's disappeared—'

Simon toed the door away from between them and grinned at him.

'Where do you think he went to?' he inquired interestedly.

His fist jolted up under the youth's jaw, and the assistant sat down and unrolled himself backwards and lay still.

The Saint massaged his knuckles contentedly, and pulled a large roll of adhesive tape from his pocket. He used it to fasten the three sleeping beauties' hands and feet together, and had enough left to fasten over their mouths in a way that would gravely handicap any loquacity to which they might be moved when they woke up.

Not that they were showing any signs of waking up for some time to come, which was another disadvantage attached to the effectiveness of that sizzling uppercut. By all the symptoms, it would be quite a while before they were in any condition to start a conversation. It was an obstacle to further developments which Simon had not previously considered, and he scratched his head over it in a moment of indecision. As a matter of fact, he had not given much previous consideration to anything beyond that brief and temporarily conclusive scuffle – he never made any definite plans on such occasions, but he had an infinite faith in impromptu action and the bountiful inspirations of Providence. Meanwhile, no harm would probably be done by making a quick and comprehensive search of the premises, or—

In the stillness of his meditation and the surrounding atmosphere of sleep, an assortment of sounds penetrated to his ears from the regions downstairs. There was some forced and pointed coughing, an impatient shuffling of feet, and the tapping of a coin on plate glass. More business had apparently arrived, and was getting restive.

A faintly thoughtful tilt edged itself into his eyebrows. He glanced round the room, and saw a slightly grubby white coat hanging behind the door. In a moment he had slipped into it and was buttoning it as he skated down the stairs.

The customer was a fat and frowsy woman in a bad temper.

'Tike yer time, dontcher?' she said scathingly. 'Think I've got all die ter wiste, young man? You're new here, aintcher? Where's Mr Osbett?'

'Some people, madam, prefer to call me fresh,' replied the Saint courteously. 'Mr Osbett is asleep at the moment, but you may confide in me with perfect confidence.'

'Confide in yer?' retorted the lady indignantly. 'None o' your sauce, young feller! I want three pennyworth of lickerish an' chlorodeen lozenges, an' that's all. Young Alf's corf is awful bad agin this morning.'

'That's too bad,' said the Saint, giving the shelves a quick once-over, and feeling somewhat helpless. 'Just a minute, auntie – I'm still finding my way around.'

'Fresh,' said the lady tartly, 'Is right.'

Liquorice and chlorodyne lozenges were fairly easy. The Saint found a large bottle of them after a short search, and proceeded to tip half of it into a paper bag.

''Ere, I don't want all that,' yelped the woman. 'Three pennyworth, I said!'

Simon pushed the bag over the counter.

'As an old and valued customer, please accept the extra quantity with Mr Osbett's compliments,' he said generously.

'Threepence is the price to you, madam, and a bottle of cough mixture thrown in. Oh, yes, and you'd better give young Alf some cod-liver oil—'

He piled merchandise towards her until she grabbed up as much as she could carry and palpitated nervously out into the street. Simon grinned to himself and hoped he had not overdone it. If the news of his sensational bargain sale spread around the district, he would have his hands full.

During the lull that followed he tried to take a survey of the stock. He would be safe enough with proprietary goods, but if anyone asked for some more complicated medicine he would have to be careful. He had no grudge to work off against the neighbourhood at large; which was almost a pity.

The next customer required nothing more difficult than aspirin, and left the shop in a kind of daze when the Saint insisted on supplying a bottle of a hundred tablets for the modest price of twopence.

Simon took a trip upstairs and found that his three prizes had still failed to progress beyond the stage of half conscious moanings and a spasmodic twitching of the lower limbs. He returned downstairs to attend to a small snotty-nosed urchin who was asking for a shilling tin of baby food. Simon blandly handed her the largest size he could see, and told her that Mr Osbett was making special reductions that morning.

'Coo!' said the small child, and added a bag of peardrops to the order.

Simon poured out a pound of them – 'No charge for that, Delilah – Mr Osbett is giving peardrops away for an adver-tisement' – and the small child sprinted out as if it was afraid of waking up before it got home.

The Saint lighted another cigarette and waited thought-fully. Supplying everybody who came in with astounding quantities of Mr Osbett's goods at cut-throat prices was amusing enough, admittedly, but it was not getting him anywhere. And yet a hunch that was growing larger every minute kept him standing behind the counter.

Maybe it wasn't such a waste of time . . . The package of Miracle Tea in which he had found fifteen hundred testimonials to the lavish beneficence of his guardian angel had come from that shop; presumably it had been intended for some special customer; presumably also it was not the only eccentric transaction that had taken place there, and there was no reason why it should be the last. Maybe no other miracles of the same kind were timed to take place that day; and yet . . .

Mr Osbett's boxes of extra special toilet soap, usually priced at seven and sixpence, were reduced for the benefit of a charming young damsel to a shilling each. The charming damsel was so impressed that she tentatively inquired the price of a handsome bottle of bath salts.

'What, this?' said the Saint, taking the flagon down and wrapping it up. 'As a special bargain this morning, sweetheart, we're letting it go for sixpence.'

It went for sixpence, quickly. The Saint handed over her change without encouraging further orders – as a matter of fact, he was rather anxious to get rid of the damsel, in spite of her charm and obvious inclination to be friendly, for a man with a thin weasel face under a dirty tweed cap already overdue for the dustbin had come in, and was earnestly inspecting a showcase full of safety razors and other articles which are less widely advertised. Quite obviously the man was not anxious to draw attention to himself while there was another customer in the shop; and while there was at least one perfectly commonplace explanation for that kind of bashfulness the Saint felt a spectral tingle of expectation slide over his scalp as the girl went out and Weasel Face angled over to the counter.

'I haven't seen you before,' he stated.

His manner was flatly casual, but his small beady eyes flitted over Simon's face like flies hovering.

'Then you should be enjoying the view,' said the Saint affably. 'What can I sell you today, comrade? Hot water bottles? Shaving cream? Toothpaste? We have a special bargain line of castor oil—'

'Where's Ossy?'

'Dear old Ossy is lying down for a while – I think he's got a headache, or something. But don't let that stop you. Have you tried some of our Passion Flower lipstick, guaranteed to seduce at the first application?'

The man's eyes circled around again. He pushed out a crumpled envelope.

'Give Ossy my prescription, and don't talk so much.'

'Just a minute,' said the Saint.

He took the envelope back towards the staircase and slit it open. One glance even in the dim light that penetrated there was enough to show him that whatever else the thin sheet of paper it contained might mean, it was not a prescription that any ordinary pharmacist could have filled.

He stuffed the sheet into his pocket and came back.

'Will you call again at six o'clock?' he said, and his flippancy was no longer obtrusive. 'I'll have it ready for you then.'

'Awright.'

The beady eyes sidled over him once more, a trifle puzzledly, and the man went out.

Simon took the paper back into the dispensing room and spread it out under a good light. It was a scale plan of a building, with every detail plainly marked even to the positions of the larger pieces of furniture, and provided in addition with a closely-written fringe of marginal notes which to the Saint's professional scrutiny provided every item of information that a careful burglar could have asked for; and the first fascinating but still incomplete comprehension of Mr Osbett's extraordinary business began to reveal itself to him as he studied it.

9

The simple beauty of the system made his pulses skip. Plans like that could be passed over in the guise of prescriptions; boodle, cash payments for services rendered, or almost anything else, could be handed over the counter enclosed in tubes of cold cream or packets of Miracle Tea; and it could all be done openly and with impunity even while other genuine customers were in the shop waiting to be served. Even if the man who did it were suspected and under surveillance, the same transactions could take place countless times under the very eyes of a watcher, and be dismissed as an entirely unimportant feature of the suspect's daily activities. Short of deliberate betrayal, it left no loophole through which Osbett himself could be involved at all – and even that risk, with a little ingenuity, could probably be manipulated so as to leave someone like the shifty-eyed young assistant to hold the baby. It was foolproof and puncture-proof – except against such an unforeseen train of accidents as had delivered one fatal package of Miracle Tea into Chief Inspector Teal's unwitting paws, and tumbled it from his pocket into Simon Templar's car.

The one vast and monumental question mark that was left was wrapped all the way round the mystery of what was the motive focus of the whole machinery.

A highly organized and up-to-date gang of thieves, directed by a Master Mind and operating with the efficiency of a big business? The answer seemed trite but possible. And yet . . .

All the goods he could see round him were probably as genuine as patent slimming salts and mouth washes can be – any special packages would cetainly be kept aside. And there was nothing noticeably out of place at that time. He examined the cash register. It contained nothing but a small amount of money, which he transferred to a hospital collecting box on the counter. The ancient notes and invoices and prescriptions speared on to hook files in the dispensing compartment were obviously innocuous – nothing incriminating was likely to be left lying about there.

The first brisk spell of trade seemed to have fallen off, and no one else had entered the shop since the visit of Weasel Face. Simon went back upstairs, and investigated the room into which he had dodged when he followed the shifty-eyed youth up the stairs. He remembered it as having had the air of a storeroom of some kind, and he was right. It contained various large jars, packing cases, and cardboard cartons labelled with assorted names and cryptic signs, some of them prosaically familiar, stacked about in not particularly methodical piles. But the whole rear half of the room, in contrasting orderliness, was stacked from floor to ceiling with mounds of small yellow packages that he could recognize at a glance.

He looked around again, and on one wall he found in a cheap frame the official certificate which announced to all whom it might concern that Mr Henry Osbett had dutifully complied with the Law and registered the fact that he was trading under the business name of The Miracle Tea Company.

'Well, well, *well*!' said the Saint dreamily. 'What a small world it is after all . . .'

He fished out his cigarette case and smoked part of the way through a cigarette while he stood gazing abstractedly over the unilluminating contents of the room, and his brain was a whirlpool of new and startling questions.

Then he pulled himself together and went back to the office.

The three men he had left there were all awake again by then and squirming ineffectually. Simon shook his head at them.

'Relax, boys,' he said soothingly. 'You're only wearing yourselves out. And think what a mess you're making of your clothes.'

Their swollen eyes glared at him mutely with three individual renderings of hate and malevolence intensified by different degrees of fear; but if the Saint had been susceptible to the cremating power of the human eye he would have been a walking cinder many years ago.

Calmly he proceeded to empty their pockets and examine every scrap of paper he found on them; but except for a driving licence which gave him Mr Nancock's name and address in Croydon he was no wiser when he had finished.

After that he turned his attention to the filing cabinet; but as far as a lengthy search could tell it contained nothing but a conventional collection of correspondence on harmless matters concerned with the legitimate business of the shop and the marketing of Miracle Tea. He sat down in Mr Osbett's swivel chair and went systematically through the drawers of the desk, but they also provided him with no enlightenment. The net result of his labours was a magnificent and symmetrically rounded zero.

The Saint's face showed no hint of his disappointment. He sat for a few seconds longer, tilting himself gently back and forth; and then he stood up.

'It's a pity you don't keep more money on the premises, Henry,' he remarked. 'You could have saved yourself a stamp.'

He picked up a paperknife from the desk and tested the blade with his thumb. It was sharp enough. The eyes of the bound men dilated as they watched him.

The Saint smiled.

'From the way you were talking when I first came in, it looks as if you know my business,' he said. 'And I hope you've realized by this time that I know yours. It isn't a very nice business; but that's something for you to worry about. All I'm concerned with is to make sure that you pay the proper luxury tax to the right person, which happens to be me. So will you attend to it as soon as possible, Henry? I should think about ten thousand pounds will do for a first instalment. I shall expect it in one-pound notes, delivered by messenger before two-thirty pm tomorrow. And it had better not be late.' The Saint's blue eyes were as friendly as frozen vitriol. 'Because if it is, Chief Inspector Teal will be calling here again – and next time it won't be an accident . . . Meanwhile' – the knife spun from his hands like a whirling white flame, and the three men flinched wildly as the point buried itself with a thud in the small space of carpet centrally between them – 'if one of you gets to work with that, you ought to be up and about again in a few minutes. Goodbye, girls; and help yourself to some sal volatile when you get down stairs.'

It was nearing one o'clock by his watch when he reached the street; and Patricia was ordering herself a second Martini when he strolled into the cocktail room at Quaglino's.

She leaned back and closed her eyes.

'I know,' she said. 'Teal and the Flying Squad are about two blocks behind you. I can tell by the smug look on your face.'

'For once in your life you're wrong,' he said as he lowered himself into a chair. 'They're so far behind that if Einstein is right they ought to have been here an hour ago.'

Over lunch he gave her an account of his morning.

'But what *is* it all about?' she said.

He frowned.

'I just wish I knew, darling. But it's something bigger than burglary – you can take bets on that. If Henry Osbett is the Miracle Teapot in person, the plot is getting so thick you could float rocks on it. If I haven't got mixed on what Claud Eustace told me last night, they run a radio programme, and that costs plenty of dough and trouble. No gang of burglars would bother to go as far as that, even to keep up appearances. Therefore this is some racket in which the dough flows like water; and I wish I could think what that could be. And it's run by experts. In the whole of that shop there wasn't a single clue. I'll swear that Claud Eustace himself could put it through a sieve and not find anything . . . I was just bluffing Henry, of course, but I think I made a good job of it.'

'You don't think he'll pay, do you?'

'Stranger things have happened,' said the Saint hopefully. 'But if you put it like that – no. That was just bait. There wasn't anything else useful that I could do. If I'd had them somewhere else I might have beaten it out of them, but I couldn't do it there, and I couldn't put them in a bag and bring them home with me. Anyhow, this may be a better way. It means that the next move is up to the ungodly, and they've got to make it fast. And that may give us our break.'

'Of course it may,' she agreed politely. 'By the way, where did you tell me once you wanted to be buried?'

He chuckled.

'Under the foundation stone of a brewery,' he said. 'But don't worry. I'm going to take a lot of care of myself.'

His idea of taking care of himself for that afternoon was to drive the Hirondel down to the factory at an average speed of about sixty miles an hour to discuss the installation of a new type of supercharger designed to make the engine several degrees more lethal than it was already, and afterwards to drive back to London at a slightly higher speed in order to be punctual for his appointment with Mr Teal. Considering that ride in retrospect, he sometimes wondered whether he would have any chance of claiming that the astounding quality of care which it showed could be credited entirely to his own inspired forethought.

It was on the stroke of four when he sailed into the May Fair and espied the plump and unromantic shape of Chief Inspector Teal dumped into a pink brocade armchair and looking rather like a bailiff in a boudoir.

Teal got up as the Saint breezed towards him; and something in the way he straightened and stood there almost checked Simon in the middle of a stride. Simon forced himself to keep coming without a flaw in the smooth surface of his outward tranquillity; but a sixth sense was rocketing red danger signals through his brain even before he heard the detective's unnaturally hard gritty voice.

'I've been waiting for you, Saint!'

'Then you must have been early, Claud,' said the Saint. His smile was amiable and unruffled, but there was an outlaw's watchfulness at the back of his bantering eyes. 'Is that any excuse for the basilisk leer? Anyone would think you'd eaten something—'

'I don't want to hear any more of that,' Teal said crunchily. 'You know damned well why I'm waiting for you. Do you know what this is?'

He flourished a piece of paper in Simon's face.

The Saint raised his eyebrows.

'Not another of those jolly old warrants?' he murmured. 'You must be getting quite a collection of them.'

'I'm not going to need to collect any more,' Teal said grimly. 'You went too far when you left your mark on the dead man you threw out of your car in Richmond Park this afternoon. I'm taking you into custody on a charge of wilful murder!'

10

Simon took Mr Teal by the arm and led him back to a seat. He was probably the only man in the world who could have got away with such a thing, but he did it without the faintest sign of effort. He switched on about fifty thousand watts of his personality, and Mr Teal was sitting down beside him before he recovered from it.

'Damn it, Templar, what the hell do you think you're doing?' he exploded wrathfully. 'You're under arrest!'

'All right, I'm under arrest,' said the Saint accommodatingly, as he stretched out his long legs. 'So what?'

'I'm taking you into custody—'

'You said that before. But why the hurry? It isn't early closing day at Vine Street, is it? Let's have our tea first, and you can tell me all about this bird I'm supposed to have moidered. You say he was thrown out of a car—'

'Your Hirondel!'

'But why mine? After all, there are others. I don't use enough of them to keep the factory going by myself.'

The detective's jaws clamped on his chewing gum.

'You can say all that to the magistrate in the morning,' he retorted dourly. 'It isn't my job to listen to you. It's my job to take you to the nearest police station and leave you there, and that's what I'm going to do. I've got a car and a couple of men at each of the entrances, so you'd better not give any trouble. I had an idea you'd be here at four o'clock—'

'So I spent the afternoon moidering people and chucking

them out of cars, and then rush off to meet you so you needn't even have the trouble of looking for me. I even use my own famous Hirondel so that any cop can identify it, and put my trademark on the deceased to make everything easy for the prosecution. You know, Claud,' said the Saint pensively, 'there are times when I wonder whether I'm quite sane.'

Teal's baby blue eyes clung to him balefully.

'Go on,' he grated. 'Let's hear the new alibi. It'll give me plenty of time to get it torn down before you come up for trial!'

'Give me a chance,' Simon protested. 'I don't even know what time I'm supposed to have been doing all these exciting things.'

'You know perfectly well—'

'Never mind. You tell me, and let's see if we agree. What time did I sling this stiff out of my car?'

'A few minutes after three – and he was only killed a few minutes before that.'

The Saint opened his cigarette case.

'That rather tears it,' he said slowly; and Teal's eye kindled with triumph.

'So you weren't quite so smart—'

'Oh, no,' said the Saint diffidently. 'I was just thinking of it from your point of view. You see, just at that time I was at the Hirondel factory at Staines, talking about a new blower that I'm thinking of having glued on to the old buzz-wagon. We had quite a conference over it. There was the works manager, and the service manager, and the shop foreman, and a couple of mechanics thrown in, so far as I remember. Of course, everybody knows that the whole staff down there is in my pay, but the only thing I'm worried about is whether you'll be able to make a jury believe it.'

A queerly childish contraction warped itself across Mr Teal's rubicund features. He looked as if he had been suddenly seized with an acute pain below the belt, and was about to burst into tears.

Both of these diagnoses contained a fundament of truth. But they were far from telling the whole story.

The whole story went too far to be compressed into a space less than volumes. It went far back into the days when Mr Teal had been a competent and contented and common-place detective, adequately doing a job in which miracles did not happen and the natural laws of the universe were respected and cast-iron cases were not being perennially disintegrated under his nose by a bland and tantalizing buccaneer whose elusiveness had almost started to convince him of the reality of black magic. It coiled through an infinite history of incredible disasters and hair breadth frustrations that would have wrung the withers of anything softer than a marble statue. It belonged to the hysterical saga of his whole hopeless duel with the Saint.

Mr Teal did not burst into tears. Nor, on this one unprecedented occasion, did he choke over his gum while a flush of apoplectic fury boiled into his round face. Perhaps there were no more such reactions left in him; or perhaps on this one occasion an inescapable foreboding of the uselessness of it all strangled the spasm before it could mature and gave him the supernatural strength to stifle his emotions under the pose of stolid somnolence that he could so rarely preserve against the Saint's fiendishly shrewd attack. But however he achieved the feat, he managed to sit quite still while his hot resentful eyes bored into the Saint's smiling face for a time before he struggled slothfully to his feet.

'Wait a minute,' he said thickly.

He went over and spoke to a tall cadaverous man who was hovering in the background. Then he came back and sat down again.

Simon trickled an impudent streamer of smoke towards him.

'If I were a sensitive man I should be offended, Claud. Do you have to be quite so obvious about it when you send Sergeant Barrow to find out whether I'm telling you the truth? It isn't good manners, comrade. It savours of distrust.'

Mr Teal said nothing. He sat champing soporifically, staring steadfastly at the polished toes of his regulation boots, until Sergeant Barrow returned.

Teal got up and spoke to him at a little distance; and when he rejoined the Saint the drowsiness was turgid and treacle-thick on his pink full-moon face.

'All right,' he bit out in a cracked voice, through lips that were stiff and clumsy with the bitterness of defeat. 'Now suppose you tell me how you did it.'

'But I didn't do it, Claud,' said the Saint, with a seriousness that edged through his veneer of nonchalance. 'I'm as keen as you are to get a line on this low criminal who takes my trademark in vain. Who was the bloke they picked up this afternoon?'

For some reason which was beyond his understanding, the detective stopped short on the brink of a sarcastic comeback.

'He was an Admiralty draughtsman by the name of Nancock,' he said; and the gauzy derision in the Saint's glance faded out abruptly as he realized that in that simple answer he had been given the secret of Mr Osbett's remarkable chemistry.

11

It was as if a distorting mirror had been suddenly flattened out, so that it reflected a complete picture with brilliant and lifelike accuracy. The figures in it moved like marionettes.

Simon even knew why Nancock had died. He himself, ironically for Teal's disappointment, had sealed the fat man's death-warrant without knowing it. Nancock was the man for whom the fifteen-hundred-pound packet of Miracle Tea had been intended; Nancock had been making a fuss at the shop when the Saint arrived. The fuss was due to nothing but Nancock's fright and greed, but to suspicious eyes it might just as well have looked like the overdone attempt of a guilty conscience to establish its own innocence. Nancock's money had passed into the Saint's hands, the Saint had got into the shop on the pretext of bringing the same package back, and the Saint had said: 'I know all about your business.' Simon could hear his own voice saying it. Osbett had made from that the one obvious deduction. Nancock had been a dead man when the Saint left the shop.

And to dump the body out of a Hirondel, with a Saint drawing pinned to it, was a no less obvious reply. Probably they had used one of his own authentic drawings, which had still been lying on the desk when he left them. He might have been doing any one of a dozen things that afternoon which would have left him without an alibi.

He had told Patricia that the next move was up to the ungodly, and it had come faster than he had expected. But it had also fulfilled all his other hopes.

'Claud,' he said softly, 'how would you like to make the haul of a lifetime?'

Teal sat and looked at him.

'I'll trade it,' said the Saint, 'for something that'll hardly give you any trouble at all. I was thinking of asking you to do it for me anyhow, in return for saving your life last night. There are certain reasons why I want to know the address where they have a telephone number Berkeley 3100. I can't get the information from the telephone company myself, but you can. I'll write it down for you.' He scribbled the figures on a piece of paper. 'Let me know where that number lives, and I'll give you your murderer and a lot more.'

Teal blinked suspiciously at the memorandum.

'What's this got to do with it?' he demanded.

'Nothing at all,' said the Saint untruthfully. 'So don't waste your time sleuthing around the place and trying to pick up clues. It's just some private business of my own. Is it a sale?'

The detective's eyes hardened.

'Then you do know something about all this!'

'Maybe I'm just guessing. I'll be able to tell you later. For once in your life, will you let me do you a good turn without trying to argue me out of it?'

Mr Teal fought with himself. And for no reason that he could afterwards justify to himself, he said grudgingly: 'All right. Where shall I find you?'

'I'll stay home till I hear from you.' Simon stood up, and suddenly remembered for the first time why he was there at all. He pulled a yellow package out of his pocket and dropped it in the detective's lap. 'Oh yes. And don't forget to take some of this belly balm as soon as you get the chance. It may help you to get back that sweet disposition you used to have, and stop you being so ready to think unkind thoughts about me.'

On the way home he had a few qualms about the ultimate

wisdom of that parting gesture, but his brain was too busy to dwell on them. The final patterns of the adventure were swinging into place with the regimented precision that always seemed to come to his episodes after the most chaotic beginnings, and the rhythm of it was like wine in his blood.

He had made Teal drive slowly past Cornwall House with him in a police car, in case there were any watchers waiting to see whether the attempt to saddle him with Nancock's murder would be successful. From Cannon Row police station, which is also a rear exit from Scotland Yard, he took a taxi back to his apartment, and stopped at a newsagent's on the way to buy a copy of a certain periodical in which he had hitherto taken little interest. By the time he got home it had given him the information he wanted.

Sam Outrell, the janitor, came out from behind the desk as he entered the lobby.

'Those men was here, sir, about two hours ago, like you said they would be,' he reported. 'Said you'd sent 'em to measure the winders for some new curtains. I let 'em in like you told me, an' they went through all the rooms.'

'Thanks a lot, Sam,' said the Saint, and rode up in the lift with another piece of his mosaic settled neatly into place.

He came into the living-room like a ray of sunshine and spun his hat over Patricia's head into a corner.

'Miracle Tea is on the air in about ten minutes,' he said, 'with a programme of chamber music. Could anything be more appropriate?'

Patricia looked up from her book.

'I suppose you've heard about our curtain measurers.'

'Sam Outrell told me. Do I get my diploma in advanced prophetics? After the party I had this morning, I knew it wouldn't be long before someone wanted to know what had happened to Comrade McGuire. Did you get him to Weybridge in good condition?'

'He didn't seem to like being locked in the trunk of the Daimler very much.'

The Saint grinned, and sat down at the desk to dismantle his automatic. He opened a drawer and fished out brushes and rags and cleaning oil.

'Well, I'm sure he preferred it to being nailed up in a coffin,' he said callously. 'And he's safe enough there with Orace on guard. They won't find him in the secret room, even if they do think of looking down there . . . Be a darling and start tuning in Radio Calvados, will you?'

For a short while she was busy with the dials of the radiogram; and then she came back and watched him in silence while he went over his gun with the loving care of a man who knew how much might hang on the light touch of a trigger.

'Something else has happened,' she said at last. 'And you're holding out on me.'

Simon squinted complacently up a barrel like burnished silver, and snapped the sliding jacket back into place. There was a dynamic exuberance in his repose that no artist could have captured, an aura of resilient swiftness poised on a knife-edge of balance that sent queer little feathery ripples up her spine.

'A lot more is going to happen,' he said. 'And then I'll tell you what a genius I am.'

She would have made some reply; but suddenly he fell into utter stillness, with a quick lift of his hand.

Out of the radio, which had been briefly silent, floated the opening bars of the *Spring Song*. And his watch told him that it was the start of the Miracle Tea Company's contribution to the load that the twentieth-century ether has to bear.

Shortly the music faded to form a background for a delicate Oxford accent informing the world that this melody fairly portrayed the sensations of a sufferer from indigestion after drinking a nice big cup of Miracle Tea. There followed an unusually nauseating dissertation on the manifold virtues of the product, and then a screeching slaughter of the Grand March from *Tannhäuser* played by the same string quartet. Patricia got up pallidly and poured herself out a drink.

'I suppose we do have to listen to this?' she said.

'Wait,' said the Saint.

The rendition came to its awful end, and the voice of Miracle Tea polluted the air once again.

'Before we continue our melody programme, we should like to read you a few extracts from our file of unsolicited letters from sufferers who have tried Miracle Tea. Tonight we are choosing letters one thousand and six, one thousand and fourteen, and one thousand and twenty-seven . . .'

The unsolicited letters were read with frightful enthusiasm, and the Saint listened with such intentness that he was obviously paying no attention to the transparently bogus effusions. He sat with the gun turning gently in his hands and a blindingly beatific smile creeping by hesitant degrees into the lines of his chiselled fighting mouth, so that the girl looked at him in uncomprehending wonderment.

'. . . And there, ladies and gentlemen, you have the opinions of the writers whose letters are numbered one thousand and six, one thousand and fourteen, and one thousand and twenty-seven in our files,' said the voice of the announcer, speaking with tedious deliberation. 'These good people cured themselves by drinking Miracle Tea. Let me urge you to buy Miracle Tea – tonight. Buy Miracle Tea! . . . And now the string quartet will play *Drink to Me Only*—'

There were two more short numbers and the broadcast was over. Simon switched off the radio as the next advertiser plunged into his act.

'Well,' said Patricia mutinously, 'are you going to talk?'

'You heard as much as I did.'

'I didn't hear anything worth listening to.'

'Nor did I. That's the whole point. There wasn't anything

worth listening to. I was looking for an elaborate code message. An expert like me can smell a code message as far off as a venerable gorgonzola – there's always a certain clumsiness in the phrasing. This was so simple that I nearly missed it.'

Patricia gazed into the depths of her glass.

She said: 'Those numbers—'

He nodded.

'The "thousand" part is just coverage. Six, fourteen, and twenty-seven are the operative words. They have to buy Miracle Tea – tonight. Nothing else in the programme means a thing. But according to that paper I brought in, Miracle Tea broadcasts every night of the week; and that means that any night the Big Shot wants to he can send out a call for the men he wants to come and get their orders or anything else that's waiting for them. It's the last perfect touch of organization. There's no connecting link that any detective on earth could trace between a broadcast and any particular person who listens to it. It means that even if one of his operatives should be under suspicion, the Big Shot can contact him without the shadow of a chance of transferring suspicion to himself. You could think of hundreds of ways of working a few numbers into an advertising spiel, and I'll bet they have a new one every time.'

She looked at him steadily.

'But you still haven't told me what—'

The telephone rang before he could answer.

Simon picked it up.

'Metropolitan Police Maternity Home,' he said.

'Teal speaking,' said a familiar voice with an unnecessarily pugnacious rasp in it. 'I've got the information you asked for about that phone number. The subscriber is Baron Inescu, 16 North Ashley Street, Berkeley Square. Now what was that information you were going to give me in return?'

The Saint unpuckered his lips from a long inaudible whistle.

'Okay, Claud,' he said, and the words lilted. 'I guess you've earned it. You can start right now. Rush one of your squads to Osbett's Drug Store, 909 Victoria Street – the place where you bought your Miracle Tea. Three other guys will be there shopping for Miracle Tea at any moment from now on. I can't give you any description of them, but there's one sure way to pick them out. Have one of your men go up to every-one who comes out of the shop and say: "Are you six, four-teen, or twenty-seven?" If the guy jumps halfway out of his skin, he's one of the birds you want. And see that you get his Miracle Tea as well!'

'Miracle Tea!' sizzled the detective, with such searing savagery that the Saint's ribs suddenly ached with awful intu-ition. 'I wish—' He stopped. Then he said: 'What's this about Miracle Tea? Are you trying to be funny?'

'I was never so serious in my life, Claud. Get those three guys, and get their packets of Miracle Tea. You'll find some-thing interesting in them.'

Teal's silence reeked of tormented indecision.

'If I thought—'

'But you never have, Claud. Don't spoil your record now. Just send that Squad out and tell 'em to hustle. You stay by the telephone, and I ought to be able to call you within an hour to collect the Big Shot.'

'But you haven't told me—' Again Teal's voice wailed off abruptly. Something like a stifled groan squeezed into the gap. He spoke again in a fevered gabble. 'All right all right I'll do it I can't stop now to argue but God help you—'

The connection clicked off even quicker than the sentence could finish.

Simon fitted his automatic into the spring clip holster under his coat, and stood up with a slow smile of ineffable impishness creeping up to his eyes.

12

16 North Ashley Street stood in the middle of one of those rows of crowded but discreetly opulent dwellings which provide the less squalid aspect of certain parts of Mayfair. Lights could be seen in some of the windows, indicating that someone was at home; but the Saint was not at all troubled about that. It was, in fact, a stroke of luck which he had hoped for.

He stepped up to the front door with the easy aplomb of an invited guest, arriving punctually for dinner, and put his finger on the bell. He looked as cool as if he had come straight off the ice, but under the rakish brim of his hat the hell-for-leather mischief still rollicked in his eyes. One hand rested idly between the lapels of his coat, as if he were adjusting his tie . . .

The door opened, exposing a large and overwhelming butler. The Saint's glance weighed him with expert penetration. Butlers are traditionally large and overwhelming, but they are apt to run large in the wrong places. This butler was large in the right places. His shoulders looked as wide as a wardrobe, and his biceps stretched tight wrinkles into the sleeves of his well-cut coat.

'Baron Inescu?' inquired the Saint pleasantly.

'The Baron is not—'

Simon smiled, and pressed the muzzle of his gun a little more firmly into the stomach in front of him.

The butler recoiled, and the Saint stepped after him. He pushed the door shut with his heel.

'Turn round.'

Tensely the butler started to obey. He had not quite finished the movement when Simon lifted his gun and jerked it crisply down again. The barrel made a sharp smacking sound on the back of the butler's bullet head; and the result, from an onlooker's point of view, was quite comical. The butler's legs bowed outwards, and he rolled down on to his face with a kind of resigned reluctance, and lay motionless.

For a second the Saint stood still, listening. But except for that single clear-cut smack there had been no disturbance, and the house remained quiet and peaceful.

Simon's eyes swept round the hall. In the corner close to the front door there was a door which looked as if it belonged to a coat cupboard. It was a coat cupboard. The Saint pocketed his gun for long enough to drag the butler across the marble floor and shove him in. He locked the door on him and took the key – he was a pretty accurate judge of the comparative toughness of gun-barrels and skulls, and he was confident that the butler would not be constituting a vital factor in anybody's life for some time.

He travelled past the other doors on the ground floor like a voyaging wraith, listening at each one of them, but he could hear no signs of life in any of the rooms beyond. From the head of the basement stairs he heard an undisturbed clink of dishes and mutter of voices which reassured him that the rest of the staff were strictly minding their own business.

In another moment he was on his way up the main staircase.

On the first wide landing he knew he was near his destination. Under one door there was a thin streak of light, and as he inched noiselessly up to it he heard the faint syncopated patter of a typewriter. Then the soft burr of a telephone interrupted it.

A voice said: 'Yes . . . Yes.' There was a slight pause; then:

'Vernon! Here is your copy for the special nine o'clock broad-cast. Take it down. "Why suffer from indigestion when relief is so cheap? Two cups will make your pains vanish – only two. Four cups will set you on the road to a complete cure – so why not take four? But after sixteen cups you will forget that indigestion ever existed. Think of that. Sixteen cups will make you feel ten years younger. Wouldn't *you* like to feel ten years younger in a few days? Buy Miracle Tea – tonight!" . . . Have you got that? . . . Splendid. Goodnight!'

The receiver rattled back. And the latch of the door rattled as Simon Templar closed it behind him.

The man at the desk spun round as if a snake had bitten him.

'Good evening, Baron,' said the Saint.

He stood there smiling, blithe and elegant and indescrib-ably dangerous.

The Baron stared frozenly back at him. He was a tall, clean-shaven man with dark hair greying at the temples, and he wore impeccable evening clothes with the distinction of an ambassador: but he had spoken on the telephone in a voice that was quite strangely out of keeping with his appearance. And the Saint's smile deepened with the joy of final certainty as he held his gun steadily aligned on the pearl stud in the centre of the Baron's snowy shirt-front.

The first leap of fear across the Baron's dark eyes turned into a convincing blaze of anger.

'What is the meaning of this?'

'At a rough guess, I should say about fifteen years – for you,' answered the Saint equably. 'It'll be quite a change from your usual environment, I'm afraid. That is, if I can judge by the pictures I've seen of you in the society papers. Baron Inescu driving off the first tee at St Andrew's – Baron Inescu at the wheel of his yacht at Cowes – Baron Inescu climbing into his new racing monoplane. I'm afraid you'll find the sporting facilities rather limited at Dartmoor, Baron . . . or would you rather I called you – Henry?'

The Baron sat very still.

'You know a great deal, Mr Templar.'

'Just about all I need to know, I think. I know you've been running the most efficient espionage organization that poor old Chief Inspector Teal has had to scratch his head over for a long time. I know that you had everything lined up so well that you might have got away with it for years if it hadn't been for one of those Acts of God that the insurance companies never want to underwrite. I told you I knew all about it this morning, but you didn't believe me. By the way, how does the jaw feel tonight?'

The other watched him unwinkingly.

'I'm afraid I did find it hard to believe you,' he said evenly. 'What else do you know?'

'I know all about your phoney broadcasts. And if it's of any interest to you, there will be a squad of large flat-footed bogey-men waiting for numbers six, fourteen, and twenty-seven when they stop by for their Miracle Tea . . . I know that instead of getting ready to pay me the tax I asked for, you tried to frame me for the murder of Nancock this afternoon and I resent that, Henry.'

'I apologize,' said the Baron suavely. 'You shall have your money tomorrow—'

The Saint shook his head, and his eyes were glacially blue.

'You had your chance, and you passed it up. I shall help myself to the money.' He saw the other's eyes shift fractionally to the safe in the corner, and laughed softly. 'Give me the keys, Henry.'

The Baron hesitated a moment before he moved.

Then he put his hand slowly into his trouser pocket and pulled out a bunch of keys on a platinum chain. He detached them and threw them on to the desk.

'You have the advantage, Mr Templar,' he said smoothly. 'I give you the keys because you could easily take them yourself if I refused. But you're very foolish. There are only about three thousand pounds in the safe. Why not be sensible and wait until the morning?'

'In the morning you'll be too busy trying to put up a defence at the police court to think about me,' said the Saint coldly.

He moved towards the desk; but he did not pick up the keys at once. His eyes strayed to the sheet of paper in the typewriter; and yet they did it in such a way that the Baron still knew that the first move he made would call shattering death out of the trim unwavering automatic.

Simon read:

In conjunction with numbers 4, 10, and 16 you will proceed at once to Cheltenham and establish close watch on Sir Roland Hale who is on holiday there. Within 24 hours you will send report on the method by which urgent War Office messages—

Simon's eyes returned to the Baron's face.

'What more evidence do you think Chief Inspector Teal will need?' he said.

'With a name like mine?' came the scornful answer. 'When I tell them that you held me at the point of a gun while you wrote that message on my typewriter—'

'I'm sure they'll be very polite,' said the Saint. 'Especially when they find that yours are the only fingerprints on the keys.'

'If you made me write it under compulsion—'

'And the orders in the packets of Miracle Tea which numbers six, fourteen, and twenty-seven are going to buy tonight came from the same machine.'

The Baron moistened his lips.

'Let us talk this over,' he said.

The Saint said: 'You talk.'

He picked up the telephone and dialled 'O'.

He said: 'I want to make a call to France – Radio Calvados.'

The Baron swallowed.

'Wait a minute,' he said desperately. 'I—'

'Incidentally,' said the Saint, 'there'll be a record that you had a call to Radio Calvados this evening, and probably on lots of other evenings as well. And I'm sure we shall find that Henry Osbett moustache of yours somewhere in the house – not to mention the beard you wore when you were dealing with Red McGuire. I suppose you needed some thug outside the organization in case you wanted to deal drastically with any of the ordinary members, but you picked the wrong man in Red. He doesn't like hot curling-irons.'

Inescu's fists clenched until the knuckles were bleached. His face had gone pale under its light tan.

The Saint's call came through.

'Mr Vernon, please,' he said.

He took out his cigarette case, opening it, and lighted a cigarette with the hand that held his gun, all in some astonishing manner that never allowed the muzzle to wander for an instant from its aim on the Baron's shirt stud; and then an unmistakable Oxford accent said: 'Hullo?'

'Vernon?' said the Saint, and his voice was so exactly like the voice affected by Mr Henry Osbett that its originator could scarcely believe his ears. 'I've got to make a change in that copy I just gave you. Make it read like this: "They say there is safety in numbers. In that case, you can't go wrong with Miracle Tea. There are many numbers in our files, but they all praise Miracle Tea. *Every number has the same message.* Why should you be left out? *All of you*, buy Miracle Tea – tonight!" ... Have you got it? ... Good. See that it goes in without fail.'

Simon pressed the spring bracket down with his thumb, still holding the microphone.

The Baron's stare was wide and stupefied.

'You're mad!' he said hoarsely. 'You're throwing away a fortune—'

Simon laughed at him, and lifted the microphone to his ear again. He dialled the number of Scotland Yard.

'Give me Chief Inspector Teal,' he said. 'The Saint calling.'

There was some delay on the switchboard.

The Saint looked at Baron Inescu and said: 'There's one thing you forget, Baron. I like money as much as anybody else, and I use more of it than most people. But that's a side line. I also deliver justice. When you get to Dartmoor, you'll meet some other men that I've sent there. Ask them about it. And then you in your turn will be able to tell the same story.'

The voice of Chief Inspector Teal blared short-windedly in his ear.

'Yes?'

'Oh, Claud? How's the old tum-tum getting— . . . All right, if it's a sore subject; but I wondered— . . . Yes, of course I have. Just a minute. Did you get six, fourteen, and twenty-seven?' Simon listened, and the contentment ripened on his face. 'Well, didn't I tell you? And now you can have some more for the bag. At any time after nine o'clock there's going to be a perfect stampede of blokes asking for Miracle Tea, so you can send your squad back for more. They'd better take over the shop and grab everyone who tries to buy Miracle Tea. And while they're doing that I've got the Big Shot waiting for you. Come and get him. The address is— Excuse me.'

The Saint had the telephone in one hand and a gun in the other, and it seemed impossible for him to have done it, but a narrow-bladed ivory-hilted knife stuck quivering in the desk half an inch from the Baron's fingers as they slid towards a concealed bell. And the Saint went on talking as if nothing had happened.

'Sixteen North Ashley Street, Berkeley Square; and the name is Inescu . . . Yes, isn't that a coincidence? But there's all the evidence you'll need to make you happy, so I don't see why you should complain. Come along over and I'll show you.'

'I'll send someone over,' Teal said stiffly. 'And thanks very much.'

Simon frowned a little.

'Why send someone?' he objected. 'I thought—'

'Because I'm busy!' came a tortured howl that nearly shattered the receiver. 'I can't leave the office just now. I – I'll have to send someone.'

The Saint's eyebrows slowly lifted.

'But *why*?' he persisted.

Eventually Mr Teal told him.

Simon Templar sat on the desk in Chief Inspector Teal's office a fortnight later. The police court proceedings had just concluded after a remand, and Baron Inescu, *alias* Henry Osbett, had been committed for trial in company with some three dozen smaller cogs in his machine. The report was in the evening paper which Simon had bought, and he pointed it out to Teal accusingly.

'At least you could have rung me up and thanked me again for making you look like a great detective,' he said.

Mr Teal stripteased a slice of chewing gum and fed it into his mouth. 'I'm sorry,' he said. 'I meant to do it, but there was a lot of clearing-up work to do on the case. Anyway, it's out of my hands now, and the Public Prosecutor is pretty satisfied. It's a pity there wasn't enough direct evidence to charge Inescu with the murder of Nancock, but we haven't done badly.'

'You're looking pretty cheerful,' said the Saint.

This was true. Mr Teal's rosy face had a fresh pink glow, and his cherubic blue eyes were clear and bright under his sleepily drooping lids.

'I'm feeling better,' he said. 'You know, that's the thing that really beats me about this case. Inescu could have made a fortune out of Miracle Tea without ever going in for espionage—'

The Saint's mouth fell open.

'You don't mean to say—' he ejaculated, and couldn't go on. He said: 'But I thought you were ready to chew the blood out of everyone who had anything to do with Miracle Tea, if you could only have got away from—'

'I know it was rather drastic,' Teal said sheepishly. 'But it did the trick. Do you know, I haven't had a single attack of indigestion since I took that packet; and I even had roast pork for dinner last night!'

Simon Templar drew a long deep breath and closed his eyes. There were times when even he felt that he was standing on holy ground.

The Invisible Millionaire

I

The girl's eyes caught Simon Templar as he entered the room, ducking his head instinctively to pass under the low lintel of the door; and they followed him steadily across to the bar. They were blue eyes with long lashes, and the face to which they belonged was pretty without any distinctive feature, crowned with curly yellow hair. And besides anything else, the eyes held an indefinable hint of strain.

Simon knew all this without looking directly at her. But he had singled her out at once from the double handful of riverside weekenders who crowded the small bar-room as the most probable writer of the letter which he still carried in his pocket – the letter which had brought him out to the Bell that Sunday evening on what anyone with a less incorrigibly optimistic flair for adventure would have branded from the start as a fool's errand. She was the only girl in the place who seemed to be unattached; there was no positive reason why the writer of that letter should have been unattached, but it seemed likely that she would be. Also she was the best looker in a by no means repulsive crowd; and that was simply no clue at all except to Simon Templar's own unshakeable faith in his guardian angel, who had never thrown any other kind of damsel in distress into his buccaneering path.

But she was still looking at him. And even though he couldn't help knowing that women often looked at him with more than ordinary interest, it was not usually done quite so fixedly. His hopes rose a notch, tentatively; but it was her turn to make the next move. He had done all that had been asked of him when he walked in there punctually on the stroke of eight.

He leaned on the counter, with his wide shoulders seeming to take up half the length of the bar, and ordered a pint of beer for himself and a bottle of Vat 69 for Hoppy Uniatz, who trailed up thirstily at his heels. With the tankard in his hands, he waited for one of those inevitable moments when all the customers had paused for breath at the same time.

'Anyone leave a message for me?' he asked.

His voice was quiet and casual, but just clear enough for everyone in the room to hear. Whoever had sent for him, unless it was merely some pointless practical joker, should need no more confirmation than that . . . He hoped it would be the girl with the blue troubled eyes. He had a weakness for girls with eyes of that shade, the same colour as his own.

The barman shook his head.

'No, sir. I haven't had any messages.'

Simon went on gazing at him reflectively, and the barman misinterpreted his expression. His mouth broadened and said: 'That's all right, sir, I'd know if there was anything for you.'

Simon's fine brows lifted puzzledly.

'I've seen your picture often enough, sir. I suppose you could call me one of your fans. You're the Saint, aren't you?'

The Saint smiled slowly.

'You don't look frightened.'

'I never had the chance to be a rich racketeer, like the people you're always getting after. Gosh, though, I've had a kick out of some of the things you've done to 'em! And the way you're always putting it over on the police – I'll bet they'd give anything for an excuse to lock you up . . .'

Simon was aware that the general buzz of conversation, after starting to pick up again, had died a second time and was staying dead. His spine itched with the feel of stares fastening on his back. And at the same time the barman became feverishly conscious of the audience which had been captured by his runaway enthusiasm. He began to stammer, turned red, and plunged confusedly away to obliterate himself in some unnecessary fussing over the shelves of bottles behind him.

The Saint grinned with his eyes only, and turned tranquilly round to lean his back against the bar and face the room.

The collected stares hastily unpinned themselves and the voices got going again; but Simon was as oblivious of those events as he would have been if the rubber-necking had continued. At that moment his mind was capable of absorbing only one fearful and calamitous realization. He had turned to see whether the girl with the fair curly hair and the blue eyes had also been listening, and whether she needed any more encouragement to announce herself. And the girl was gone.

She must have got up and gone out even in the short time that the barman had been talking. The Saint's glance swept on to identify the other faces in the room – faces that he had noted and automatically catalogued as he came in. They were all the same, but her face was not one of them. There was an empty glass beside her chair, and the chair itself was already being taken by a dark slender girl who had just entered.

Interest lighted the Saint's eyes again as he saw her, awakened instantly as he appreciated the subtle perfection of the sculptured cascade of her brown hair, crystallized as he approved the contours of her slim yet mature figure revealed by a simple flowered cotton dress. Then he saw her face for the first time, and held his tankard a shade tighter. Here, indeed, was something to call beautiful, something on which the word could be used without hesitation even under his most dispassionate scrutiny. She was like – 'Peaches in autumn,' he said to himself, seeing the fresh bloom of her cheeks against the russet shades of her hair. She raised her head with a smile, and his blood sang carillons. Perhaps after all . . .

And then he saw that she was smiling and speaking to an ordinarily good-looking young man in a striped blazer who stood possessively over her; and inward laughter overtook him before he could feel the sourness of disappointment.

He loosened one elbow from the bar to run a hand through his dark hair, and his eyes twinkled at Mr Uniatz.

'Oh, well, Hoppy,' he said. 'It looks as if we can still be taken for a ride, even at our age.'

Mr Uniatz blinked at him. Even in isolation, the face that Nature had planted on top of Mr Uniatz's bull neck could never have been mistaken for that of a matinée idol with an inclination towards intellectual pursuits and the cultivation of the soul; but when viewed in exaggerating contrast with the tanned piratical chiselling of the Saint's features it had a grotesqueness that was sometimes completely shattering to those who beheld it for the first time. To compare it with the face of a gorilla which had been in violent contact with a variety of blunt instruments during its formative years would be risking the justifiable resentment of any gorilla which had been in violent contact with a variety of blunt instruments during its formative years. The best that can be said of it is that it contained in mauled and primitive form all the usual organs of sight, smell, hearing, and ingestion, and prayerfully let it go at that. And yet it must also be said that Simon Templar had come to regard it with a fondness which even its mother could scarcely have shared. He watched it with good-humoured patience, waiting for it to answer.

'I dunno, boss,' said Mr Uniatz.

He had not thought over the point very deeply. Simon knew this, because when Mr Uniatz was thinking his face screwed itself into even more frightful contortions than were stamped on it in repose. Thinking of any kind was an activity which caused Mr Uniatz excruciating pain. On this occasion he had clearly escaped much suffering because his mind – if such a word can be used without blasphemy in connection with any of Mr Uniatz's cerebral processes – had been elsewhere.

'Something is bothering you, Hoppy,' said the Saint. 'Don't keep it to yourself, or your head will start aching.'

'Boss,' said Mr Uniatz gratefully, 'do I have to drink dis wit' de paper on?'

He held up the parcel he was nursing.

Simon looked at him blankly for a moment, and then felt weak in the middle.

'Of course not,' he said. 'They only wrapped it up because they thought we were going to take it home. They haven't got to know you yet, that's all.'

An expression of sublime relief spread over Mr Uniatz's homely countenance as he pawed off the wrapping paper from the bottle of Vat 69. He pulled out the cork, placed the neck of the bottle in his mouth, and tilted his head back. The soothing fluid flowed in a cooling stream down his asbestos gullet. All his anxieties were at rest.

For the Saint, consolation was not quite so easy. He finished his tankard and pushed it across the bar for a refill. While he was waiting for it to come back, he pulled out of his pocket and read over again the note that had brought him there. It was on a plain sheet of good notepaper, with no address.

Dear Saint,

　I'm not going to write a long letter, because if you aren't going to believe me it won't make any difference how many pages I write.

I'm only writing to you at all because I'm utterly desperate. How can I put it in the baldest possible way? I'm being
forced into making myself an accomplice in one of the
most gigantic frauds that can ever have been attempted,
and I can't go to the police for the same reason that I'm
being forced to help.

There you are. It's no use writing any more. If you can
be at the Bell at Hurley at eight o'clock on Sunday evening
I'll see you and tell you everything. If I can only talk to you
for half an hour, I know I can make you believe me.

Please, for God's sake, at least let me talk to you.

My name is

                                                    Nora Prescott

Nothing there to encourage too many hopes in the imagination of any one whose mail was as regularly cluttered with
crank letters as the Saint's; and yet the handwriting looked
neat and sensible, and the brief blunt phrasing had somehow
carried more conviction than a ream of protestations. All the
rest had been hunch – that supernatural affinity for the dark
trail of ungodliness which had pitchforked him into the
middle of more brews of mischief than any four other free-
booters of his day.

And for once the hunch had been wrong. If only it hadn't
been for that humdrumly handsome excrescence in the
striped blazer . . .

Simon looked up again for another tantalizing eyeful of
the dark slender girl.

He was just in time to get a parting glimpse of her back as
she made her way to the door, with the striped blazer hovering over her like a motherly hen. Then she was gone; and
everyone else in the bar suddenly looked nondescript and
obnoxious.

The Saint sighed.

He took a deep draught of his beer, and turned back to Hoppy Uniatz. The neck of the bottle was still firmly clamped in Hoppy's mouth, and there was no evidence to show that it had ever been detached therefrom since it was first inserted. His Adam's apple throbbed up and down with the regularity of a slow pulse. The angle of the bottle indicated that at least a pint of its contents had already reached his interior.

Simon gazed at him with reverence.

'You know, Hoppy,' he remarked, 'when you die we shan't even have to embalm you. We'll just put you straight into a glass case, and you'll keep for years.'

The other customers had finally returned to their own business, except for a few who were innocently watching for Mr Uniatz to stiffen and fall backwards; and the talkative young barman edged up again with a show of wiping off the bar.

'Nothing much here to interest you tonight, sir, is there?' he began chattily.

'There was,' said the Saint ruefully. 'But she went home.'

'You mean the dark young lady, sir?'

'Who else?'

The man nodded knowingly.

'You ought to come here more often, sir. I've often seen her in here alone. Miss Rosemary Chase, that is. Her father's Mr Marvin Chase, the millionaire. He just took the New Manor for the season. Had a nasty motor accident only a week ago . . .'

Simon let him go on talking, without paying much attention. The dark girl's name wasn't Nora Prescott, anyhow. That seemed to be the only important item of information – and with it went the last of his hopes. The clock over the bar crept on to twenty minutes past eight. If the girl who had written to him had been as desperate as she said, she wouldn't come as late as that – she'd have been waiting there when he arrived. The girl with the strained blue eyes had probably been suffering from nothing worse than biliousness or thwarted love. Rosemary Chase had happened merely by accident. The real writer of the letter was almost certainly some fat and frowsy female among those he had passed over without a second thought, who was doubtless still gloating over him from some obscure corner, gorging herself with the spectacle of her inhibition's hero in the flesh.

A hand grasped his elbow, turning him round, and a lightly accented voice said: 'Why, Mr Templar, what are you looking so sad about?'

The Saint's smile kindled as he turned.

'Giulio,' he said, 'if I could be sure that keeping a pub would make anyone as cheerful as you, I'd go right out and buy a pub.'

Giulio Trapani beamed at him teasingly.

'Why should you need anything to make you cheerful? You are young, strong, handsome, rich – and famous. Or perhaps you are only waiting for a new romance?'

'Giulio,' said the Saint, 'that's a very sore point, at the moment.'

'Ah! Perhaps you are waiting for a love-letter which has not arrived?'

The Saint straightened up with a jerk. All at once he laughed. Half incredulous sunshine smashed through his despondency, lighted up his face. He extended his palm.

'You old son-of-a-gun! Give!'

The landlord brought his left hand from behind his back, holding an envelope. Simon grabbed it and ripped it open. He recognized the handwriting at a glance. The note was on a sheet of hotel paper.

Thank God you came. But I daren't be seen speaking to you after the barman recognized you.

Go down to the lock and walk up the towpath. Not very far along on the left there's a boathouse with green doors. I'll wait for you there. Hurry.

The Saint raised his eyes, and sapphires danced in them.

'Who gave you this, Giulio?'

'Nobody. It was lying on the floor outside when I came through. You saw the envelope – *Deliver at once to Mr Templar in the bar*. So that's what I do. Is it what you were waiting for?'

Simon stuffed the note into his pocket, and nodded. He drained his tankard.

'This is the romance you were talking about – maybe,' he said. 'I'll tell you about it later. Save some dinner for me. I'll be back.' He clapped Trapani on the shoulder and swung round newly awakened, joyously alive again. Perhaps, in spite of everything, there was still adventure to come . . . 'Let's go, Hoppy!'

He took hold of Mr Uniatz's bottle and pulled it down. Hoppy came upright after it with a plaintive gasp.

'Chees, boss—'

'Have you no soul?' demanded the Saint sternly, as he herded him out of the door. 'We have a date with a damsel in distress. The moon will be mirrored in her beautiful eyes, and she will pant out a story while we fan the gnats away from her snowy brow. Sinister eggs are being hatched behind the scenes. There will be villains and mayhem and perhaps even moider . . .'

He went on talking lyrical nonsense as he set a brisk pace down the lane towards the river; but when they reached the towpath even he had dried up. Mr Uniatz was an unresponsive audience, and Simon found that some of the things he was saying in jest were oddly close to the truth that he believed. After all, such fantastic things had happened to him before . . .

He didn't fully understand the change in himself as he turned off along the river bank beside the dark shimmering sleekness of the water. The ingrained flippancy was still with him – he could feel it like a translucent film over his mind – but underneath it he was all open and expectant, a receptive void in which anything might take shape. And something was beginning to take shape there – something still so nebulous and formless that it eluded any conscious survey, and yet something as inescapably real as a promise of thunder in the air. It was as if the hunch that had brought him out to the Bell in the first place had leapt up from a whisper to a great shout; and yet everything was silent. Far away, to his sensitive ears, there was the ghostly hum of cars on the Maidenhead road; close by, the sibilant lap of the river, the lisp of leaves, the stertorous breathing and elephantine footfalls of Mr Uniatz; but those things were only phases of the stillness that was everywhere. Everything in the world was quiet, even his own nerves, and they were almost too quiet. And ahead of him, presently, loomed the shape of a building like a boathouse. His pencil flashlight stabbed out for a second and caught the front of it. It had green doors.

Quietly, he said: 'Nora.'

There was no answer, no hint of movement anywhere. And he didn't know why, but in the same quiet way his right hand slid up to his shoulder rig and loosened the automatic in the spring clip under his arm.

He covered the last two yards in absolute silence, put his hand to the knob of the door, and drew it back quickly as his fingers slid on a sticky dampness. It was queer, he thought even then, even as his left hand angled the flashlight down, that it should have happened just like that, when everything in him was tuned and waiting for it, without knowing what it was waiting for. Blood – on the door.

2

Simon stood for a moment, and his nerves seemed to grow even calmer and colder under an edge of sharp bitterness.

Then he grasped the doorknob again, turned it, and went in. The inside of the building was pitch dark. His torch needled the blackness with a thin jet of light that splashed dim reflections from the glossy varnish on a couple of punts and an electric canoe. Somehow he was quite sure what he would find, so sure that the certainty chilled off any rise of emotion. He knew what it must be; the only question was, who? Perhaps even that was not such a question. He was never quite sure about that. A hunch that had almost missed its mark had become stark reality with a suddenness that disjointed the normal co-ordinates of time and space: it was as if instead of discovering things, he was trying to remember things he had known before and had forgotten. But he saw her at last, almost tucked under the shadow of the electric canoe, lying on her side as if she were asleep.

He stepped over and bent his light steadily on her face, and knew then that he had been right. It was the girl with the troubled blue eyes. Her eyes were open now, only they were not troubled any more. The Saint stood and looked down at her. He had been almost sure when he saw the curly yellow hair. But she had been wearing a white blouse when he saw her last, and now there was a splotchy crimson pattern on the front of it. The pattern glistened as he looked at it.

Beside him, there was a noise like an asthmatic foghorn loosening up for a burst of song.

'Boss,' began Mr Uniatz.

'Shut up.'

The Saint's voice was hardly more than a whisper, but it cut like a razorblade. It cut Hoppy's introduction cleanly off from whatever he had been going to say; and at the same moment as he spoke Simon switched off his torch, so that it was as if the same tenuous whisper had sliced off even the ray of light, leaving nothing around them but blackness and silence.

Motionless in the dark, the Saint quested for any betraying breath of sound. To his tautened eardrums, sensitive as a wild animal's, the hushed murmurs of the night outside were still an audible background against which the slightest stealthy movement even at a considerable distance would have stood out like a bugle call. But he heard nothing then, though he waited for several seconds in uncanny stillness.

He switched on the torch again.

'Okay, Hoppy,' he said. 'Sorry to interrupt you, but that blood was so fresh that I wondered if someone mightn't still be around.'

'Boss,' said Mr Uniatz aggrievedly, 'I was doin' fine when ya stopped me.'

'Never mind,' said the Saint consolingly. 'You can go ahead now. Take a deep breath and start again.'

He was still partly listening for something else, wondering if even then the murderer might still be within range.

'It ain't no use now,' said Mr Uniatz dolefully.

'Are you going to get temperamental on me?' Simon demanded sufferingly. 'Because if so—'

Mr Uniatz shook his head.

'It ain't dat, boss. But you gotta start wit' a full bottle.'

Simon focused him through a kind of fog. In an obscure

and apparently irrelevant sort of way, he became aware that
Hoppy was still clinging to the bottle of Vat 69 with which he
he been irrigating his tonsils at the Bell, and that he was holding it up against the beam of the flashlight as though brooding over the level of the liquid left in it. The Saint clutched at
the buttresses of his mind.

'What in the name of Adam's grandfather,' he said, 'are
you talking about?'

'Well, boss, dis is an idea I get out of a book. De guy walks
in a saloon, he buys a bottle of Scotch, he pulls de cork, an'
he drinks de whole bottle straight down wit'out stopping. So
I was tryin' de same t'ing back in de pub, an' I was doin' fine
when ya stopped me. Lookit, I ain't left more 'n two-t'ree
swallows. But it ain't no use goin' on now,' explained Mr
Uniatz, working back to the core of his grievance. 'You gotta
start wit' a full bottle.'

Nothing but years of training and self-discipline gave
Simon Templar the strength to recover his sanity.

'Next time, you'd better take the bottle away somewhere
and lock yourself up with it,' he said, with terrific moder-
ation. 'Just for the moment, since we haven't got another
bottle, is there any danger of your noticing that someone has
been murdered around here?'

'Yeah,' said Mr Uniatz brightly. 'De wren.'

Having contributed his share of illumination, he relapsed
into benevolent silence. This, his expectant self-effacement
appeared to suggest, was not his affair. It appeared to be
something which required thinking about; and Thinking was
a job for which the Saint possessed an obviously supernatural aptitude which Mr Uniatz had come to lean upon with a
childlike faith that was very much akin to worship.

The Saint was thinking. He was thinking with a level and
passionless detachment that surprised even himself. The girl
was dead. He had seen plenty of men killed before,

sometimes horribly; but only one other woman. Yet that must not make any difference. Nora Prescott had never meant anything to him: he would never even have recognized her voice. Other women of whom he knew just as little were dying everywhere, in one way or another, every time he breathed; and he could think about it without the slightest feeling. Nora Prescott was just another name in the world's long roll of undistinguished dead.

But she was someone who had asked him for help, who had perhaps died because of what she had wanted to tell him. She hadn't been just another twittering fluffhead going into hysterics over a mouse. She really had known something – something that was dangerous enough for someone else to commit murder rather than have it revealed.

'*One of the most gigantic frauds that can ever have been attempted . . .*'

The only phrase out of her letter which gave any information at all came into his head again, not as a merely provocative combination of words, but with some of the clean-cut clarity of a sober statement of fact. And yet the more he considered it, the closer it came to clarifying precisely nothing.

And he was still half listening for a noise that it seemed as if he ought to have heard. The expectation was a subtle nagging at the back of his mind, the fidget for attention of a thought that still hadn't found conscious shape.

His torch panned once more around the interior of the building. It was a plain wooden structure, hardly more than three walls and a pair of double doors which formed the fourth, just comfortably roomy for the three boats which it contained. There was a small window on each side, so neglected as to be almost opaque. Overhead, his light went straight up to the bare rafters which supported the shingle roof. There was no place in it for anybody to hide except under one of the boats; and his light probed along the floor and eliminated that possibility.

The knife lay on the floor near the girl's knees – an ordinary cheap kitchen knife, but pointed and sharp enough for what it had had to do. There was a smear of blood on the handle; and some of it must have gone on the killer's hand, or more probably on his glove, and in that way been left on the doorknob. From the stains and rents on the front of the girl's blouse, the murderer must have struck two or three times; but if he was strong he could have held her throat while he did it, and there need have been no noise.

'Efficient enough,' the Saint summed it up aloud, 'for a rush job.'

He was thinking: 'It must have been a rush job, because he couldn't have known she was going to meet me here until after she'd written that note at the Bell. Probably she didn't even know it herself until then. Did he see the note? Doesn't seem possible. He could have followed her. Then he must have had the knife on him already. Not an ordinary sort of knife to carry about with you. Then he must have known he was going to use it before he started out. Unless it was here in the boathouse and he just grabbed it up. No reason why a knife like that should be lying about in a place like this. Bit too convenient. Well, so he knew she'd got in touch with me, and he'd made up his mind to kill her. Then why not kill her before she even got to the Bell? She might have talked to me there, and he couldn't have stopped her – could he? Was he betting that she wouldn't risk talking to me in public? He could have been. Good psychology, but the hell of a nerve to bet on it. Did he find out she'd written to me? Then I'd probably still have the letter. If I found her murdered, he'd expect me to go to the police with it. Dangerous. And he knew I'd find her. Then why—'

The Saint felt something like an inward explosion as he

realized what his thoughts were leading to. He knew then why half of his brain had never ceased to listen – searching for what intuition had scented faster than reason.

Goose-pimples crawled up his spine on to the back of his neck.

And at the same moment he heard the sound.

It was nothing that any other man might have heard at all. Only the gritting of a few tiny specks of gravel between a stealthy shoe sole and the board stage outside. But it was what every nerve in his body had unwittingly been keyed for ever since he had seen the dead girl at his feet. It was what he inevitably had to hear, after everything else that had happened. It spun him round like a jerk of the string wound round a top.

He was in the act of turning when the gun spoke.

Its bark was curt and flat and left an impression of having been curiously thin, though his ears rang with it afterwards. The bullet zipped past his ear like a hungry mosquito; and from the hard fierce note that it hummed he knew that if he had not been starting to turn at the very instant when it was fired it would have struck him squarely in the head. Pieces of shattered glass rattled on the floor.

Lights smashed into his eyes as he whirled at the door, and a clear clipped voice snapped at him: 'Drop that gun! You haven't got a chance!'

The light beam beat on him with blinding intensity from the lens of a pocket searchlight that completely swallowed up the slim ray of his own torch. He knew that he hadn't a chance. He could have thrown bullets by guesswork; but to the man behind the glare he was a target on which patterns could be punched out.

Slowly his fingers opened off the big Luger, and it plonked on the boards at his feet.

His hand swept across and bent down the barrel of the

automatic which Mr Uniatz had whipped out like lightning when the first shot crashed between them.

'You too, Hoppy,' he said resignedly. 'All that Scotch will run away if they make a hole in you now.'

'Back away,' came the next order.

Simon obeyed.

The voice said: 'Go on, Rosemary – pick up the guns. I'll keep 'em covered.'

A girl came forward into the light. It was the dark slender girl whose quiet loveliness had unsteadied Simon's breath at the Bell.

3

She bent over and collected the two guns by the butts, holding them aimed at Simon and Hoppy, not timidly, but with a certain stiffness which told the Saint's expert eye the feel of them was unfamiliar. She moved backwards and disappeared again behind the light.

'Do you mind,' asked the Saint ceremoniously, 'if I smoke?'

'I don't care.' The clipped voice, he realized now, could only have belonged to the young man in the striped blazer. 'But don't try to start anything, or I'll let you have it. Go on back in there.'

The Saint didn't move at once. He took out his cigarette case first, opened it, and selected a cigarette. The case came from his breast pocket, but he put it back in the pocket at his hip, slowly and deliberately and holding it lightly, so that his hand was never completely out of sight and a nervous man would have no cause to be alarmed at the movement. He had another gun in that pocket, a light but beautifully balanced Walther; but for the time being he left it there, sliding the cigarette case in behind it and bringing his hand back empty to get out his lighter.

'I'm afraid we weren't expecting to be held up in a place like this,' he remarked apologetically. 'So we left the family jools at home. If you'd only let us know—'

'Don't be funny. If you don't want to be turned over to the police you'd better let *me* know what you're doing here.'

The Saint's brows shifted a fraction of an inch.

'I don't see what difference it makes to you, brother,' he said slowly. 'But if you're really interested, we were just taking a stroll in the moonlight to work up an appetite for dinner, and we happened to see the door of this place open—'

'So that's why you both had to pull out guns when you heard us.'

'My dear bloke,' Simon argued reasonably, 'what do you expect anyone to do when you creep up behind them and start sending bullets whistling round their heads?'

There was a moment's silence.

The girl gasped.

The man spluttered: 'Good God you've got a nerve! After you blazed away at us like that – why, you might have killed one of us!'

The Saint's eyes strained uselessly to pierce beyond the light. There was an odd hollow feeling inside him, making his frown unnaturally rigid.

Something was going wrong. Something was going as immortally cockeyed as it was possible to go. It was taking him a perceptible space of time to grope for a bearing in the reeling void. Somewhere the scenario had gone as paralysingly off the rails as if a Wagnerian soprano had bounced into a hotcha dance routine in the middle of *Tristan*.

'Look,' he said. 'Let's be quite clear about this. Is your story going to be that you thought I took a shot at you?'

'I don't have to think,' retorted the other. 'I heard the bullet whizz past my head. Go on – get back in that boathouse.'

Simon dawdled back.

His brain felt as if it was steaming. The voice behind the light, now that he was analysing its undertones, had a tense unsophistication that didn't belong in the script at all. And the answers it gave were all wrong. Simon had had it all figured out one ghostly instant before it began to happen. The murderer hadn't just killed Nora Prescott and faded away, of course. He had killed her and waited outside, knowing that Simon Templar must find her in a few minutes, knowing that that would be his best chance to kill the Saint as well and silence whatever the Saint knew already and recover the letter. That much was so obvious that he must have been asleep not to have seen it from the moment when his eyes fell on the dead girl. Well, he had seen it now. And yet it wasn't clicking. The dialogue was all there, and yet every syllable was striking a false note.

And he was back inside the boathouse, as far as he could go, with the square bow of a punt against his calves and Hoppy beside him.

The man's voice said: 'Turn a light on, Rosemary.'

The girl came round and found a switch. Light broke out from a naked bulb that hung by a length of flex from one of the rafters, and the young man in the striped blazer flicked off his torch.

'Now,' he started to say, 'we'll—'

'*Jim!*'

The girl didn't quite scream, but her voice tightened and rose to within a semitone of it. She backed against the wall, one hand to her mouth, with her face and her eyes dilated with horror. The man began to turn towards her, and then followed her wide and frozen stare. The muzzle of the gun he was holding swung slack from its aim on the Saint's chest as he did so; it was an error that in some situations would have cost him his life, but Simon let him live. The Saint's head was whirling with too many questions, just then, to have any interest in the opportunity. He was looking at the gun which the girl was still holding, and recognizing it as the property of Mr Uniatz.

'It's Nora,' she gasped. 'She's—'

He saw her gather herself with an effort, force herself to go forward and kneel beside the body. Then he stopped watching her. His eyes went to the gun that was still wavering in the young man's hand—

'Jim,' said the girl brokenly, 'she's dead!'

The man took a half step towards the Saint.

'You swine!' he grunted. 'You killed her—'

'Go on,' said the Saint gently. 'And then I took a pot at you. So you fired back in self-defence, and just happened to kill us. It'll make a swell story even if it isn't a very new one, and you'll find yourself quite a hero. But why all the play-acting for our benefit? We know the gag.'

There was complete blankness behind the anger in the other's eyes. And all at once the Saint's somersaulting cosmos stabilized itself with a jolt – upside down, but solid.

He was looking at the gun which was pointing at his chest, and realizing that it was his own Luger.

And the girl had got Hoppy's gun. And there was no other artillery in sight.

The arithmetic of it smacked him between the eyes and made him dizzy. Of course there was an excuse for him, in the shape of the first shot and the bullet that had gone snarling past his ear. But even with all that, for him out of all people in the world, at his time of life—

'Run up to the house and call the police, Rosemary,' said the striped blazer in a brittle bark.

'Wait a minute,' said the Saint.

His brain was not fogged any longer. It was turning over as swiftly and smoothly as a hair-balanced flywheel, registering every item with the mechanical infallibility of an adding machine. His nerves were tingling.

His glance whipped from side to side. He was standing again approximately where he had been when the shot cracked out, but facing the opposite way. On his right quarter was the window that had been broken, with the shards of glass scattered on the floor below it – he ought to have understood everything when he heard them hit the floor. Turning the other way, he saw that the line from the window to himself continued on through the open door.

He took a long drag on his cigarette.

'It kind of spoils the scene,' he said quietly, 'but I'm afraid we've both been making the same mistake. You thought I fired at you—'

'I don't have—'

'All right, you don't have to think. You heard the bullet whizz past your head. You said that before. You're certain I shot at you. Okay. Well, I was just as certain that you shot at me. But I know now I was wrong. You never had a gun until you got mine. It was that shot that let you bluff me. I'd heard the bullet go past *my* head, and so it never occurred to me that you were bluffing. But we were both wrong. The shot came through that window – it just missed me, went on out through the door, and just missed you. And somebody else fired it!'

The other's face was stupid with stubborn incredulity.

'Who fired it?'

'The murderer.'

'That means you,' retorted the young man flatly. 'Hell, I don't want to listen to you. You see if you can make the police believe you. Go on and call them, Rosemary. I can take care of these two.'

The girl hesitated.

'But, Jim—'

'Don't worry about me, darling. I'll be all right. If either of these two washouts tries to get funny, I'll give him plenty to think about.'

The Saint's eyes were narrowing.

'You lace-pantie'd bladder of hot air,' he said in a cold even voice that seared like vitriol. 'It isn't your fault if God didn't give you a brain, but he did give you eyes. Why don't you use them? I say the shot was fired from outside, and you can see for yourself where the broken window-pane fell. Look at it. It's all on the floor in here. If you can tell me how I could shoot at you in the doorway and break a window behind me, and make the broken glass fall inwards, I'll pay for your next marcel wave. Look at it, nitwit—'

The young man looked.

He had been working closer to the Saint, with his free fist clenched and his face flushed with wrath, since the Saint's first sizzling insult smoked under his skin. But he looked. Somehow, he had to do that. He was less than five feet away when his eyes shifted. And it was then that Simon jumped him.

The Saint's lean body seemed to lengthen and swoop across the intervening space. His left hand grabbed the Luger, bent the wrist behind it agonizingly inwards, while the heel of his open right hand settled under the other's chin. The gun came free; and the Saint's right arm straightened jarringly and sent the young man staggering back.

Simon reversed the automatic with a deft flip and held it on him. Even while he was making his spring, out of the corner of his eye he had seen Hoppy Uniatz flash away from him with an electrifying acceleration that would have stunned anyone who had misguidedly judged Mr Uniatz on the speed of his intellectual reactions; now he glanced briefly aside and saw that Hoppy was holding his gun again and keeping the girl pinioned with one arm.

'Okay, Hoppy,' he said. 'Keep your Betsy and let her go. She's going to call the police for us.'

Hoppy released her, but the girl did not move. She stood against the wall, rubbing slim wrists that had been bruised by Mr Uniatz's untempered energy, looking from Simon to the striped blazer, with scared desperate eyes.

'Go ahead,' said the Saint impatiently. 'I won't damage little Jimmy unless he makes trouble. If this was one of my murdering evenings, you don't think I'd bump him and let you get away, do you? Go on and fetch your policemen – and we'll see whether the boy friend can make them believe *his* story!'

4

They had to wait for some time . . .

After a minute, Simon turned the prisoner over to Hoppy and put his Luger away under his coat. He reached for his cigarette case again and thoughtfully helped himself to a smoke. With the cigarette curling blue drifts past his eyes, he traced again the course of the bullet that had so nearly stamped finale on all his adventures. There was no question that it had been fired from outside the window – and that also explained the peculiarly flat sound of the shot which had faintly puzzled him. The cleavage lines on the few scraps of glass remaining in the frame supplied the last detail of incontrovertible proof. He devoutly hoped that the shining lights of the local constabulary would have enough scientific knowledge to appreciate it.

Mr Uniatz, having brilliantly performed his share of physical activity, appeared to have been snared again in the unfathomable quagmires of the Mind. The tortured grimace that had cramped itself into his countenance indicated that some frightful eruption was taking place in the small core of grey matter which formed a sort of glutinous marrow inside his skull. He cleared his throat, producing a noise like a piece of sheet iron getting between the blades of a lawn mower, and gave the fruit of his travail to the world.

'Boss,' he said, 'I dunno how dese mugs t'ink dey can get away wit' it.'

'How which mugs think they can get away with what?' asked the Saint somewhat vacantly.

'Dese mugs,' said Mr Uniatz, 'who are tryin' to take us for a ride, like ya tell me in de pub.'

Simon had to stretch his memory backwards almost to breaking point to hook up again with Mr Uniatz's train of thought; and when he had finally done so he decided that it was wisest not to start any argument.

'Others have made the same mistake,' he said casually, and hoped that would be the end of it.

Mr Uniatz nodded sagely.

'Well, dey all get what's comin' to dem,' he said with philosophic complacency. 'When do I give dis punk de woiks?'

'When do you—What?'

'Dis punk,' said Mr Uniatz, waving his Betsy at the prisoner. 'De mug who takes a shot at us.'

'You don't,' said the Saint shortly.

The equivalent of what on anybody else's face would have been a slight frown carved its fearsome corrugations into Hoppy's brow.

'Ya don't mean he gets away wit' it after all?'

'We'll see about that.'

'Dijja hear what he calls us?'

'What was that?'

'He calls us washouts.'

'That's too bad.'

'Yeah, dat's too bad.' Mr Uniatz glowered disparagingly at the captive. 'Maybe I better go over him wit' a paddle foist. Just to make sure he don't go to sleep.'

'Leave him alone,' said the Saint soothingly. 'He's young, but he'll grow up.'

He was watching the striped blazer with more attention than a chance onlooker would have realized. The young man stood glaring at them defiantly – not without fear, but that was easy to explain if one wanted to. His knuckles tensed up involuntarily from time to time; but a perfectly understandable anger would account for that. Once or twice he glanced at the strangely unreal shape of the dead girl half hidden in the shadows, and it was at those moments that Simon was studying him most intently. He saw the almost conventionalized horror of death that takes the place of practical thinking with those who have seen little of it, and a bitter disgust that might have had an equally conventional basis. Beyond that, the sullen scowl which disfigured the other's face steadily refused him the betraying evidence that might have made everything so much simpler. Simon blew placid and meditative smoke rings to pass the time; but there was an irking bafflement behind the cool patience of his eyes.

It took fifteen minutes by his watch for the police to come, which was less than he had expected.

They arrived in the persons of a man with a waxed moustache, in plain clothes, and two constables in uniform. After them, breathless when she saw the striped blazer still inhabited by an apparently undamaged owner, came Rosemary Chase. In the background hovered a man who even without his costume could never have been mistaken for anything but a butler.

Simon turned with a smile.

'Glad to see you, Inspector,' he said casily.

'Just "Sergeant",' answered the plainclothes man, in a voice that sounded as if it should have been 'sergeant-major.'

He saw the automatic that Mr Uniatz was still holding, and stepped forward with a rather hollow but courageous belligerence.

'Give me that gun!' he said loudly.

Hoppy ignored him, and looked inquiringly at the only man whom he took orders from; but Simon nodded. He politely offered his own Luger as well. The sergeant took the two guns, squinted at them sapiently, and stuffed them into his side pockets. He looked relieved, and rather clever.

'I suppose you've got licences for these firearms,' he said temptingly.

'Of course,' said the Saint, in a voice of saccharine virtue.

He produced certificate and permit to carry from his pocket. Hoppy did the same. The sergeant pored over the documents with surly suspicion for some time before he handed them to one of the constables to note down the particulars. He looked so much less clever that Simon had difficulty in keeping a straight face. It was as if the Official Mind, jumping firmly to a foregone conclusion, had spent the journey there developing an elegantly graduated approach to the obvious climax, and therefore found the entire structure staggering when the first step caved in under his feet.

A certain awkwardness crowded itself into the scene.

With a businesslike briskness that was only a trifle too elaborate, the sergeant went over to the body and brooded over it with portentous solemnity. He went down on his hands and knees to peer at the knife, without touching it. He borrowed a flashlight from one of the constables to examine the floor around it. He roamed about the boathouse and frowned into dark corners. At intervals, he cogitated. When he could think of nothing else to do, he came back and faced his audience with dogged valour.

'Well,' he said, less aggressively, 'while we're waiting for the doctor I'd better take your statements.' He turned. 'You're Mr Forrest, sir?'

The young man in the striped blazer nodded.

'Yes.'

'I've already heard the young lady's story, but I'd like to hear your version.'

Forrest glanced quickly at the girl, and almost hesitated. He said: 'I was taking Miss Chase home, and we saw a light moving in here. We crept up to find out what it was, and one of these men fired a shot at us. I turned my torch on them and pretended I had a gun too, and they surrendered. We took their guns away; and then this man started arguing and trying to make out that somebody else had fired the shot, and he managed to distract my attention and get his gun back.'

'Did you hear any noise as you were walking along? The sort of noise this – er – deceased might have made as she was being attacked?'

'No.'

'I – did – not hear – the – noise – of – the – deceased – being – attacked,' repeated one of the constables with a notebook and pencil, laboriously writing it down.

The sergeant waited for him to finish, and turned to the Saint.

'Now, Mr Templar,' he said ominously. 'Do you wish to make a statement? It is my duty to warn you—'

'Why?' asked the Saint blandly.

The sergeant did not seem to know the answer to that.

He said gruffly: 'What statement do you wish to make?'

'Just what I told Comrade Forrest when we were arguing. Mr Uniatz and I were ambling around to work up a thirst, and we saw this door open. Being rather inquisitive and not having anything better to do, we just nosed in, and we saw the body. We were just taking it in when somebody fired at us; and then Comrade Forrest turned on the spotlight and yelled "Hands up!" or words to that effect, so to be on the safe side we handed up, thinking he'd fired the first shot. Still, he looked kind of nervous when he had hold of my gun, so I took it away from him in case it went off. Then I told Miss Chase to go ahead and fetch you. Incidentally, as I tried to tell Comrade Forrest, I've discovered that we were both wrong about that shooting. Somebody else did it from outside the window. You can see for yourself if you take a look at the glass.'

The Saint's voice and manner were masterpieces of matter-of-fact veracity. It is often easy to tell the plain truth and be disbelieved; but Simon's pleasant imperturbality left the sergeant visibly nonplussed. He went and inspected the broken glass at some length, and then he came back and scratched his head.

'Well,' he admitted grudgingly, 'there doesn't seem to be much doubt about that.'

'If you want any more proof,' said the Saint nonchalantly, 'you can take our guns apart. Comrade Forrest will tell you that we haven't done anything to them. You'll find the magazines full and the barrels clean.'

The sergeant adopted the suggestion with morbid eagerness, but he shrugged resignedly over the result.

'That seems to be right,' he said with stoic finality. 'It looks as if both you gentlemen were mistaken.' He went on scrutinizing the Saint grimly. 'But it still doesn't explain why you were in here with the deceased.'

'Because I found her,' answered the Saint reasonably. 'Somebody had to.'

The sergeant took another glum look around. He did not audibly acknowledge that all his castles in the air had settled soggily back to earth, but the morose admission was implicit in the majestic stolidity with which he tried to keep anything that might have been interpreted as a confession out of his face. He took refuge in an air of busy inscrutability, as if he had just a little more up his sleeve than he was prepared to share with anyone else for the time being; but there was at least one member of his audience who was not deceived, and who breathed a sigh of relief at the lifting of what might have been a dangerous suspicion.

'Better take down some more details,' he said gruffly to the constable with the notebook, and turned to Rosemary Chase. 'The deceased's name is Nora Prescott – is that right, miss?'

'Yes.'

'You knew her quite well?'

'Of course. She was one of my father's personal secretaries,' said the dark girl; and the Saint suddenly felt as if the last knot in the tangle had been untied.

5

He listened with tingling detachment while Rosemary Chase talked and answered questions. The dead girl's father was a man who had known and helped Marvin Chase when they were both young, but who had long ago been left far behind by Marvin Chase's sensational rise in the financial world. When Prescott's own business was failing, Chase had willingly lent him large sums of money, but the failure had still not been averted. Illness had finally brought Prescott's misfortunes to the point where he was not even able to meet the interest on the loan, and when he refused further charity Chase had sent him to Switzerland to act as an entirely superfluous 'representative' in Zurich and had given Nora Prescott a job himself. She had lived more as one of the family than as an employee. No, she had given no hint of having any private troubles or being afraid of anyone. Only she had not seemed to be quite herself since Marvin Chase's motor accident . . .

The bare supplementary facts clicked into place in the framework that was already there, as if into accurately fitted sockets, filling in sections of the outline without making much of it more recognizable. They filed themselves away in the Saint's memory with mechanical precision; and yet the closeness which he felt to the mystery that hid behind them was more intuitive than methodical, a weird sensitivity that sent electric shivers coursing up his spine.

A grey-haired ruddy-cheeked doctor arrived and made his matter-of-fact examination and report.

'Three stab wounds in the chest – I'll be able to tell you more about them after I've made the post-mortem, but I should think any one of them might have been fatal. Slight contusions on the throat. She hasn't been dead much more than an hour.'

He stood glancing curiously over the other faces.

'Where's that ambulance?' said the sergeant grumpily.

'They've probably gone to the house,' said the girl. 'I'll send them down if I see them – you don't want us getting in your way any more, do you?'

'No, miss. This isn't very pleasant for you, I suppose. If I want any more information I'll come up and see you in the morning. Will Mr Forrest be there if we want to see him?'

Forrest took a half step forward.

'Wait a minute,' he blurted. 'You haven't—'

'They aren't suspicious of you, Jim,' said the girl, with a quiet firmness. 'They might just want to ask some more questions.'

'But you haven't said anything about Templar's—'

'Of course.' The girl's interruption was even firmer. Her voice was still quiet and natural, but the undercurrent of determined warning in it was as plain as a siren to the Saint's ears. 'I know we owe Mr Templar an apology, but we don't have to waste Sergeant Jesser's time with it. Perhaps he'd like to come up to the house with us and have a drink – that is, if you don't need him any more, Sergeant.'

Her glance only released the young man's eye after it had pinned him to perplexed and scowling silence. And once again Simon felt that premonitory crisping of his nerves.

'All this excitement certainly does dry out the tonsils,' he remarked easily. 'But if Sergeant Jesser wants me to stay—'

'No, sir.' The reply was calm and ponderous. 'I've made a note of your address, and I don't think you could run away. Are you going home tonight?'

'You might try the Bell first, in case we decide to stop over.'

Simon buttoned his coat and strolled towards the door with the others; but as they reached it he stopped and turned back.

'By the way,' he said blandly, 'do you mind if we take our lawful artillery?'

The sergeant gazed at him, and dug the guns slowly out of his pocket. Simon handed one of them to Mr Uniatz, and leisurely fitted his own automatic back into the spring holster under his arm. His smile was very slight.

'Since there still seems to be a murderer at large in the neighbourhood,' he said, 'I'd like to be ready for him.'

As he followed Rosemary Chase and Jim Forrest up a narrow footpath away from the river, with Hoppy Uniatz beside him and the butler bringing up the rear, he grinned inwardly over that delicately pointed line, and wondered whether it had gone home where he intended it to go. Since his back had been turned to the real audience, he had been unable to observe their reaction; and now their backs were turned to him in an equally uninformative reversal. Neither of them said a word on the way, and Simon placidly left the silence to get tired of itself. But his thoughts were very busy as he sauntered after them along the winding path and saw the lighted windows of a house looming up through the thinning trees that had hidden it from the river bank. This, he realized with a jolt, must be the New Manor, and therefore the boathouse where Nora Prescott had been murdered was presumably a part of Marvin Chase's property. It made no difference to the facts, but the web of riddles seemed to draw tighter around him . . .

They crossed a lawn and mounted some steps to a flagged terrace. Rosemary Chase led them through open french windows into an inoffensively furnished drawing-room, and the butler closed the windows behind him as he followed. Forrest threw himself sulkily into an armchair, but the girl had regained a composure that was just a fraction too detailed to be natural.

'What kind of drinks would you like?' she asked.

'Beer for me,' said the Saint, with the same studied urbanity. 'Scotch for Hoppy. I'm afraid I should have warned you about him – he likes to have his own bottle. We're trying to wean him, but it isn't going very well.'

The butler bowed and oozed out.

The girl took a cigarette from an antique lacquer box, and Simon stepped forward politely with his lighter. He had an absurd feeling of unreality about this new atmosphere that made it a little difficult to hide his sense of humour, but all his senses were vigilant. She was even lovelier than he had thought at first sight, he admitted to himself as he watched her face over the flame – it was hard to believe that she might be an accomplice to wilful and messy and apparently mercenary murder. But she and Forrest had certainly chosen a very dramatic moment to arrive . . .

'It's nice of you to have us here,' he murmured, 'after the way we've behaved.'

'My father told me to bring you up,' she said. 'He seems to be quite an admirer of yours, and he was sure you couldn't have had anything to do with – with the murder.'

'I noticed – down in the boathouse – you knew my name,' said the Saint thoughtfully.

'Yes – the sergeant used it.'

Simon looked at the ceiling.

'Bright lads, these policemen, aren't they? I wonder how *he* knew?'

'From – your gun licence, I suppose.'

Simon nodded.

'Oh, yes. But before that. I mean, I suppose he must have told your father who I was. Nobody else could have done it, could they?'

The girl reddened and lost her voice; but Forrest found his. He jerked himself angrily out of his chair.

'What's the use of all this beating about the bush, Rosemary?' he demanded impatiently. 'Why don't you tell him we know all about that letter that Nora wrote him?'

The door opened, and the butler came back with a tray of bottles and glasses and toured the room with them. There was a strained silence until he had gone again. Hoppy Uniatz stared at the newly opened bottle of whisky which had been put down in front of him, with a rapt and menacing expression which indicated that his grey matter was in the throes of another paroxysm of Thought.

Simon raised his glass and gazed appreciatively at the sparkling brown clearness within it.

'All right,' he said. 'If you want it that way. So you knew Nora Prescott had written to me. You came to the Bell to see what happened. Probably you watched through the windows first; then when she went out, you came in to watch me. You followed one of us to the boathouse—'

'And we ought to have told the police—'

'Of course.' The Saint's voice was mild and friendly. 'You ought to have told them about the letter. I'm sure you could have quoted what was in it. Something about how she was being forced to help in putting over a gigantic fraud, and how she wanted me to help her. Sergeant Jesser would have been wild with excitement about that. Naturally, he'd 've seen at once that that provided an obvious motive for me to murder her, and none at all for the guy whose fraud was going to be given away. It really was pretty noble of you both to take so much trouble to keep me out of suspicion, and I appreciate it a lot. And now that we're all pals together, and there aren't any policemen in the audience, why don't you save me a lot of headaches and tell me what the swindle is?'

The girl stared at him.

'Do you know what you're saying?'

'I usually have a rough idea,' said the Saint coolly and deliberately. 'I'll make it even plainer, if that's too subtle for you. Your father's a millionaire, they tell me. And when there are any gigantic frauds in the wind, I never expect to find the big shot sitting in a garret toasting kippers over a candle.'

Forrest started towards him.

'Look here, Templar, we've stood about enough from you—'

'And I've stood plenty from you,' said the Saint, without moving. 'Let's call it quits. We were both misunderstanding each other at the beginning, but we don't have to go on doing it. I can't do anything for you if you don't put your cards on the table. Let's straighten it out now. Which of you two cooled off Nora Prescott?'

He didn't seem to change his voice, but the question came with a sharp stinging clarity like the flick of a whip. Rosemary Chase and the young man gaped at him frozenly, and he waited for an answer without a shift of his lazily negligent eyes. But he didn't get it.

The rattle of the doorhandle made everyone turn, almost in relief at the interruption. A tall cadaverous man, severely dressed in a dark suit and high old-fashioned collar, his chin bordered with a rim of black beard, pince-nez on a loop of black ribbon in his hand, came into the room and paused hesitantly.

Rosemary Chase came slowly out of her trance.

'Oh, Dr Quintus,' she said in a quiet forced voice. 'This is Mr Templar and – er—'

'Hoppy Uniatz,' Simon supplied.

Dr Quintus bowed; and his black sunken eyes clung for a moment to the Saint's face.

'Delighted,' he said in a deep burring bass; and turned back to the girl. 'Miss Chase, I'm afraid the shock has upset your father a little. Nothing at all serious, I assure you, but I think it would be unwise for him to have any more excitement just yet. However, he asked me to invite Mr Templar to stay for dinner. Perhaps later . . .'

Simon took another sip at his beer, and his glance swung idly over to the girl with the first glint of a frosty sparkle in its depths.

'We'd be delighted,' he said deprecatingly. 'If Miss Chase doesn't object—'

'Why, of course not.' Her voice was only the minutest shred of a decibel out of key. 'We'd love to have you stay.'

The Saint smiled his courteous acceptance, ignoring the wrathful half movement that made Forrest's attitude rudely obvious. He would have stayed anyway, whoever had objected. It was just dawning on him that out of the whole fishy set-up, Marvin Chase was the one man he had still to meet.

6

'Boss,' said Mr Uniatz, rising to his feet with an air of firm decision, 'should I go to de terlet?'

It was not possible for Simon to pretend that he didn't know him; nor could he take refuge in temporary deafness. Mr Uniatz's penetrating accents were too peremptory for that to have been convincing. Simon swallowed, and took hold of himself with the strength of despair.

'I don't know, Hoppy,' he said bravely. 'How do you feel?'

'I feel fine, boss. I just t'ought it might be a good place.'

'It might be,' Simon conceded feverishly.

'Dat was a swell idea of yours, boss,' said Mr Uniatz, hitching up his bottle.

Simon took hold of the back of a chair for support.

'Oh, not at all,' he said faintly. 'It's nothing to do with me.'

Hoppy looked puzzled.

'Sure, you t'ought of it foist, boss,' he insisted generously. 'Ya said to me, de nex time I should take de bottle away some place an' lock myself up wit' it. So I t'ought I might take dis one in de terlet. I just t'ought it might be a good place,' said Mr Uniatz, rounding off the résumé of his train of thought.

'Sit down!' said the Saint, with paralysing ferocity.

Mr Uniatz lowered himself back on to his hams with an expression of pained mystification, and Simon turned to the others.

'Excuse us, won't you?' he said brightly. 'Hoppy's made a sort of bet with himself about something, and he has a rather one-track mind.'

Forrest glared at him coldly. Rosemary half put on a gracious smile, and took it off again. Dr Quintus almost bowed, with his mouth open. There was a lot of silence, in which Simon could feel the air prickling with pardonable speculations on his sanity. Every other reaction that he had been deliberately building up to provoke had had time to disperse itself under cover of the two consecutive interruptions. The spell was shattered, and he was back again where he began. He knew it, and resignedly slid into small talk that might yet lead to another opening.

'I heard that your father had a nasty motor accident, Miss Chase,' he said.

'Yes.'

The brief monosyllable offered nothing but the baldest affirmation; but her eyes were fixed on him with an expression that he tried unavailingly to read.

'I hope he wasn't badly hurt?'

'Quite badly burned,' rumbled the doctor. 'The car caught fire, you know. But fortunately his life isn't in danger. In fact, he would probably have escaped with nothing worse than a few bruises if he hadn't made such heroic efforts to save his secretary, who was trapped in the wreckage.'

'I read something about it,' lied the Saint. 'He was burned to death, wasn't he? What was his name now—'

'Bertrand Tamblin.'

'Oh, yes. Of course.'

Simon took a cigarette from his case and lighted it. He looked at the girl. His brain was still working at fighting pitch; but his manner was quite casual and disarming now – the unruffled conversational manner of an accepted friend discussing a minor matter of mutual interest.

'I just remembered something you said to the sergeant a little while ago, Miss Chase – about your having noticed that

Nora Prescott seemed to be rather under a strain since Tamblin was killed.'

She looked back at him steadily, neither denying it nor encouraging him.

He said, in the same sensible and persuasive way: 'I was wondering whether you'd noticed them being particularly friendly before the accident – as if there was any kind of attachment between them.'

He saw that the eyes of both Forrest and Dr Quintus turned towards the girl, as if they both had an unexpectedly intense interest in her answer. But she looked at neither of them.

'I can't be sure,' she answered, as though choosing her words carefully. 'Their work brought them together all the time, of course. Mr Tamblin was really father's private secretary and almost his other self, and when Nora came to us she worked for Mr Tamblin nearly as much as father. I thought sometimes that Mr Tamblin was – well, quite keen on her – but I don't know whether she responded. Of course I didn't ask her.'

'You don't happen to have a picture of Tamblin, do you?'

'I think there's a snapshot somewhere—'

She stood up and went over to an inlaid writing-table and rummaged in the drawer. It might have seemed fantastic that she should do that, obeying the Saint's suggestion as if he had hypnotized her; but Simon knew just how deftly he had gathered up the threads of his broken dominance and woven them into a new pattern. If the scene had to be played in that key, it suited him as well as any other. And with that key established, such an ordinary and natural request as he had made could not be refused. But he noticed that Dr Quintus followed her with his hollow black eyes all the way across the room.

'Here.'

She gave Simon a commonplace Kodak print that showed two men standing on the steps of a house. One of them was apparently of medium height, a little flabby, grey-haired in the small areas of his head where he was not bald. The other was a trifle shorter and leaner, with thick smooth black hair and metal-rimmed glasses.

The Saint touched his forefinger on the picture of the older man.

'Your father?'

'Yes.'

It was a face without any outstanding features, creased in a tolerant if somewhat calculating smile. But Simon knew how deceptive a face could be, particularly in that kind of reproduction.

And the first thought that was thrusting itself forward in his mind was that there were two people dead, not only one – two people who had held similar and closely associated jobs, who from the very nature of their employment must have shared a good deal of Marvin Chase's confidence and known practically everything about his affairs, two people who must have known more about the intricate details of his business life than anyone else around him. One question clanged in the Saint's head like a deep jarring bell: Was Nora Prescott's killing the first murder to which that unknown swindle had led, or only the second?

All through dinner his brain echoed the complex repercussions of that explosive idea, under the screen of superficial conversation which lasted through the meal. It gave that part of the evening a macabre spookiness. Hoppy Uniatz, hurt and frustrated, toyed halfheartedly with his food, which is to say that he did not ask for more than two helpings of any one dish. From time to time he washed down a mouthful with a gulp from the bottle which he had brought in with him, and put it down again to leer at it malevolently, as if it had personally welshed on him; Simon watched him anxiously when he seemed to lean perilously close to the candles which lighted the table, thinking that it would not take much to cause his breath to ignite and burn with a blue flame. Forrest had given up his efforts to protest at the whole procedure. He ate most of the time in sulky silence, and when he spoke at all he made a point of turning as much of his back to the Saint as his place at the table allowed: plainly he had made up his mind that Simon Templar was a cad on whom good manners would be wasted. Rosemary Chase talked very little, but she spoke to the Saint when she spoke at all, and she was watching him all the time with enigmatic intentness. Dr Quintus was the only one who helped to shoulder the burden of maintaining an exchange of urbane trivialities. His reverberant basso bumbled obligingly into every conversational opening, and said nothing that was worth remembering. His eyes were like pools of basalt at the bottom of dry caverns, never altering their expression, and yet always moving, slowly, in a way that seemed to keep everyone under ceaseless surveillance.

Simon chatted genially and emptily, with faintly mocking calm. He had shown his claws once, and now it was up to the other side to take up the challenge in their own way. The one thing they could not possibly do was ignore it, and he was ready to wait with timeless patience for their lead. Under his pose of idle carelessness he was like an arrow on a drawn bow with ghostly fingers balancing the string.

Forrest excused himself as they left the dining-room. Quintus came as far as the drawing-room, but didn't sit down. He pulled out a large gold watch and consulted it with impressive deliberation.

'I'd better have another look at the patient,' he said. 'He may have settled down again by now.'

The door closed behind him.

Simon leaned himself against the mantelpiece. Except for

the presence of Mr Uniatz, who in those circumstances was no more obtrusive than a piece of primitive furniture, he was alone with Rosemary Chase for the first time since so many things had begun to happen. And he knew that she was also aware of it.

She kept her face averted from his tranquil gaze, taking out a cigarette and lighting it for herself with impersonal unapproachability, while he waited. And then suddenly she turned on him as if her own restraint had defeated itself.

'Well?' she said, with self-consciously harsh defiance. 'What are you thinking, after all this time?'

The Saint looked her in the eyes. His own voice was contrastingly even and unaggressive.

'Thinking,' he said, 'that you're either a very dangerous crook or just a plain damn fool. But hoping you're just the plain damn fool. And hoping that if that's the answer, it won't be much longer before your brain starts working again.'

'You hate crooks, don't you?'

'Yes.'

'I've heard about you,' she said. 'You don't care what you do to anyone you think is a crook. You've even – killed them.'

'I've killed rats,' he said. 'And I'll probably do it again. It's the only treatment that's any good for what they've got.'

'Always?'

Simon shrugged.

'Listen,' he said, not unkindly. 'If you want to talk theories we can have a lot of fun, but we shan't get very far. If you want me to admit that there are exceptions to my idea of justice, you can take it as admitted; but we can't go on from there without getting down to cases. I can tell you this, though. I've heard that there's something crooked being put over here; and from what's happened since, it seems to be true. I'm going to find out what the swindle is and break it up if it takes fifty years. Only it won't take me nearly as long as that. Now, if you know something that you're afraid to tell me because of what it might make me do to you or somebody else who matters to you, all I can say is that it'll probably be a lot worse if I have to dig it out for myself. Is that any use?'

She moved closer towards him, her brown eyes searching his face.

'I wish—'

It was all she had time to say. The rush of sounds that cut her off hit both of them at the same time, muffled by distance and the closed door of the room, and yet horribly distinct, stiffening them both together as though they had been clutched by invisible clammy tentacles. A shrill incoherent yell, hysterical with terror but unmistakably masculine. A heavy thud. A wild shout of '*Help!*' in the doctor's deep thundery voice. And then a ghostly inhuman wailing gurgle that choked off into deathly silence.

7

Balanced on a knife-edge of uncanny self-control, the Saint stood motionless, watching the girl's expression for a full long second before she turned away with a gasp and rushed at the door. Hoppy Uniatz flung himself after her like a wild bull awakened from slumber: he could have remained comatose through eons of verbal fencing, but this was a call to action, clear and unsullied, and such simple clarions had never found him unresponsive. Simon started the thin edge of an instant later than either of them; but it was his hand that reached the doorknob first.

He threw the door wide and stepped out with a smooth combination of movements that brought him through the opening with a gun in his hand and his eyes streaking over the entire scene outside in one whirling survey. But the hall was empty. At the left and across from him, the front door was closed; at the opposite end, a door which obviously communicated with the service wing of the house was thrown open to disclose the portly emerging figure of the butler with the white frightened faces of other servants peering from behind him.

The Saint's glance swept on upwards. The noises that had brought him out had come from upstairs, he was certain: that was also the most likely place for them to have come from, and it was only habitual caution that had made him pause to scan the hall as he reached it. He caught the girl's arm as she came by him.

'Let me go up first,' he said. He blocked Hoppy's path on his other side, and shot a question across at the butler without raising his voice. 'Are there any other stairs, Jeeves?'

'Y-yes, sir—'

'All right. You stay here with Miss Chase. Hoppy, you find those back stairs and cover them.'

He raced on up the main stairway.

As he took the treads three at a time, on his toes, he was trying to find a niche for one fact of remarkable interest. Unless Rosemary Chase was the greatest natural actress that a generation of talent scouts had overlooked, or unless his own judgment had gone completely cockeyed, the interruption had hit her with the same chilling shock as it had given him. It was to learn that that he had stayed to study her face before he moved: he was sure that he would have caught any shadow of deception, and yet if there had really been no shadow there to catch it meant that something had happened for which she was totally unprepared. And that in its turn might mean that all his suspicions of her were without foundation. It gave a jolt to the theories he had begun to put together that threw them into new and fascinating outlines, and he reached the top of the stairs with a glint of purely speculative delight shifting behind the grim alertness of his eyes.

From the head of the staircase the landing opened off in the shape of a squat long-armed T. All the doors that he saw at first were closed; he strode lightly to the junction of the two arms, and heard a faint movement down the left-hand corridor. Simon took a breath, and jumped out on a quick slant that would have been highly disconcerting to any marksman who might have been waiting for him round the corner. But there was no marksman.

The figures of two men were piled together on the floor, in the middle of a sickening mess; and only one of them moved.

The one who moved was Dr Quintus, who was groggily trying to scramble up to his feet as the Saint reached him. The one who lay still was Jim Forrest; and Simon did not need to look at him twice to see that his stillness was permanent. The mess was blood – pools and gouts and splashes of blood, in hideous quantity, puddling on the floor, dripping down the walls, soddening the striped blazer and mottling the doctor's clothes. The gaping slash that split Forrest's throat from ear to ear had almost decapitated him.

The Saint's stomach turned over once. Then he was grasping the doctor's arm and helping him up. There was so much blood on him that Simon couldn't tell what his injuries might be.

'Where are you hurt?' he snapped.

The other shook his head muzzily. His weight was leaden on Simon's supporting grip.

'Not me,' he mumbled hoarsely. 'All right. Only hit me – on the head. Forrest—'

'Who did it?'

'Dunno. Probably same as – Nora. Heard Forrest . . . yell—'

'Where did he go?'

Quintus seemed to be in a daze through which outside promptings only reached him in the same form as outside noises reach the brain of a sleepwalker. He seemed to be making a tremendous effort to retain some sort of consciousness, but his eyes were half closed and his words were thick and rambling, as if he were dead drunk.

'Suppose Forrest was – going to his room – for something . . . Caught murderer – sneaking about . . . Murderer – stabbed him . . . I heard him yell . . . Rushed out . . . Got hit with – something . . . Be all right – soon. Catch him—'

'Well, where did he go?'

Simon shook him, roughly slapped up the sagging head.

The doctor's chest heaved as though it were taking part in his terrific struggle to achieve coherence. He got his eyes wide open.

'Don't worry about me,' he whispered with painful clarity. 'Look after – Mr Chase.'

His eyelids fluttered again.

Simon let him go against the wall, and he slid down almost to a sitting position, clasping his head in his hands.

The Saint balanced his Luger in his hand, and his eyes were narrowed to chips of sapphire hardness. He glanced up and down the corridor. From where he stood, he could see the length of both passages which formed the arms of the T-plan of the landing. The arm on his right finished with a glimpse of the banisters of a staircase leading down – obviously the back stairs whose existence the butler had admitted, at the foot of which Hoppy Uniatz must already have taken up his post. But there had been no sound of disturbance from that direction. Nor had there been any sound from the front hall where he had left Rosemary Chase with the butler. And there was no other normal way out for anyone who was upstairs. The left-hand corridor, where he stood, ended in a blank wall; and only one door along it was open.

Simon stepped past the doctor and over Forrest's body, and went silently to the open door.

He came to it without any of the precautions that he had taken before exposing himself a few moments before. He had a presentiment amounting to conviction that they were unnecessary now. He remembered with curious distinctness that the drawing-room curtains had not been drawn since he entered the house. Therefore anyone who wanted to could have shot at him from outside long ago. No one had shot at him. Therefore—

He was looking into a large white-painted airy bedroom. The big double bed was empty, but the covers were thrown open and rumpled. The table beside it was loaded with medicine bottles. He opened the doors in the two side walls. One belonged to a spacious built-in cupboard filled with clothing; the other was a bathroom. The wall opposite the entrance door was broken by long casement windows, most of them wide open. He crossed over to one of them and looked out. Directly beneath him was the flat roof of a porch.

The Saint put his gun back in its holster, and felt an unearthly cold dry calm sinking through him. Then he climbed out over the sill on to the porch roof below, which almost formed a kind of blind balcony under the window. He stood there recklessly, knowing that he was silhouetted against the light behind, and lighted a cigarette with leisured, tremorless hands. He sent a cloud of blue vapour drifting towards the stars; and then with the same leisured passivity he sauntered to the edge of the balustrade, sat on it, and swung his legs over. From there it was an easy drop on to the parapet which bordered the terrace along the front of the house, and an even easier drop from the top of the parapet to the ground. To an active man, the return journey would not present much more difficulty.

He paused long enough to draw another lungful of night air and tobacco smoke, and then strolled on along the terrace. It was an eerie experience, to know that he was an easy target every time he passed a lighted window, to remember that the killer might be watching him from a few yards away, and still to hold his steps down to the same steady pace; but the Saint's nerves were hardened to an icy quietness, and all his senses were working together in taut-strung vigilance.

He walked three-quarters of the way round the building, and arrived at the back door. It was unlocked when he tried it; and he pushed it open and looked down the barrel of Mr Uniatz's Betsy.

'I bet you'll shoot somebody one of these days, Hoppy,' he

remarked; and Mr Uniatz lowered the gun with a faint tinge of disappointment.

'What ya find, boss?'

'Quite a few jolly and interesting things.' The Saint was only smiling with his lips. 'Hold the fort a bit longer, and I'll tell you.'

He found his way through the kitchen, where the other servants were clustered together in dumb and terrified silence, back to the front hall where Rosemary Chase and the butler were standing together at the foot of the stairs. They jumped as if a gun had been fired when they heard his footsteps; and then the girl ran towards him and caught him by the lapels of his coat.

'What is it?' she pleaded frantically. 'What happened?'

'I'm sorry,' he said, as gently as he could.

She stared at him. He meant her to read his face, for everything except the fact that he was still watching her like a spectator on the dark side of the footlights.

'Where's Jim?'

He didn't answer.

She caught her breath suddenly, with a kind of sob, and turned towards the stairs. He grabbed her elbows and turned her back and held her.

'I wouldn't go up,' he said evenly. 'It wouldn't do any good.'

'Tell me, then. For God's sake, tell me! Is he—' She choked on the word – 'dead?'

'Jim, yes.'

Her face was whiter than chalk, but she kept her feet. Her eyes dragged at his knowledge through a brightness of unheeded tears.

'Why do you say it like that? What else is there?'

'Your father seems to have disappeared,' he said, and held her as she went limp in his arms.

8

Simon carried her into the drawing-room and laid her down on the sofa. He stood gazing at her introspectively for a moment; then he bent over her again quickly and stabbed her in the solar plexus with a stiff forefinger. She didn't stir a muscle.

The monotonous *cheep-cheep* of a telephone bell ringing somewhere outside reached his ears, and he saw the butler starting to move mechanically towards the door. Simon passed him, and saw the instrument half hidden by a curtain on the other side of the hall. He took the receiver off the hook and said: 'Hullo.'

'May I speak to Mr Templar, please?'

The Saint put a hand on the wall to save himself from falling over.

'Who wants him?'

'Mr Trapani.'

'Giulio!' Simon exclaimed. The voice was familiar now, but its complete unexpectedness had prevented him from recognizing it before. 'It seems to be about sixteen years since I saw you – and I never came back for dinner.'

'That's quite all right, Mr Templar. I didn't expect you, when I knew what had happened. I only called up now because it's getting late and I didn't know if you would want a room for tonight.'

The Saint's brows drew together.

'What the hell is this?' he demanded slowly. 'Have you taken up crystal-gazing, or something?'

Giulio Trapani chuckled.

'No, I am not any good at that. The police sergeant stopped here on his way back, and he told me. He said you had got mixed up with a murder, and Miss Chase had taken you home with her. So, of course, I knew you would be very busy. Has she asked you to stay?'

'Let me call you back in a few minutes, Giulio,' said the Saint. 'Things have been happening, and I've got to get hold of the police again.' He paused, and a thought struck him. 'Look, is Sergeant Jesser still there, by any chance?'

There was no answer.

Simon barked: 'Hullo.'

Silence. He jiggled the hook. The movements produced no corresponding clicks in his ear. He waited a moment longer, while he realized that the stillness of the receiver was not the stillness of a broken connection, but a complete inanimate muteness that stood for something less easily remedied than that.

He hung the receiver up and traced the course of the wiring with his eyes. It ran along the edge of the wainscoting to the frame of the front door, and disappeared into a hole bored at the edge of the wood. Simon turned right round with another abrupt realization. He was alone in the hall – the butler was no longer in sight.

He slipped his pencil flashlight out of his breast pocket with his left hand, and let himself out of the front door. The telephone wires ran up outside along the margin of the door-frame, and continued up over the exterior wall. The beam of his torch followed them up, past a lighted window over the porch from which he had climbed down a few minutes ago, to where they were attached to a pair of porcelain insulators under the eaves. Where the wires leading on from the insulators might once have gone was difficult to decide: they dangled slackly downwards now, straddling the balcony and trailing away into the darkness of the drive.

The Saint switched off his light and stood motionless. Then he flitted across the terrace, crossed the drive, and merged himself into the shadow of a big clump of laurels on the edge of the lawn. Again he froze into breathless immobility. The blackness ahead of him was stygian, impenetrable, even to his noctambulant eyes, but hearing would serve his temporary purpose almost as well as sight. The night had fallen so still that he could even hear the rustle of the distant river; and he waited for minutes that seemed like hours to him, and must have seemed like weeks to a guilty prowler who could not have travelled very far after the wires were broken. And while he waited, he was trying to decide at exactly what point in his last speech the break had occurred. It could easily have happened at a place where Trapani would think he had finished and rung off . . . But he heard nothing while he stood there – not the snap of a twig or the rustle of a leaf.

He went back to the drawing-room and found the butler standing there, wringing his hands in a helpless sort of way.

'Where have you been?' he inquired coldly.

The man's loose bloodhound jowls wobbled.

'I went to fetch my wife, sir.' He indicated the stout red-faced woman who was kneeling beside the couch, chafing the girl's nerveless wrists. 'To see if she could help Miss Chase.'

Simon's glance flickered over the room like a rapier blade, and settled pricklingly on an open french window.

'Did you have to fetch her in from the garden?' he asked sympathetically.

'I – I don't understand, sir.'

'Don't you? Neither do I. But that window was closed when I saw it last.'

'I opened it just now, sir, to give Miss Chase some fresh air.'

The Saint held his eyes ruthlessly, but the butler did not try to look away.

'All right,' he said at length. 'We'll check up on that presently. Just for the moment, you can both go back to the kitchen.'

The stout woman got to her feet with the laboured motions of a rheumatic camel.

' 'Oo do you think you are,' she demanded indignantly, 'to be bossing everybody about in this 'ouse?'

'I am the Grand Gugnunc of Waziristan,' answered the Saint pleasantly. 'And I said – get back to the kitchen.'

He followed them back himself, and went on through to find Hoppy Uniatz. The other door of the kitchen conveniently opened into the small rear hall into which the back stairs came down and from which the back door also opened. Simon locked and bolted the back door, and drew Hoppy into the kitchen doorway and propped him up against the jamb.

'If you stand here,' he said, 'you'll be able to cover the back stairs and this gang in the kitchen at the same time. And that's what I want you to do. None of them is to move out of your sight – not even to get somebody else some fresh air.'

'Okay, boss,' said Mr Uniatz dimly. 'If I only had a drink—'

'Tell Jeeves to buy you one.'

The Saint was on his way out again when the butler stopped him.

'Please, sir, I'm sure I could be of some use—'

'You are being useful,' said the Saint, and closed the door on him.

Rosemary Chase was sitting up when he returned to the drawing-room.

'I'm sorry,' she said weakly. 'I'm afraid I fainted.'

'I'm afraid you did,' said the Saint. 'I poked you in the tummy to make sure it was real, and it was. It looks as if I've been wrong about you all the evening. I've got a lot of apologies to make, and you'll have to imagine most of them. Would you like a drink?'

She nodded; and he turned to the table and operated with a bottle and siphon. While he was doing it, he said with matter-of-fact naturalness: 'How many servants do you keep here?'

'The butler and his wife, a housemaid, and a parlourmaid.'

'Then they're all rounded up and accounted for. How long have you known them?'

'Only about three weeks – since we've been here.'

'So that means nothing. I should have had them corralled before, but I didn't think fast enough.' He brought the drink over and gave it to her. 'Anyway, they're corralled now, under Hoppy's thirsty eye, so if anything else happens we'll know they didn't have anything to do with it. If that's any help . . . Which leaves only us – and Quintus.'

'What happened to him?'

'He said he got whacked on the head by our roving bogey-man.'

'Hadn't you better look after him?'

'Sure. In a minute.'

Simon crossed the room and closed the open window, and drew the curtains. He came back and stood by the table to light a cigarette. There had been so much essential activity during the past few minutes that he had had no time to do any constructive thinking; but now he had to get every possible blank filled in before the next move was made. He put his lighter away and studied her with cool and friendly encouragement, as if they had a couple of years to spare in which to straighten out misunderstandings.

She sipped her drink and looked up at him with dark stricken eyes from which, he knew, all pretence and concealment had now been wiped away. They were eyes that he would have liked to see without the grief in them; and the pallor of her face made him remember its loveliness as he had first seen it. Her red lips formed bitter words without flinching.

'I'm the one who ought to have been killed. If I hadn't been such a fool this might never have happened. I ought to be thrown in the river with a weight round my neck. Why don't you say so?'

'That wouldn't be any use now,' he said. 'I'd rather you made up for it. Give me the story.'

She brushed the hair off her forehead with a weary gesture.

'The trouble is – I can't. There isn't any story that's worth telling. Just that I was – trying to be clever. It all began when I read a letter that I hadn't any right to read. It was in this room. I'd been out. I came in through the french windows, and I sat down at the desk because I'd just remembered something I had to make a note of. The letter was on the blotter in front of me – the letter you got. Nora must have just finished it, and then left the room for a moment, just before I came in, not thinking anyone else would be around. I saw your name on it. I'd heard of you, of course. It startled me so much that I was reading on before I knew what I was doing. And then I couldn't stop. I read it all. Then I heard Nora coming back. I lost my head and slipped out through the window again without her seeing me.'

'And you never spoke to her about it?'

'I couldn't – later. After all that, I couldn't sort of come out and confess that I'd read it. Oh, I know I was a damn fool. But I was scared. It seemed as if she must know something dreadful that my father was involved in. I didn't know anything about his affairs. But I loved him. If he was doing something crooked, whatever it was, I'd have been hurt to death; but still I wanted to try and protect him. I couldn't talk about it to anybody but Jim. We decided the only thing was to find out what it was all about. That's why we followed Nora to the Bell, and then followed you to the boathouse.'

'Why didn't you tell me this before?'

She shrugged hopelessly.

'Because I was afraid to. You remember I asked you about how much you hated crooks? I was afraid that if my father was mixed up in – anything wrong – you'd be even more merciless than the police. I wanted to save him. But I didn't think – all this would happen. It was hard enough not to say anything when we found Nora dead. Now that Jim's been killed, I can't go on with it any more.'

The Saint was silent for a moment, weighing her with his eyes; and then he said: 'What do you know about this guy Quintus?'

9

'Hardly anything,' she said. 'He happened to be living close to where the accident happened, and father was taken to his house. Father took such a fancy to him that when they brought him home he insisted on bringing Dr Quintus along to look after him – at least, that's what I was told. I know what you're thinking.' She looked at him steadily. 'You think there's something funny about him.'

' "Phoney" is the way I pronounce it,' answered the Saint bluntly.

She nodded.

'I wondered about him too – after I read that letter. But how could I say anything?'

'Can you think of anything that might have given him a hold over your father?'

She moved her hands desperately.

'How could I know? Father never talked business at home. I never heard anything – discreditable about him. But how could I know?'

'You've seen your father since he was brought home?'

'Of course. Lots of times.'

'Did he seem to have anything on his mind?'

'I can't tell—'

'Did he seem to be worried, or frightened?'

'It's so *hard*,' she said. 'I don't know what I really saw and what I'm making myself imagine. He was badly hurt, you know, and he was still trying to keep some of his business affairs going, so that took a lot out of him, and Dr Quintus never let me stay with him very long at a time. And then he didn't feel like talking much. Of course he seemed shaky, and not a bit like himself; but after an accident like that you wouldn't expect anything else . . . I don't know what to think about anything. I thought he always liked Jim, and now . . . Oh, God, what a mess I've made!'

The Saint smothered the end of his cigarette in an ashtray, and there was an odd kind of final contentment in his eyes. All the threads were in his hands now, all the questions answered – except for the one answer that would cover all the others. Being as he was, he could understand Rosemary Chase's story, forgetting the way it had ended. Others might have found it harder to forgive; but to him it was just the old tale of amateur adventuring leading to tragic disaster. And even though his own amateur adventures had never led there, they were still close enough for him to realize the hair-breadth margin by which they had escaped it . . . And the story she told him gathered up many loose ends.

He sat down beside her and put his hand on her arm.

'Don't blame yourself too much about Jim,' he said steadyingly. 'He made some of the mess himself. If he hadn't thrown me off the track by the way he behaved, things might have been a lot different. Why the hell did he have to do that?'

'He'd made up his mind that you'd only come into this for what you could get out of it – that if you found out what Nora knew, you'd use it to blackmail father, or something like that. He wasn't terribly clever. I suppose he thought you'd killed her to keep the information to yourself—'

The Saint shrugged wryly.

'And I thought one of you had killed her to keep her mouth shut. None of us has been very clever – yet.'

'What are we going to do?' she said.

Simon thought. And he may have been about to answer

when his ears caught a sound that stopped him. His fingers tightened on the girl's wrist for an instant, while his eyes rested on her like bright steel; and then he got up.

'Give me another chance,' he said, in a soft voice that could not even have been heard across the room.

And then he was walking across to greet the doctor as the footsteps that had stopped him arrived at the door and Quintus came in.

'Dr Quintus!' The Saint's air was sympathetic, his face full of concern. He took the doctor's arm. 'You shouldn't have come down alone. I was just coming back for you, but there've been so many other things—'

'I know. And they were probably more valuable than anything you could have done for me.'

The blurry resonance of the other's voice was nearly normal again. He moved firmly over to the table on which the tray of drinks stood.

'I'm going to prescribe myself a whisky and soda,' he said.

Simon fixed it for him. Quintus took the glass and sat down gratefully on the edge of a chair. He rubbed a hand over his dishevelled head as though trying to clear away the lingering remnants of fog. He had washed his face and hands, but the darkening patches of red stain on his clothing were still gruesome reminders of the man who had not come down.

'I'm sorry I was so useless, Mr Templar,' he said heavily. 'Did you find anything?'

'Not a thing.' The Saint's straightforwardness sounded completely ingenuous. 'Mr Chase must have been taken out of the window – I climbed down from there myself, and it was quite easy. I walked most of the way round the house, and nothing happened. I didn't hear a sound, and it was too dark to see anything.'

Quintus looked across at the girl.

'There isn't anything I can say, Miss Chase. I can only tell you that I would have given my own right hand to prevent this.'

'But *why*?' she said brokenly. 'Why are all these things happening? What is it all about? First Nora and then – Jim . . . And now my father. What's happened to him? What have they done with him?'

The doctor's lips tightened.

'Kidnapped, I suppose,' he said wretchedly. 'I suppose everything has been leading up to that. Your father's a rich man. They'd expect him to be worth a large ransom – large enough to run any risks for. Jim's death was . . . well, just a tragic accident. He happened to run into one of them in the corridor, so he was murdered. If that hadn't confused them, they'd probably have murdered me.'

'They?' interposed the Saint quickly. 'You saw them, then.'

'Only one man, the one who hit me. He was rather small, and he had a handkerchief tied over his face. I didn't have a chance to notice much. I'm saying "they" because I don't see how one man alone could have organized and done all this . . . It must be kidnapping. Possibly they were trying to force or bribe Nora to help them from the inside, and she was murdered because she threatened to give them away.'

'And they tried to kill me in case she had told me about the plot.'

'Exactly.'

Simon put down the stub of his cigarette and searched for a fresh one.

'Why do you think they should think she might have told me anything?' he inquired.

Quintus hesitated expressionlessly. He drank slowly from his glass, and brought his cavernous black eyes back to the Saint's face.

'With your reputation – if you will forgive me – finding you on the scene . . . I'm only theorizing, of course—'

Simon nodded good humouredly.

'Don't apologize,' he murmured. 'My reputation is a great asset. It's made plenty of clever crooks lose their heads before this.'

'It *must* be kidnapping,' Quintus repeated, turning to the girl. 'If they'd wanted to harm your father, they could easily have done it in his bedroom when they had him at their mercy. They wouldn't have needed to take him away. You must be brave and think about that. The very fact that they took him away proves that they must want him alive.'

The Saint finished chain-lighting the fresh cigarette and strolled over to the fireplace to flick away the butt of the old one. He stood there for a moment, and then turned thoughtfully back to the room.

'Talking of this taking away,' he said, 'I did notice something screwy about it. I didn't waste much time getting upstairs after I heard the commotion. And starting from the same commotion, our kidnapping guy or guys had to dash into the bedroom, grab Mr Chase, shove him out of the window, and lower him to the ground. All of which must have taken a certain amount of time.' He looked at the doctor. 'Well, I wasted a certain amount of time myself in the corridor, finding out whether you were hurt, and so forth. So those times begin to cancel out. Then, when I got in the bedroom, I saw at once that the bed was empty. I looked in the cupboard and the bathroom, just making sure the old boy was really gone; but that can't have taken more than a few seconds. Then I went straight to the window. And then, almost immediately, I climbed out of it and climbed down to the ground to see if I could see anything, because I knew Marvin Chase could only have gone out that way. Now, you remember what I told you? *I didn't hear a sound.* Not so much as the dropping of a pin.'

'What do you mean?' asked the girl.

'I mean this,' said the Saint. 'Figure out our timetables for yourselves – the kidnappers' and mine. They can't have been more than a few seconds ahead of me. And from below the window they had to get your father to a car, shove him in, and take him away – *if they took him away*. But I told you! I walked all round the house, slowly, listening, and I didn't hear anything. When did they start making these completely noiseless cars?'

Quintus half rose from his chair.

'You mean – they might still be in the grounds? Then we're sure to catch them! As soon as the police get here – you've sent for them, of course—'

Simon shook his head.

'Not yet. And that's something else that makes me think I'm right. I haven't called the police yet because I can't. I can't call them because the telephone wires have been cut. And they were cut *after* all this had happened – after I'd walked round the house, and come back in, and told Rosemary what had happened!'

The girl's lips were parted, her wide eyes fastened on him with a mixture of fear and eagerness. She began to say: 'But they might—'

The crash stopped her.

Her eyes switched to the left, and Simon saw blank horror leap into her face as he whirled towards the sound. It had come from one of the windows, and it sounded like smashing glass . . . It was the glass. He saw the stir of the curtains, and the gloved hand that came between them under a shining gun-barrel, and flung himself fiercely backwards.

10

He catapulted himself at the main electric light switches beside the door – without conscious decision, but knowing that his instinct must be right. More slowly, while he was moving, his mind reasoned it out: the unknown man who had broken the window had already beaten him to the draw, and in an open gun battle with the lights on, the unknown had a three-to-one edge in choice of targets . . . Then the Saint's shoulder hit the wall, and his hand sliced up over the switches just as the invader's revolver spoke once, deafeningly.

Blam!

Simon heard the spang of the bullet some distance from him, and more glass shattered. Quintus gasped deeply. The Saint's ears sang with the concussion, but through the buzzing he was trying to determine whether the gunman had come in.

He moved sideways, noiselessly, crouching, his Luger out in his hand. Nothing else seemed to move. His brain was working again in a cold fever of precision. Unless the pot-shot artist had hoped to settle everything with the first bullet, he would expect the Saint to rush the window. Therefore the Saint would not rush the window . . . The utter silence in the room was battering his brain with warnings.

His fingers touched the knob of the door, closed on it and turned it without a rattle until the latch disengaged. Gathering his muscles, he whipped it suddenly open, leapt through it out into the hall, and slammed it behind him. In the one red-hot instant when he was clearly outlined against the lights of the hall, a second shot blasted out of the dark behind him and splintered the woodwork close to his shoulder; but his exposure was too swift and unexpected for the sniper's marksmanship. Without even looking back, Simon dived across the hall and let himself out the front door.

He raced around the side of the house, and dropped to a crouch again as he reached the corner that would bring him in sight of the terrace outside the drawing-room windows. He slid an eye round the corner, prepared to yank it back on an instant's notice, and then left it there with the brow over it lowering in a frown.

It was dark on the terrace, but not too dark for him to see that there was no one standing there.

He scanned the darkness on his right, away from the house; but he could find nothing in it that resembled a lurking human shadow. And over the whole garden brooded the same eerie stillness, the same incredible absence of any hint of movement, that had sent feathery fingers creeping up his spine when he was out there before.

The Saint eased himself along the terrace, flat against the wall of the house, his forefinger tight on the trigger and his eyes probing the blackness of the grounds. No more shots came at him. He reached the french windows with the broken pane, and stretched out a hand to test the handle. They wouldn't open. They were still fastened on the inside – as he had fastened them.

He spoke close to the broken pane.

'All clear, souls. Don't put the lights on yet, but let me in.'

Presently the window swung back. There were shutters outside, and he folded them across the opening and bolted them as he stepped in. Their hinges were stiff from long disuse. He did the same at the other window before he groped his way back to the door and relit the lights.

'We'll have this place looking like a fortress before we're through,' he remarked cheerfully; and then the girl ran to him and caught his sleeve.

'Didn't you see anyone?'

He shook his head.

'Not a soul. The guy didn't even open the window – just stuck his gun through the broken glass and sighted from outside. I have an idea he was expecting me to charge through the window after him, and then he'd 've had me cold. But I fooled him. I guess he heard me coming round the house, and took his feet off the ground.' He smiled at her reassuringly. 'Excuse me a minute while I peep at Hoppy – he might be worried.'

He should have known better than to succumb to that delusion. In the kitchen, a trio of white-faced women and one man who was not much more sanguine jumped round with panicky squeals and goggling eyes as he entered; but Mr Uniatz removed the bottle which he was holding to his lips with dawdling reluctance.

'Hi, boss,' said Mr Uniatz, with as much phlegmatic cordiality as could be expected of a man who had been interrupted in the middle of some important business; and the Saint regarded him with new respect.

'Doesn't anything ever worry you, Hoppy?' he inquired mildly.

Mr Uniatz waved his bottle with liberal nonchalance.

'Sure, boss, I hear de firewoiks,' he said. 'But I figure if anyone is gettin' hoit it's some udder guy. How are t'ings?'

'T'ings will be swell, so long as I know you're on the job,' said the Saint reverently, and withdrew again.

He went back to the drawing-room with his hands in his pockets, not hurrying; and in spite of what had happened he felt more composed than he had been all the evening. It was as if he sensed that the crescendo was coming to a climax beyond which it could go no further, while all the time his own unravellings were simplifying the tangled undercurrents towards one final resolving chord that would bind them all together. And the two must coincide and blend. All he wanted was a few more minutes, a few more answers . . . His smile was almost indecently carefree when he faced the girl again.

'All is well,' he reported, 'and I'm afraid Hoppy is ruining your cellar.'

She came up to him, her eyes searching him anxiously.

'That shot when you ran out,' she said. 'You aren't hurt?'

'Not a bit. But it's depressing to feel so unpopular.'

'What makes you think you're the only one who's unpopular?' asked the doctor dryly.

He was still sitting in the chair where Simon had left him, and Simon followed his glance as he screwed his neck round indicatively. Just over his left shoulder, a picture on the wall had a dark-edged hole drilled in it, and the few scraps of glass that still clung to the frame formed a jagged circle around it.

The Saint gazed at the bullet scar, and for a number of seconds he said nothing. He had heard the impact, of course, and heard the tinkle of glass; but since the shot had missed him he hadn't given it another thought. Now that its direction was pointed out to him, the whole sequence of riddles seemed to fall into focus.

The chain of alibis was complete.

Anyone might have murdered Nora Prescott – even Rosemary Chase and Forrest. Rosemary Chase herself could have fired the shot at the boathouse, an instant before Forrest switched on his torch, and then rejoined him. But Forrest wasn't likely to have cut his own throat; and even if he had done that, he couldn't have abducted Marvin Chase afterwards. And when Forrest was killed, the Saint himself was Rosemary's alibi. The butler might have done all these things; but after that he had been shut in the kitchen with

Hoppy Uniatz to watch over him, so that the Saint's own precaution acquitted him of having fired those last two shots a few minutes ago. Dr Quintus might have done everything else, might never have been hit on the head upstairs at all; but he certainly couldn't have fired those two shots either – and one of them had actually been aimed at him. Simon went back to his original position by the fireplace to make sure of it. The result didn't permit the faintest shadow of doubt. Even allowing for his dash to the doorway, if the first shot had been aimed at the Saint and had just missed Quintus instead, it must have been fired by someone who couldn't get within ten feet of the bull's-eye at ten yards' range – an explanation that wasn't even worth considering.

And that left only one person who had never had an alibi – who had never been asked for one because he had never seemed to need one. The man around whom all the commotion was centred – and yet the one member of the cast, so far as the Saint was concerned, who had never yet appeared on the scene. Someone who, for all obvious purposes, might just as well have been nonexistent.

But if Marvin Chase himself had done all the wild things that had been done that night, it would mean that the story of his injuries must be entirely fictitious. And it was hardly plausible that any man would fabricate and elaborate such a story at a time when there was no conceivable advantage to be gained from it.

Simon thought about that, and everything in him seemed to be standing still.

The girl was saying: 'These people wouldn't be doing all this if they just wanted to kidnap my father. Unless they were maniacs. They can't get any ransom if they kill off everyone who's ever had anything to do with him, and that's what they seem to be trying to do—'

'Except you,' said the Saint, almost inattentively. 'You haven't been hurt yet.'

He was thinking: 'The accident happened a week ago – days before Nora Prescott wrote to me, before there was ever any reason to expect me on the scene. But all these things that a criminal might want an alibi for have happened *since* I came into the picture, and probably on my account. Marvin Chase might have been a swindler, and he might have rubbed out his secretary in a phoney motor accident because he knew too much; but for all he could have known that would have been the end of it. He didn't need to pretend to be injured himself, and take the extra risk of bringing in a phoney doctor to build up the atmosphere. Therefore he didn't invent his injuries. Therefore his alibi is as good as anyone else's. Therefore we're right back where we started.'

Or did it mean that he was at the very end of the hunt? In a kind of trance, he walked over to the broken window and examined the edges of the smashed pane. On the point of one of the jags of glass clung a couple of kinky white threads – such as might have been ripped out of a gauze bandage. Coming into the train of thought that his mind was following, the realization of what they meant gave him hardly any sense of shock. He already knew that he was never going to meet Marvin Chase.

Dr Quintus was getting to his feet.

'I'm feeling better now,' he said. 'I'll go for the police.'

'Just a minute,' said the Saint quietly. 'I think I can have someone ready for them to arrest when they get here.'

11

He turned to the girl and took her shoulders in his hands. 'I'm sorry, Rosemary,' he said. 'You're going to be hurt now.'

Then, without stopping to face the bewildered fear that came into her eyes, he went to the door and raised his voice.

'Send the butler along, Hoppy. See that the curtains are drawn where you are, and keep an eye on the windows. If anyone tries to rush you from any direction give 'em the heat first and ask questions afterwards.'

'Okay, boss,' replied Mr Uniatz obediently.

The butler came down the hall as if he were walking on eggs. His impressively fleshy face was pallid and apprehensive, but he stood before the Saint with a certain ineradicable dignity.

'Yes, sir?'

Simon beckoned him to the front door; and this time the Saint was very careful. He turned out all the hall lights before he opened the door, and then drew the butler quickly outside without fully closing it behind them. They stood where the shadow of the porch covered them in solid blackness.

'Jeeves,' he said, and in contrast with all that circumspection his voice was extraordinarily clear and carrying, 'I want you to go to the nearest house and use their phone to call the police station. Ask for Sergeant Jesser. I want you to give him a special message.'

'Me, sir?'

Simon couldn't see the other's face, but he could imagine

the expression on it from the tremulous tone of the reply. He smiled to himself, but his eyes were busy on the dark void of the garden.

'Yes, you. Are you scared?'

'No-no, sir. But—'

'I know what you mean. It's creepy, isn't it? I'd feel the same way myself. But don't let it get you down. Have you ever handled a gun?'

'I had a little experience during the War, sir.'

'Swell. Then here's a present for you.' Simon felt for the butler's flabby hand and pressed his own Luger into it. 'It's all loaded and ready to talk. If anything tries to happen, use it. And this is something else. I'll be with you. You won't hear me and you won't see me, but I'll be close by. If anyone tries to stop you or do anything to you, he'll get a nasty surprise. So don't worry. You're going to get through.'

He could hear the butler swallow.

'Very good, sir. What was the message you wished me to take?'

'It's for Sergeant Jesser,' Simon repeated, with the same careful clarity. 'Tell him about the murder of Mr Forrest, and the other things that have happened. Tell him I sent you. And tell him I've solved the mystery, so he needn't bother to bring back his gang of coroners and photographers and fingerprint experts and what not. Tell him I'm getting a confession now, and I'll have it all written out and signed for him by the time he gets here. Can you remember that?'

'Yes, sir.'

'Okay, Jeeves. On your way.'

He slipped his other automatic out of his hip pocket and stood there while the butler crossed the drive and melted into the inky shadows beyond. He could hear the man's softened footsteps even when he was out of sight, but they kept regularly on until they faded in the distance, and there was no disturbance. When he felt as sure as he could hope to be that the butler was beyond the danger zone, he put the Walther away again and stepped soundlessly back into the darkened hall.

Rosemary Chase and the doctor stared blankly at him as he re-entered the drawing-room; and he smiled blandly at their mystification.

'I know,' he said. 'You heard me tell Jeeves that I was going to follow him.'

Quintus said: 'But why—'

'For the benefit of the guy outside,' answered the Saint calmly. 'If there is a guy outside. The guy who's been giving us so much trouble. If he's hung around as long as this, he's still around. He hasn't finished his job yet. He missed the balloon pretty badly on the last try, and he daren't pull out and leave it missed. He's staying right on the spot, wondering like hell what kind of a fast play he can work to save his bacon. So he heard what I told the butler. I meant him to. And I think it worked. I scared him away from trying to head off Jeeves with another carving-knife performance. Instead of that, he decided to stay here and try to clean up before the police arrive. And that's also what I meant him to do.'

The doctor's deep-set eyes blinked slowly.

'Then the message you sent was only another bluff?'

'Partly. I may have exaggerated a little. But I meant to tickle our friend's curiosity. I wanted to make sure that he'd be frantic to find out more about it. So he had to know what's going on in this room. I'll bet money that he's listening to every word I'm saying now.'

The girl glanced at the broken window, beyond which the venetian shutters hid them from outside but would not silence their voices, and then glanced at the door; and she shivered. She said: 'But then he knows you didn't go with the butler—'

'But he knows it's too late to catch him up. Besides, this is much more interesting now. He wants to find out how much I've really got up my sleeve. And I want to tell him.'

'But you said you were only bluffing,' she protested huskily. 'You don't really know anything.'

The Saint shook his head.

'I only said I was exaggerating a little. I haven't got a confession yet, but I'm hoping to get one. The rest of it is true. I know everything that's behind tonight's fun and games. I know why everything has been done, and who did it.'

They didn't try to prompt him, but their wide-open eyes clung to him almost as if they had been hypnotized. It was as if an unreasoned fear of what he might be going to say made them shrink from pressing him, while at the same time they were spellbound by a fascination beyond their power to break.

The Saint made the most of his moment. He made them wait while he sauntered to a chair, and settled himself there, and lighted a cigarette, as if they were only enjoying an ordinary casual conversation. The theatrical pause was deliberate, aimed at the nerves of the one person whom he had to drive into self-betrayal.

'It's all so easy, really, when you sort it out,' he said at length. 'Our criminal is a clever guy, and he'd figured out a swindle that was so simple and audacious that it was practically foolproof – barring accidents. And to make up for the thousandth fraction of risk, it was bound to put millions into his hands. Only the accident happened; and one accident led to another.'

He took smoke from his cigarette, and returned it through musingly half smiling lips.

'The accident was when Nora Prescott wrote to me. She had to be in on the swindle, of course; but he thought he could keep her quiet with the threat that if she exposed him

her father would lose the sinecure that was practically keeping him alive. It wasn't a very good threat, if she'd been a little
more sensible, but it scared her enough to keep her away
from the police. It didn't scare her out of thinking that a guy
like me might be able to wreck the scheme somehow and still
save something out of it for her. So she wrote to me. Our
villain found out about that, but wasn't able to stop the letter.
So he followed her to the Bell tonight, planning to kill me as
well, because he figured that once I'd received that letter I'd
keep prying until I found something. When Nora led off to
the boathouse, it looked to be in the bag. He followed her,
killed her, and waited to add me to the collection. Only on
account of another accident that happened then, he lost his
nerve and quit.'

Again the Saint paused.

'Still, our villain knew he had to hang on to me until I
could be disposed of,' he went on with the same leisured
confidence. 'He arranged to bring me up here to be got rid of
as soon as he knew how. He stalled along until after dinner,
when he'd got a plan worked out. He'd just finished talking it
over with his accomplice—'

'Accomplice?' repeated the doctor.

'Yes,' said the Saint flatly. 'And just to make sure we understand each other, I'm referring to a phoney medico who goes
under the name of Quintus.'

The doctor's face went white, and his hands whitened on
the arms of his chair; but the Saint didn't stir.

'I wouldn't try it,' he said. 'I wouldn't try anything, brother,
if I were you. Because if you do, I shall smash you into
soup-meat.'

Rosemary Chase stared from one to the other.

'But – you don't mean—'

'I mean that that motor accident of your father's was a lie
from beginning to end.' Simon's voice was gentle. 'He needed

a phoney doctor to back up the story of those injuries. He couldn't have kept it up with an honest one, and that would have wrecked everything. It took me a long time to see it, but that's because we're all ready to take too much for granted. You told me you'd seen your father since it happened, so I didn't ask any more questions. Naturally, you didn't feel you had to tell me that when you saw him he was smothered in bandages like a mummy, and his voice was only a hoarse croak; but he needed Quintus to keep him that way.'

'You must be out of your mind!' Quintus roared hollowly.

The Saint smiled.

'No. But you're out of a job. And it was an easy one. I said we all take too much for granted. You're introduced as a doctor, and so everybody believes it. Now you're going to have another easy job – signing the confession I promised Sergeant Jesser. You'll do it to save your own skin. You'll tell how Forrest wasn't quite such a fool as he seemed – how he listened outside Marvin Chase's room, and heard you and your pal cooking up a scheme to have your pal bust this window here and take a shot at you, just for effect, and then kill me and Hoppy when we came dashing into the fight – how Forrest got caught there, and how he was murdered so he couldn't spill the beans—'

'And what else?' said a new voice.

Simon turned his eyes towards the doorway and the man who stood there – a man incongruously clad in dark wine-coloured silk pyjamas and bedroom slippers whose head was swathed in bandages so that only his eyes were visible, whose gloved right hand held a revolver aimed at the Saint's chest. The Saint heard Rosemary come to her feet with a stifled cry and answered to her rather than to anyone else.

'I told you you were going to be hurt, Rosemary,' he said. 'Your father was killed a week ago. But you'll remember his secretary. This is Mr Bertrand Tamblin.'

12

'You're clever, aren't you?' Tamblin said viciously.

'Not very,' said the Saint regretfully. 'I ought to have tumbled to it long ago. But as I was saying, we all take too much for granted. Everyone spoke of you as Marvin Chase, and so I assumed that was who you were. I got thrown off the scent a bit further when Rosemary and Forrest crashed into the boathouse at an awkward moment when you got the wind up and scrammed. I didn't get anywhere near the mark until I began to think of you as the invisible millionaire – the guy that all the fuss was about and yet who couldn't be seen. Then it all straightened out. You killed Marvin Chase, burnt his body in a fake auto crash, and had yourself brought home by Quintus in his place. Nobody argued about it; you had Quintus to keep you covered; you knew enough about his affairs to keep your end up in any conversation – you could even fool his daughter on short interviews, with your face bandaged and talking in the sort of faint unrecognizable voice that a guy who'd been badly injured might talk in. And you were all set to get your hands on as much of Marvin Chase's dough as you could squeeze out of banks and bonds before anyone got suspicious.'

'Yes?'

'Oh, yes . . . It was a grand idea until the accidents began to happen. Forrest was another accident. You got some of his blood on you – it's on you now – and you were afraid to jump back into bed when you heard me coming up the stairs. You lost your head again, and plunged into a phoney kidnapping. I don't believe that you skipped out of your window at all just then – you simply hopped into another room and hid there till the coast was clear. I wondered about that when I didn't hear any car driving off, and nobody took a shot at me when I walked round the house.'

'Go on.'

'Then you realized that someone would send for the police, and you had to delay that until you'd carried out your original plan of strengthening Quintus's alibi and killing Hoppy and me. You cut the phone wires. That was another error: an outside gang would have done that first and taken no chances, not run the risk of hanging around to do it after the job was pulled. Again, you didn't shoot at me when I went out of doors the second time, because you wanted to make it look as if Quintus was also being shot at first. Then when you chose your moment, I was lucky enough to be too fast for you. When you heard me chasing round the outside of the house, you pushed off into the night for another think. I'd 've had the hell of a time catching you out there in the dark, so I let you hear me talking to the butler because I knew it would fetch you in.'

Tamblin nodded.

'You only made two mistakes,' he said. 'Forrest would have been killed anyway, only I should have chosen a better time for it. I heard Rosemary talking to him one night outside the front door, directly under my window, when he was leaving – that is how I found out that Nora had written to you and where she was going to meet you.'

'And the other mistake?' Simon asked coolly.

'Was when you let your own cleverness run away with you. When you arranged your clever scheme to get me to walk in here to provide the climax for your dramatic revelations, and even left the front door ajar to make it easy for me. You conceited fool! You've got your confession; but did you think I'd let it do you any good? Your bluff only bothered me for a moment when I was afraid Quintus had ratted. As soon as I found he hadn't, I was laughing at you. The only difference you've made is that now I shall have to kill Rosemary as well. Quintus had ideas about her, and we could have used her to build up the story—'

'Bertrand,' said the Saint gravely, 'I'm afraid you are beginning to drivel.'

The revolver that was trained on him did not waver.

'Tell me why,' Tamblin said interestedly.

Simon trickled smoke languidly through his nostrils. He was still leaning back in his chair, imperturbably relaxed, in the attitude in which he had stayed even when Tamblin entered the room.

'Because it's your turn to be taking too much for granted. You thought my cleverness had run away with me, and so you stopped thinking. It doesn't seem to have occurred to you that since I expected you to come in, I may have expected just how sociable your ideas would be when you got here. You heard me give Jeeves a gun, and so you've jumped to the conclusion that I'm unarmed. Now will you take a look at my left hand? You notice that it's in my coat pocket. I've got you covered with another gun, Bertrand, and I'm ready to bet I can shoot faster than you. If you don't believe me, just start squeezing that trigger.'

Tamblin stood gazing motionlessly at him for a moment; and then his head tilted back and a cackle of hideous laughter came through the slit in the bandages over his mouth.

'Oh, no, Mr Templar,' he crowed. 'You're the one who took too much for granted. You decided that Quintus was a phoney doctor, and so you didn't stop to think that he might be a genuine pickpocket. When he was holding on to you in the corridor upstairs – you remember? – he took the magazines out of both your guns. You've got one shot in the chamber of the gun you've got left, and Quintus has got you covered as well now. You can't get both of us with one bullet. You've been too clever for the last time—'

It was no bluff. Simon knew it with a gambler's instinct, and knew that Tamblin had the last laugh.

'Take your hand out of your pocket,' Tamblin snarled. 'Quintus is going to aim at Rosemary. If you use that gun, you're killing her as surely as if—'

The Saint saw Tamblin's forefinger twitch on the trigger, and waited for the sharp bite of death.

The crisp thunder of cordite splintered the unearthly stillness; but the Saint felt no shock, no pain. Staring incredulously, he saw Tamblin stagger as if a battering-ram had hit him in the back; saw him sway weakly, his right arm drooping until the revolver slipped through his fingers; saw his knees fold and his body pivot slantingly over them like a falling tree ... And saw the cubist figure and pithecanthropoid visage of Hoppy Uniatz coming through the door with a smoking Betsy in its hairy hand.

He heard another thud on his right, and looked round. The thud was caused by Quintus's gun hitting the carpet. Quintus's hands waved wildly in the air as Hoppy turned towards him.

'Don't shoot!' he screamed. 'I'll give you a confession. I haven't killed anyone. Tamblin did it all. Don't shoot me—'

'He doesn't want to be shot, Hoppy,' said the Saint. 'I think we'll let the police have him – just for a change. It may help to convince them of our virtue.'

'Boss,' said Mr Uniatz, lowering his gun, 'I done it.'

The Saint nodded. He got up out of his chair. It felt rather strange to be alive and untouched.

'I know,' he said. 'Another half a second and he'd 've been the most famous gunman on earth.'

Mr Uniatz glanced cloudily at the body on the floor.

'Oh, him,' he said vaguely. 'Yeah . . . But listen, boss – I done it!'

'You don't have to worry about it,' said the Saint. 'You've done it before. And Comrade Quintus's squeal will let you out.'

Rosemary Chase was coming towards him, pale but steady. It seemed to Simon Templar that a long time had been wasted in which he had been too busy to remember how beautiful she was and how warm and red her lips were. She put out a hand to him; and because he was still the Saint and always would be, his arm went round her.

'I know it's tough,' he said. 'But we can't change it.'

'It doesn't seem so bad now, somehow,' she said. 'To know that at least my father wasn't doing all this . . . I wish I knew how to thank you.'

'Hoppy's the guy to thank,' said the Saint, and looked at him. 'I never suspected you of being a thought-reader, Hoppy, but I'd give a lot to know what made you come out of the kitchen in the nick of time?'

Mr Uniatz blinked at him.

'Dat's what I mean, boss, when I say I done it,' he explained, his brow furrowed with the effort of amplifying a statement which seemed to him to be already obvious enough. 'When you call out de butler, he is just opening me anudder bottle of Scotch. An' dis time I make de grade. I drink it down to de last drop wit'out stopping. So I come right out to tell ya.' A broad beam of ineffable pride opened up a gold mine in the centre of Mr Uniatz's face. 'I done it, boss! Ain't dat sump'n?'

The Affair of Hogsbotham

INTRODUCTION BY LESLIE CHARTERIS*

Originality in a writer is generally supposed to be an asset; although on the other side of the argument there is always the old proverb about how there is nothing new under the sun. In my very limited field I have tried to achieve a little originality; I don't know with how much success.

Within the rather conventionalised boundaries of the modern crime story, there are actually only a very small and definite number of choices for the central figure, who must be what you might call the focal point of the lens through which the reader is going to inspect the crime. He or she can be (a) an observant bystander, (b) a professional policeman, (c) a brilliant amateur, (d) a sort of Saint, or (e) the criminal. But these possibilities are even more reduced in practice. The observant bystander is necessarily negative, and to me an unsatisfactory evasion. The professional policeman, if credibly depicted, would have to be a little dull and stereotyped, for what seems to me to be the obvious reason that no one with an original personality would want to be a professional policeman – or, if he did want to be one, that no police force under the present system would encourage his ambition. The criminal, on the other hand, while his point of view might provide an interesting angle for a single story, cannot survive a series simply because the repetition of his crimes would make him an increasingly objectionable person – Raffles and

*From *The First Saint Omnibus* (1939)

Arsène Lupin got away with it in a very different age, and are pardoned now through a kind of sentimental purifying, much as we find it convenient to forget that Richard the Lion Heart probably did not take many baths.

This brings us down to two alternatives, of which the Brilliant Amateur is the most commonly chosen. Perhaps for this reason, the effort of making him original seems to get a little more shortwinded with every incarnation. He is invested with weirder and weirder attributes in a frantic attempt to distinguish him from his continually multiplying host of predecessors. He progresses from violins and cocaine to Gallic gestures and laboured malapropisms, to collections of Chinese porcelain and Egyptian scarabs, to talking like a combination menu and wine list, to quoting Oriental proverbs, to almost anything within the scope of imagination that will distinguish him as if he carried a flag. Without wanting to disparage the excellent stories that are being written by a goodly number of my contemporaries, I still feel sufficiently patriarchal in this business to admit that I sometimes visualise the agony of a new writer sitting down to the task of creating an original hero. Shall he have a glass eye and a forked red beard, and indulge the eccentricity of playing the cornet on the roof of a taxi whilst brooding over his clues? Or shall she be an overweight spinster with a passion for astrology, who can only solve her problems when she is knitting green stockings in a cemetery and being massaged by a one-armed Hindu who quotes Wordsworth with an Icelandic accent? It is getting so difficult to think of anything that hasn't been done before.

But these things, of course, are only mannerisms: they do not make a man. They are characteristics, not character. That should be a platitude, but I'm afraid it is forgotten too often.

I have done my best to remember it. As I said at the beginning, I have been trying to make a picture of a man. Changing, yes. Developing, I hope. Fantastic, improbable – perhaps. Quite worthless, quite irritating, if you feel that way. Or a slightly cockeyed ideal, if you feel differently. It doesn't matter so much, so long as you feel that you would recognise him if you met him tomorrow.

And this is the last story in this book.

Originality in a story is something else again. I'm not sure whether there are three million million plots, or fundamentally only three. There are different schools of thought on the subject. I do know that after writing more than eighty separate stories about the same character I have left myself wide open to be accused of falling into a formula. The selection of a concluding story was therefore quite a problem. It was a temptation to try to bow out with a parting burst of brilliance, a farewell display of fireworks. But on the other hand I wanted a story that in its own way would summarise them all. So it should have Patricia, and Teal, and Hoppy. And Orace, and Peter Quentin. And boodle. It should have spicings of mayhem and mystery and murder, also of romance; of Teal-baiting; and of the Saint's own outrageous brand of philosophical indignation. All those are here. So you might say that it just looks like a distillation of all the Saint stories – the mixture as before. You may be right, too. I wouldn't know. But you will get no apologies from me, because I'm afraid I still like it.

I

'There are times,' remarked Simon Templar, putting down the evening paper and pouring himself a second glass of Tio Pepe, 'when I am on the verge of swearing a great oath never to look at another newspaper as long as I live. Here you have a fascinating world full of all kinds of busy people, being born, falling in love, marrying, dying and being killed, working, starving, fighting, splitting atoms and measuring stars, inventing trick corkscrews and relativity theories, building skyscrapers and suffering hell with toothache. When I buy a newspaper I want to read all about them. I want to know what they're doing and creating and planning and striving for and going to war about – all the exciting vital things that make a picture of a real world and real people's lives. And what do I get?'

'What do you get, Saint?' asked Patricia Holm with a smile.

Simon picked up the newspaper again.

'This is what I get,' he said. 'I get a guy whose name, believe it or not, is Ebenezer Hogsbotham. Comrade Hogsbotham, having been born with a name like that and a face to match it, if you can believe a newspaper picture, has never had a chance in his life to misbehave, and has therefore naturally developed into one of those guys who feel that they have a mission to protect everyone else from misbehaviour. He has therefore been earnestly studying the subject in order to be able to tell other people how to protect themselves from it. For several weeks, apparently, he has

been frequenting the bawdiest theatres and the nudest night
clubs, discovering just how much depravity is being put out
to ensnare those people who are not so shiningly immune to
contamination as himself; as a result of which he has come
out hot and strong for a vigorous censorship of all public
entertainment. Since Comrade Hogsbotham has carefully
promoted himself to be president of the National Society
for the Preservation of Public Morals, he hits the front-page
headlines while five hundred human beings who get themselves blown to bits by honourable Japanese bombs are only
worth a three-line filler on page eleven. And this is the
immortal utterance that he hits them with: "The public has
a right to be protected," he says, "from displays of sugges-
tiveness and undress which are disgusting to all right-thinking people." . . . "Right-thinking people", of course, only
means people who think like Comrade Hogsbotham; but
it's one of those crushing and high-sounding phrases that
the Hogsbothams of this world seem to have a monopoly
on. Will you excuse me while I vomit?'

Patricia fingered the curls in her soft golden hair and
considered him guardedly.

'You can't do anything else about it,' she said. 'Even you
can't alter that sort of thing, so you might as well save your
energy.'

'I suppose so.' The Saint scowled. 'But it's just too hopeless to resign yourself to spending the rest of your life watching nine-tenths of the world's population, who've got more
than enough serious things to worry about already, being
browbeaten into a superstitious respect for the humbug of a
handful of yapping cryptorchid Hogsbothams. I feel that
somebody on the other side of the fence ought to climb over
and pin his ears back . . . I have a pain in the neck. I should
like to do something to demonstrate my unparalleled immor-
ality. I want to go out and burgle a convent; or borrow a guitar

and parade in front of Hogsbotham's house, singing obscene songs in a beery voice.'

He took his glass over to the window and stood there looking down over Piccadilly and the Green Park with a faraway dreaminess in his blue eyes that seemed to be playing with all kinds of electric and reprehensible ideas beyond the humdrum view on which they were actually focused; and Patricia Holm watched him with eyes of the same reckless blue but backed by a sober understanding. She had known him too long to dismiss such a mood as lightly as any other woman would have dismissed it. Any other man might have voiced the same grumble without danger of anyone else remembering it beyond the next drink; but when the man who was so fantastically called the Saint uttered that kind of unsaintly thought, his undercurrent of seriousness was apt to be translated into a different sort of headline with a frequency that Patricia needed all her reserves of mental stability to cope with. Some of the Saint's wildest adventures had started from less sinister openings than that, and she measured him now with a premonition that she had not yet heard the last of that random threat. For a whole month he had done nothing illegal, and in his life thirty days of untarnished virtue was a long time. She studied the buccaneering lines of his lean figure, sensed the precariously curbed restlessness under his lounging ease, and knew that even if no exterior adventure crossed his path that month of peace would come to spontaneous disruption . . .

And then he turned back with a smile that did nothing to reassure her.

'Well, we shall see,' he murmured, and glanced at his watch. 'It's time you were on your way to meet that moribund aunt of yours. You can make sure she hasn't changed her will, because we might stir up some excitement by bumping her off.'

She made a face at him and stood up.

'What are you going to do tonight?'

'I called Claud Eustace this morning and made a date to take him out to dinner – maybe he'll know about something exciting that's going on. And it's time we were on our way too. Are you ready, Hoppy?'

The rudimentary assortment of features which constituted the hairless or front elevation of Hoppy Uniatz's head emerged lingeringly from behind the bottle of Caledonian dew with which he had been making another of his indomitable attempts to assuage the chronic aridity of his gullet.

'Sure, boss,' he said agreeably. 'Ain't I always ready? Where do we meet dis dame we gotta bump off?'

The Saint sighed.

'You'll find out,' he said. 'Let's go.'

Mr Uniatz trotted placidly after him. In Mr Uniatz's mind, a delicate organ which he had to be careful not to overwork, there was room for none of the manifestations of philosophical indignation with which Simon Templar was sometimes troubled. By the time it had found space for the ever-present problems of quenching an insatiable thirst and finding a sufficient supply of lawfully bumpable targets to keep the rust from forming in the barrel of his Betsy, it really had room for only one other idea. And that other permanently comforting and omnipresent notion was composed entirely of the faith and devotion with which he clung to the intellectual pre-eminence of the Saint. The Saint, Mr Uniatz had long since realized, with almost religious awe, could Think. To Mr Uniatz, a man whose rare experiments with Thought had always given him a dull pain under the hat, this discovery had simplified life to the point where Paradise itself would have had few advantages to offer, except possibly rivers flowing with Scotch whisky. He simply did what he was told, and everything came out all right. Anything the Saint said was okay with him.

It is a lamentable fact that Chief Inspector Claud Eustace Teal had no such faith to buoy him up. Mr Teal's views were almost diametrically the reverse of those which gave so much consolation to Mr Uniatz. To Mr Teal, the Saint was a perennial harbinger of woe, an everlasting time-bomb planted under his official chair – with the only difference that when ordinary bombs blew up they were at least over and done with, whereas the Saint was a bomb with the supernatural and unfair ability to blow up whenever it wanted to without in any way impairing its capacity for future explosions. He had accepted the Saint's invitation to dinner with an uneasy and actually unjustified suspicion that there was probably a catch in it, as there had been in most of his previous encounters with the Saint; and there was a gleam of something like smugness in his sleepy eyes as he settled more firmly behind his desk at Scotland Yard and shook his head with every conventional symptom of regret.

'I'm sorry, Saint,' he said. 'I ought to have phoned you, but I've been so busy. I'm going to have to ask you to fix another evening. We had a bank holdup at Staines today, and I've got to go down there and take over.'

Simon's brows began to rise by an infinitesimal hopeful fraction.

'A bank holdup, Claud? How much did they get away with?'

'About fifteen thousand pounds,' Teal said grudgingly. 'You ought to know. It was in the evening papers.'

'I do seem to remember seeing something about it tucked away somewhere,' Simon said thoughtfully. 'What do you know?'

The detective's mouth closed and tightened up. It was as if he was already regretting having said so much, even though the information was broadcast on the streets for anyone with a spare penny to read. But he had seen that tentatively optimistic flicker of the Saint's mocking eyes too often in the past to ever be able to see it again without a queasy hollow feeling in the pit of his ample stomach. He reacted to it with a brusqueness that sprang from a long train of memories of other occasions when crime had been in the news and boodle in the wind, and Simon Templar had greeted both promises with the same incorrigibly hopeful glimmer of mischief in his eyes, and that warning had presaged one more nightmare chapter in the apparently endless sequence that had made the name of the Saint the most dreaded word in the vocabulary of the underworld and the source of more grey hairs in Chief Inspector Teal's dwindling crop than any one man had a right to inflict on a conscientious officer of the law.

'If I knew all about it I shouldn't have to go to Staines,' he said conclusively. 'I'm sorry, but I can't tell you where to go and pick up the money.'

'Maybe I could run you down,' Simon began temptingly. 'Hoppy and I are all on our own this evening, and we were just looking for something useful to do. My car's outside, and it needs some exercise. Besides, I feel clever tonight. All my genius for sleuthing and deduction—'

'I'm sorry,' Teal repeated. 'There's a police car waiting for me already. I'll have to get along as well as I can without you.' He stood up, and held out his hand. A sensitive man might almost have thought that he was in a hurry to avoid an argument. 'Give me a ring one day next week, will you? I'll be able to tell you all about it then.'

Simon Templar stood on the Embankment outside Scotland Yard and lighted a cigarette with elaborately elegant restraint.

'And that, Hoppy,' he explained, 'is what is technically known as the Bum's Rush.'

He gazed resentfully at the dingy panorama which is the total of everything that generations of London architects and

County Councils have been able to make out of their river frontages.

'Nobody loves us,' he said gloomily. 'Patricia forsakes us to be a dutiful niece to a palsied aunt, thereby leaving us exposed to every kind of temptation. We try to surround ourselves with holiness by dining with a detective, and he's too busy to keep the date. We offer to help him and array ourselves on the side of law and order, and he gives us the tax-collector's welcome. His evil mind distrusts our immaculate motives. He is so full of suspicion and uncharitableness that he thinks our only idea is to catch up with his bank holder-uppers before he does and relieve them of their loot for our own benefit. He practically throws us out on our ear, and abandons us to any wicked schemes we can cook up. What are we going to do about it?'

'I dunno, boss.' Mr Uniatz shifted from one foot to the other, grimacing with the heroic effort of trying to extract a constructive suggestion from the gummy interior of his skull. He hit upon one at last, with the trepidant amazement of another Newton grasping the law of gravity. 'Maybe we could go some place an' get a drink,' he suggested breathlessly.

Simon grinned at him and took him by the arm.

'For once in your life,' he said, 'I believe you've had an inspiration. Let us go to a pub and drown our sorrows.'

On the way he bought another evening paper and turned wistfully to the story of the bank holdup; but it gave him very little more than Teal had told him. The bank was a branch of the City & Continental, which handled the accounts of two important factories on the outskirts of the town. That morning the routine consignment of cash in silver and small notes had been brought down from London in a guarded van to meet the weekly payrolls of the two plants; and after it had been placed in the strong-room the van and the guards had departed as usual, although the factory messengers would not call for it until the afternoon. There was no particular secrecy about the arrangements, and the possibility of a holdup of the bank itself had apparently never been taken seriously. During the lunch hour the local police, acting on an anonymous telephone call, had sent a hurried squad to the bank in time to interrupt the holdup; but the bandits had shot their way out, wounding two constables in the process; and approximately fifteen thousand pounds' worth of untraceable small change had vanished with them. Their car had been found abandoned only a few blocks from the bank premises, and there the trail ended; and the Saint knew that it was likely to stay ended there for all the clues contained in the printed story. England was a small country, but it contained plenty of room for two unidentified bank robbers to hide in.

Simon refolded the newspaper and dumped it resignedly on the bar; and as he did so it lay in such a way that the headlines summarizing the epochal utterance of Mr Ebenezer Hogsbotham stared up at him with a complacent prominence that added insult to injury.

The Saint stared malevolently back at them; and in the mood which circumstances had helped to thrust upon him their effect had an almost fateful inevitability. No other man on earth would have taken them in just that way; but there never had been another man in history so harebrained as the Saint could be when his rebellious instincts boiled over. The idea that was being born to him grew momentarily in depth and richness. He put down his glass, and went to the telephone booth to consult the directory. The action was rather like the mental tossing of a coin. And it came down heads. Mr Hogsbotham was on the telephone. And accordingly, decisively, his address was in the book . . .

The fact seemed to leave no further excuse for hesitation. Simon went back to the bar, and his head sang carols with the blitheness of his own insanity.

'Put that poison away, Hoppy,' he said. 'We're going places.'

Mr Uniatz gulped obediently, and looked up with a contented beam.

'Dijja t'ink of sump'n to do, boss?' he asked eagerly.

The Saint nodded. His smile was extravagantly radiant.

'I did. We're going to burgle the house of Hogsbotham.'

2

It was one of those lunatic ideas that any inmate of an asylum might have conceived, but only Simon Templar could be relied on to carry solemnly into execution. He didn't waste any more time on pondering over it, or even stop to consider any of its legal aspects. He drove his huge cream and red Hirondel snarling over the roads to Chertsey at an average speed that was a crime in itself, and which would probably have given a nervous breakdown to any passenger less impregnably phlegmatic than Mr Uniatz; but he brought it intact to the end of the trip without any elaborations on his original idea or any attempt to produce them. He was simply on his way to effect an unlawful entry into the domicile of Mr Hogsbotham, and there to do something or other that would annoy Mr Hogsbotham greatly and at the same time relieve his own mood of general annoyance; but what that something would be rested entirely with the inspiration of the moment. The only thing he was sure about was that the inspiration would be forthcoming.

The telephone directory had told him that Mr Hogsbotham lived at Chertsey. It also located Mr Hogsbotham's home on Greenleaf Road, which Simon found to be a narrow turning off Chertsey Lane running towards the river on the far side of the town. He drove the Hirondel into a field a hundred yards beyond the turning and left it under the broad shadow of a clump of elms, and returned to Greenleaf Road on foot. And there the telephone directory's information became vague. Following the ancient custom by which the Englishman strives to preserve the sanctity of his castle from strange visitors by refusing to give it a street number, hiding it instead under a name like 'Mon Repos', 'Sea View', 'The Birches', 'Dunrovin', 'Jusweetu', and other similar whimsies the demesne of Mr Hogsbotham was apparently known simply as 'The Snuggery'. Which might have conveyed volumes to a postman schooled in tracking self-effacing citizens to their lairs, but wasn't the hell of a lot of help to any layman who was trying to find the place for the first time on a dark night.

Simon had not walked very far down Greenleaf Road when that fact was brought home to him. Greenleaf Road possessed no street lighting to make navigation easier. It was bordered by hedges of varying heights and densities, behind which lighted windows could sometimes be seen and sometimes not. At intervals, the hedges yawned into gaps from which ran well-kept drives and things that looked like cart-tracks in about equal proportions. Some of the openings had gates, and some hadn't. Some of the gates had names painted on them; and on those which had, the paint varied in antiquity from shining newness to a state of weatherbeaten decomposition which made any name that had ever been there completely illegible. When the Saint realized that they had already passed at least a dozen anonymous entrances, any one of which might have led to the threshold of Mr Hogsbotham's Snuggery, he stopped walking and spoke eloquently on the subject of town planning for a full minute without raising his voice.

He could have gone on for longer than that, warming to his subject as he developed the theme; but farther down the road the wobbling light of a lone bicycle blinked into view, and he stepped out from the side of the road as it came abreast of them and kept his hat down over his eyes and his face averted from the light while he asked the rider if he knew the home of Hogsbotham.

'Yes, sir, it's the fourth 'ouse on yer right the way yer goin'. Yer can't miss it.' said the wanderer cheerfully, with a native's slightly patronizing simplicity, and rode on.

The Saint paused to light a cigarette, and resumed his stride. The lines of his face dimly illumined in the glow of smouldering tobacco were sharp with half humorous anticipation.

'Hogsbotham may be in London investigating some more nightclubs,' he said. 'But you'd better get a handkerchief tied round your neck so you can pull it up over your dial – just in case. We don't want to be recognized, because it would worry Claud Eustace Teal, and he's busy.'

He was counting the breaks in the hedges as he walked. He counted three, and stopped at the fourth. A gate that could have closed it stood open, and he turned his pocket flashlight on it cautiously. It was one of the weatherbeaten kind, and the words that had once been painted on it were practically indecipherable, but they looked vaguely as if they might once had stood for 'The Snuggery'.

Simon killed his torch after that brief glimpse. He dropped his cigarette and trod it out under his foot.

'We seem to have arrived,' he said. 'Try not to make too much noise, Hoppy, because maybe Hogsbotham isn't deaf.'

He drifted on up the drive as if his shoes had been soled with cotton wool. Following behind him, Mr Uniatz's efforts to lighten his tread successfully reduced the total din of their advance to something less than would have been made by a small herd of buffalo; but Simon knew that the average citizen's sense of hearing is mercifully unselective. His own silent movements were more the result of habit than of any conscious care.

The drive curved around a dense mass of laurels, above which the symmetrical spires of cypress silhouetted against the dark sky concealed the house until it loomed suddenly in front of him as if it had risen from the ground. The angles of its roof-line cut a serrated pattern out of the gauzy backcloth of half-hearted stars hung behind it; the rest of the building below that angled line was merely a mass of solid blackness in which one or two knife edges of yellow light gleaming between drawn curtains seemed to be suspended disjointedly in space. But they came from ground-floor windows, and he concluded that Ebenezer Hogsbotham was at home.

He did not decide that Mr Hogsbotham was not only at home, but at home with visitors, until he nearly walked into a black closed car parked in the driveway. The car's lights were out, and he was so intent on trying to establish the topography of the lighted windows that the dull sheen of its coachwork barely caught his eye in time for him to check himself. He steered Hoppy round it, and wondered what sort of guests a man with the name and temperament of Ebenezer Hogsbotham would be likely to entertain.

And then, inside the house, a radio or gramophone began to play.

It occurred to Simon that he might have been unnecessarily pessimistic in suggesting that Mr Hogsbotham might not be deaf. From the muffled quality of the noise which reached him, it was obvious that the windows of the room in which the instrument was functioning were tightly closed; but even with that obstruction, the volume of sound which boomed out into the night was startling in its quantity. The opus under execution was the 'Ride of the Valkyries', which is admittedly not rated among the most ethereal melodies in the musical pharmacopoeia; but even so, it was being produced with a vim which inside the room itself must have been earsplitting. It roared out in a stunning fortissimo that made the Saint put his heels back on the ground and disdain even to moderate his voice.

'This is easy,' he said. 'We'll just batter the door down and walk in.'

He was not quite as blatant as that, but very nearly. He was careful enough to circle the house to the back door; and whether he would actually have battered it down remained an unanswered question, for he had no need to use any violence on it at all. It opened when he touched the handle, and he stepped in as easily as he had entered the garden.

Perhaps it was at that point that he first realized that the unplanned embryo of his adventure was taking a twist which he had never expected of it. It was difficult to pin down the exact moment of mutation, because it gathered force from a series of shocks that superimposed themselves on him with a speed that made the separate phases of the change seem somewhat blurred. And the first two or three of those shocks chased each other into his consciousness directly that unlatched back door swung inwards under the pressure of his hand.

The very fact that the door opened so easily to his exploring touch may have been one of them; but he could take that in his stride. Many householders were inclined to be absent-minded about the uses of locks and bolts. But the following blows were harder to swallow. The door opened to give him a clear view of the kitchen and that was when the rapid sequence of impacts began to make an impression on his powers of absorption.

To put it bluntly, which is about the only way anything of that kind could be put, the door opened to give him a full view of what appeared to be quite a personable young woman tied to a chair.

There was a subsidiary shock in the realization that she appeared to be personable. Without giving any thought to the subject, Simon had never expected Mr Hogsbotham to have a servant who was personable. He had automatically credited him with a housekeeper who had stringy mouse-coloured hair, a long nose inclined to redness, and a forbidding lipless mouth, a harridan in tightlaced corsets whose egregiously obvious virtue would suffice to strangle any gossip about Mr Hogsbotham's bachelor ménage – Mr Hogsbotham had to be a bachelor, because it was not plausible that any woman, unless moved by a passion which a man of Mr Hogsbotham's desiccated sanctity could never hope to inspire, would consent to adopt a name like Mrs Hogsbotham. The girl in the chair appeared to be moderately young, moderately well-shaped, and moderately inoffensive to look at; although the dishcloth which was knotted across her mouth as a gag made the last quality a little difficult to estimate. Yet she wore a neat housemaid's uniform, and therefore she presumably belonged to Mr Hogsbotham's domestic staff.

That also could be assimilated – with a slightly greater effort. It was her predicament that finally overtaxed his swallowing reflexes. It was possible that there might be some self-abnegating soul in the British Isles who was willing to visit with Mr Hogsbotham; it was possible that Mr Hogsbotham might be deaf; it was possible that he might be careless about locking his back door; it was possible, even, that he might employ a servant who didn't look like the twin sister of a Gorgon; but if he left her tied up and gagged in the kitchen while he entertained his guests with ear-shattering excerpts from Wagner, there was something irregular going on under his sanctimonious roof which Simon Templar wanted to know more about.

He stood staring into the maid's dilated eyes while a galaxy of fantastic queries and surmises skittered across his brain like the grand finale of a firework display. For one long moment he couldn't have moved or spoken if there had been a million-dollar bonus for it.

Mr Uniatz was the one who broke the silence, if any state of affairs that was so numbingly blanketed by the magnified blast of a symphony orchestra could properly be called a silence. He shifted his feet, and his voice grated conspiratorially in the Saint's ear.

'Is dis de old bag, boss?' he inquired with sepulchral sangfroid; and the interruption brought Simon's reeling imagination back to earth.

'What old bag?' he demanded blankly.

'De aunt of Patricia's,' said Mr Uniatz, no less blank at even being asked such a question, 'who we are goin' to bump off.'

The Saint took a firmer grip of material things.

'Does she look like an old bag?' he retorted.

Hoppy inspected the exhibit again, dispassionately.

'No,' he admitted. He seemed mystified. Then a solution dawned dazzlingly upon him. 'Maybe she has her face lifted, boss,' he suggested luminously.

'Or maybe she isn't anybody's aunt,' Simon pointed out.

This kind of extravagant speculation was too much for Mr Uniatz. He was unable to gape effectively on account of the handkerchief over his mouth, but the exposed area between the bridge of his nose and the brim of his hat hinted that the rest of his face was gaping.

'And maybe we've run into something,' said the Saint.

The rest of his mind was paying no attention to Hoppy's problems. He was not even taking much notice of the maid's panic-stricken eyes as they widened still further in mute terror at the conversation that was passing over her head. He was listening intently to the music that still racketed stridently in his eardrums, three times louder now that he was inside the house. There had been a time in the history of his multitudinous interests when he had had a spell of devotion to grand opera, and his ears were as analytically sensitive as those of a trained musician. And he was realizing, with a melodramatic suddenness that prickled the hairs on the nape of his neck, that the multisonous shrillness of the 'Ride of the Valkyries' had twice been mingled with a brief high-pitched shriek that Wagner had never written into the score.

His fingers closed for an instant on Hoppy's arm.

'Stay here a minute,' he said.

He went on past the trussed housemaid, out of the door on the far side of the kitchen. The screeching fanfares of music battered at him with redoubled savagery as he opened the door and emerged into the cramped over-furnished hall beyond it. Aside from its clutter of fretwork mirror-mountings, spindly umbrella stands and etceteras, and vapid Victorian chromos, it contained only the lower end of a narrow staircase and three other doors, one of which was the front entrance. Simon had subconsciously observed a serving hatch in the wall on his left as he opened the kitchen door, and on that evidence he automatically attributed the left-hand door in the hallway to the dining-room. He moved towards the right-hand door. And as he reached it the music stopped, in the middle of a bar, as if it had been sheared off with a knife, leaving the whole house stunned with stillness.

The Saint checked on one foot, abruptly conscious even of his breathing in the sudden quiet. He was less than a yard from the door that must have belonged to the living-room. Standing there, he heard the harsh rumble of a thick brutal voice on the other side of the door, dulled in volume but perfectly distinct.

'All right,' it said. 'That's just a sample. Now will you tell us what you did with that dough, or shall we play some more music?'

3

Simon lowered his spare foot to the carpet, and bent his leg over it until he was down on one knee. From that position he could peer through the keyhole and get a view of part of the room.

Directly across from him, a thin small weasel-faced man stood over a radiogram beside the fireplace. A cigarette dangled limply from the corner of his mouth, and the eyes that squinted through the smoke drifting past his face were beady and emotionless like a snake's. Simon placed the lean cruel face almost instantly in his encyclopedic mental records of the population of the underworld, and the recognition walloped into his already tottering awareness to register yet another item in the sequence of surprise punches that his phenomenal resilience was trying to stand up to. The weasel-faced man's name was Morris Dolf; and he was certainly no kind of guest for anyone with the reputation of Ebenezer Hogsbotham to entertain.

The Saint's survey slid off him on to the man who sat in front of the fireplace. This was someone whom the Saint did not recognize, and he knew he was not Mr Hogsbotham. He was a man with thin sandy hair and a soft plump face that would have fitted very nicely on somebody's pet rabbit. At the moment it was a very frightened rabbit. The man sat in a stiff-backed chair placed on the hearthrug, and pieces of clothesline had been used to keep him there. His arms had been stretched round behind him and tied at the back of the chair so that his shoulders were hunched slightly forward by the strain. His shirt had been ripped open to the waist, so that his chest was bare; and his skin was very white and insipid, as if it had never seen daylight since he was born. It was so white that two irregular patches of inflammation on it stood out like blotches of dull red paint. His lips were trembling, and his eyes bulged in wild orbs of dread.

'I don't know!' he blubbered. 'I tell you, you're making a mistake. I don't know anything about it. I haven't got it. Don't burn me again!'

Morris Dolf might not have heard. He stood leaning boredly against the radiogram and didn't move.

Someone else did. It was a third man, whose back was turned to the door. The back was broad and fitted tightly into his coat, so that the material wrinkled at the armpits, and the neck above it was short and thick and reddish, running quickly into close-cropped wiry black hair. The whole rear view had a hard coarse physical ruthlessness that made it unnecessary to see its owner's face to make an immediate summary of his character. It belonged without a shadow of doubt to the thick brutal voice that Simon had heard first – and equally without doubt, it could not possibly have belonged to Mr Ebenezer Hogsbotham.

The same voice spoke again. It said: 'Okay, Verdean. But you're the one who made the mistake. You made it when you thought you'd be smart and try to doublecross us. You made it worse when you tried to turn us in to the cops, so we could take the rap for you and leave you nothing to worry about. Now you're going to wish you hadn't been so damn smart.'

The broad back moved forward and bent towards the fire-place. The gas fire was burning in the grate, although the evening was warm; and all at once the Saint understood why he had heard through the music those screechy ululations which no orchestral instrument could have produced. The man with the broad back straightened up again, and his powerful hand was holding an ordinary kitchen ladle of which the bowl glowed bright crimson.

'You have it just how you like, rat,' he said. 'I don't mind how long you hold out. I'm going to enjoy working on you. We're going to burn your body a bit more for a start, and then we'll take your shoes and socks off and put your feet in the fire and see how you like that. You can scream your head off if you want to, but nobody 'll hear you over the gramophone . . . Let's have some more of that loud stuff, Morrie.'

Morris Dolf turned back to the radiogram, without a flicker of expression, and moved the pick-up arm. The 'Ride of the Valkyries' crashed out again with a fearful vigour that would have drowned anything less than the howl of a hurricane; and the broad back shifted towards the man in the chair.

The man in the chair stared in delirious horror from the glowing ladle to the face of the man who held it. His eyes bulged until there were white rims all round the pupils. His quivering lips fluttered into absurd jerky patterns, pouring out frantic pleas and protestations that the music swamped into inaudibility.

Simon Templar removed his eye from the keyhole and loosened the gun under his arm. He had no fanciful ideas about rushing to the rescue of a hapless victim of persecution. In fact, all the more subtle aspects of the victim looked as guilty as hell to him – if not of the actual doublecrossing that seemed to be under discussion, at least of plenty of other reprehensible things. No entirely innocent householder would behave in exactly that way if he were being tortured by a couple of invading thugs. And the whole argument as Simon had overheard it smelled ripely with the rich fragrance of dishonour and dissension among thieves. Which was an odour that had perfumed some of the most joyous hours of the Saint's rapscallion life. By all the portents, he was still a puzzlingly long way from getting within kicking distance of the elusive Mr Hogsbotham; but here under his very nose was a proposition that looked no less diverting and a lot more mysterious; and the Saint had a sublimely happy-go-lucky adaptability to the generous vagaries of Fate. He took his gun clear out of the spring harness where he carried it, and opened the door.

He went in without any stealth, which would have been entirely superfluous. The operatic pandemonium would have made his entrance mouselike if he had ridden in on a capering elephant. He walked almost nonchalantly across the room; and its occupants were so taken up with their own business that he was within a couple of yards of them before any of them noticed that he was there.

Morris Dolf saw him first. His beady eyes swivelled incuriously towards the movement that must have finally caught the fringes of their range of vision, and became petrified into glassy blankness as they fastened on the Saint's tall figure. His jaw dropped so that the cigarette would have fallen out of his mouth if the adhesive dampness of the paper hadn't kept it hanging from his lower lip. He stood as horripilantly still as if a long icy needle had shot up out of the floor and impaled him from sacrum to occiput.

That glazed paralysis lasted for about a breath and a half. And then his right hand whipped towards his pocket.

It was nothing but an involuntary piece of sheer stupidity born out of shock, and the Saint was benevolent enough to treat it that way. He simply lifted the gun in his hand a little, bringing it more prominently into view; and Dolf stopped himself in time.

The man with the beefy neck, in his turn, must have caught some queer impression from Dolf's peculiar movements out of the corner of his eye. He turned and looked at his companion's face, froze for an instant, and then went on turning more quickly, straightening as he did so. He let go the red-hot ladle, and his right hand started to make the same instinctive grab that Dolf had started – and stopped in mid-air for the same reason. His heavy florid features seemed to bunch into knots of strangulated viciousness as he stood glowering numbly at the Saint's masked face.

Simon stepped sideways, towards the blaring radiogram, and lifted the needle off the record. The nerve-rasping bombardment of sound broke off into blissful silence.

'That's better,' he murmured relievedly. 'Now we can all talk to each other without giving ourselves laryngitis. When did you discover this passion for expensive music, Morrie?'

Morris Dolf's eyes blinked once at the jar of being addressed by name, but he seemed to find it hard to work up an enthusiasm for discussing his cultural development. His tongue slid over his dry lips without forming an answering syllable.

Simon turned to the big florid man. Now that he had seen his face, he had identified him as well.

'Judd Kaskin, I believe?' he drawled, with the delicate suavity of an ambassador of the old régime. 'Do you know that you're burning the carpet?'

Kaskin looked at the fallen ladle. He bent and picked it up, rubbing the sole of his shoe over the smouldering patch of rug. Then, as if he suddenly realized that he had done all that in mechanical obedience to a command that the Saint hadn't even troubled to utter directly, he threw it clattering into the fireplace and turned his savage scowl back to the Saint.

'What the hell do you want?' he snarled.

'You know, I was just going to ask you the same question,' Simon remarked mildly. 'It seemed to me that you were feel-ing your oats a bit, Judd. I suppose you get that way after doing five years on the Moor. But you haven't been out much more than three months, have you? You shouldn't be in such a hurry to go back.'

The big man's eyes gave the same automatic reaction as Dolf's had given to the accuracy of the Saint's information, and hardened again into slits of unyielding suspicion.

'Who the hell are you?' he grated slowly. 'You aren't a cop. Take that rag off your face and let's see who you are.'

'When I'm ready,' said the Saint coolly. 'And then you may wish I hadn't. Just now, I'm asking the questions. What is this doublecross you're trying to find out about from Comrade Verdean?'

There was a silence. Morris Dolf's slight expression was fading out again. His mouth closed, and he readjusted his cigarette. Simon knew that behind that silent hollow-cheeked mask a cunning brain was getting back to work.

Kaskin's face, when he wanted to play tricks with it, could put on a ruddy rough-diamond joviality that was convincing enough to deceive most people who did not know too much about his criminal record. But at this moment he was making no effort to put on his stock disguise. His mouth was buttoned up in an ugly down-turned curve.

'Why don't you find out, if you're so wise?'

'I could do that,' said the Saint.

He moved on the arc of a circle towards Verdean's chair, keeping Dolf and Kaskin covered all the time. His left hand dipped into his coat pocket and took out a penknife. He opened it one-handed, bracing it against his leg, and felt around to cut the cords from Verdean's wrists and ankles without shifting his eyes for an instant from the two men at the other end of his gun.

'We can go on with the concert,' he explained gently. 'And I'm sure Comrade Verdean would enjoy having a turn as Master of Ceremonies. Put the spoon back in the fire, Verdean, and let's see how Comrade Kaskin likes his chops broiled.'

Verdean stood up slowly, and didn't move any farther. His gaze wavered idiotically over the Saint, as if he was too dazed to make up his mind what he ought to do. He pawed at his burned chest and made helpless whimpering noises in his throat, like a sick child.

Kaskin glanced at him for a moment, and slowly brought his eyes back to the Saint again. At the time, Simon thought that it was Verdean's obvious futility that kindled the stiffening belligerent defiance in Kaskin's stare. There was something almost like tentative domination in it.

Kaskin sneered: 'See if he'll do it. He wouldn't have the guts. And *you* can't, while you've got to keep that gun on us. I'm not soft enough to fall for that sort of bluff. You picked the wrong show to butt in on, however you got here. You'd better get out again in a hurry before you get hurt. You'd better put that gun away and go home, and forget you ever came here—'

And another voice said: 'Or you can freeze right where you are. Don't try to move, or I'll let you have it.'

The Saint froze.

The voice was very close behind him – too close to take any chances with. He could have flattened Kaskin before it could carry out its threat, but that was as far as he would get. The Saint had a coldblooded way of estimating his chances in any situation; and he was much too interested in life just then to make that kind of trade. He knew now the real reason for Kaskin's sudden gathering of confidence, and why the big man had talked so fast in a strain that couldn't help centring his attention. Kaskin had taken his opportunity well. Not a muscle of his face had betrayed what he was seeing; and his loud bullying voice had effectively covered any slight noise that the girl might have made as she crept up.

The girl. Yes. Simon Templar's most lasting startlement clung to the fact that the voice behind him unmistakably belonged to a girl.

4

'Drop that gun,' she said, 'and be quick about it.' Simon dropped it. His ears were nicely attuned to the depth of meaning behind a voice, and this voice meant what it said. His automatic plunked on the carpet; and Morris Dolf stooped into the scene and snatched it up. Even then, Dolf said nothing. He propped himself back on the radiogram and kept the gun levelled, watching Simon in silence with sinister lizard eyes. He was one of the least talkative men that Simon had ever seen.

'Keep him covered,' Kaskin said unnecessarily. 'We'll see what he looks like.'

He stepped forward and jerked the handkerchief down from the Saint's smile.

And then there was a stillness that prolonged itself through a gamut of emotions which would have looked like the most awful kind of ham acting if they had been faithfully recorded on celluloid. Neither Dolf nor Kaskin had ever met the Saint personally; but his photograph had at various times been published in almost every newspaper on earth, and verbal descriptions of him had circulated through underworld channels so often that they must have worn a private groove for themselves. Admittedly there were still considerable numbers of malefactors to whom the Saint was no more than a dreaded name; but Messrs Dolf and Kaskin were not among them. Recognition came to them slowly, which accounted for the elaborate and longdrawn detail of their changing expressions; but it came with a frightful certainty. Morris Dolf's fleshless visage seemed to grow thinner and meaner, and his fingers twitched hungrily around the butt of Simon's gun. Judd Kaskin's sanguine complexion changed colour for a moment, and then his mouth twisted as though tasting its own venom.

'The Saint!' he said hoarsely.

'I told you you might be sorry,' said the Saint.

He smiled at them pleasantly, as if nothing had happened to disturb his poise since he was holding the only weapon in sight. It was a smile that would have tightened a quality of desperation into the vigilance of certain criminals who knew him better than Dolf and Kaskin did. It was the kind of smile that only touched the Saint's lips when the odds against him were most hopeless – and when all the reckless fighting vitality that had written the chapter headings in his charmed saga of adventure was blithely preparing to thumb its nose at them . . .

Then he turned and looked at the girl.

She was blonde and blue-eyed, with a small face like a very pretty baby doll; but the impression of vapid immaturity was contradicted by her mouth. Her mouth had character – not all of it very good, by conventional standards, but the kind of character that has an upsetting effect on many conventional men. It was a rather large mouth, with a sultry lower lip that seemed to have been fashioned for the express purpose of reviving the maximum amount of the Old Adam in any masculine observer. The rest of her, he noticed, carried out the theme summarized in her mouth. Her light dress moulded itself to her figure with a snugness that vouched for the fragility of her underwear, and the curves that it suggested were stimulating to the worst kind of imagination.

'Angela,' said the Saint genially, 'you're looking very well for your age. I ought to have remembered that Judd always worked with a woman, but I didn't think he'd have one with him on a job like this. I suppose you were sitting in the car outside, and saw me arrive.'

'You know everything, don't you?' Kaskin gibed.

He was recovering from the first shock of finding out whom he had captured; and the return of his self-assurance was an ugly thing.

'Only one thing puzzles me,' said the Saint equably. 'And that is why they sent you to Dartmoor instead of putting you in the Zoo. Or did the RSPCA object on behalf of the other animals?'

'You're smart,' Kaskin said lividly. His ugliness had a hint of bluster in it that was born of fear – a fear that the legends about the Saint were capable of inspiring even when he was apparently disarmed and helpless. But the ugliness was no less dangerous for that reason. Perhaps it was more danger- ous . . . 'You're smart, like Verdean,' Kaskin said 'Well, you saw what he got. I'm asking the questions again now, and I'll burn you the same way if you don't answer. And I'll burn you twice as much if you make any more funny answers. Now do your talking, smart guy. How did you get here?'

'I flew in,' said the Saint, 'with my little wings.'

Kaskin drew back his fist.

'Wait a minute,' said the girl impatiently. 'He had another man with him.'

Kaskin almost failed to hear her. His face was contorted with the blind rage into which men of his type are fatally easy to tease. His fist had travelled two inches before he stopped it. The girl's meaning worked itself into his intelligence by visibly slow degrees, as if it had to penetrate layers of gum. He turned his head stiffly.

'What's that?'

'There were two of them. I saw them.'

'Then where's the other one?' Kaskin said stupidly.

Simon was asking himself the same question; but he had more data to go on. He had left the kitchen door open, and also left the living-room door open behind him when he came in. The girl had come in through the door without touching it; and she must have entered the house at the front, or she would have met Hoppy before. The chances were, therefore, that Hoppy had heard most of the conversation since the music stopped. But with the living-room door still open, and three of the ungodly in the room facing in different directions, it would be difficult for him to show himself and go into action without increasing the Saint's danger. He must have been standing in the hall by that time, just out of sight around the edge of the doorway, waiting for Simon to make him an opening. At least, Simon hoped he was. He had to gamble on it, for he was never likely to get a better break.

Kaskin swung back on him to repeat the question in a lower key.

'Where's your pal, smart guy?'

'You haven't looked at the window lately, have you?' said the Saint blandly.

At any other time it might not have worked; but this time the ungodly were at a disadvantage because one of their own number had brought up the subject. They had another disadvantage, because they didn't realize until a second later that the room contained more than one window. And their third misfortune was that they all gave way simultaneously to a natural instinct of self-preservation that the Saint's indescribably effortless serenity did everything in its power to encourage. All of them looked different ways at once, while all of them must have assumed that somebody else was continuing to watch the Saint. Which provided a beautiful example of one of those occasions when unanimity is not strength.

Kaskin was nearly between Simon and the girl, and the Saint's swift sidestep perfected the alignment. The Saint's right foot drove at the big man's belt buckle, sent Kaskin staggering back against her. She was caught flat-footed, and started moving too late to dodge him. They collided with a thump; but Kaskin's momentum was too great to be completely absorbed by the impact. They reeled back together, Kaskin's flailing arms nullifying the girl's desperate effort to regain her balance. The small nickelled automatic waved wildly in her hand.

Simon didn't wait to see how the waltz worked out. He had only a matter of split seconds to play with, and they had to be crowded ones. He was pivoting on his left foot, with his right leg still in the air, even as Kaskin started caroming backwards from the kick; and Morris Dolf was a fraction of an instant slow in sorting out the situation. The Saint's left hand grabbed his automatic around the barrel before the trigger could tighten, twisting it sideways out of line; it exploded once, harmlessly, and then the Saint's right fist slammed squarely on the weasel-faced man's thin nose. Morris Dolf's eyes bleared with agony, and his fingers went limp with the stunning pain. Simon wrenched the gun away and reversed the butt swiftly into his right hand.

The Saint spun around. Hoppy's chunky outline loomed in the doorway, his massive automatic questing for a target, a pleased warrior smile splitting the lower half of his face. But Kaskin was finding solid ground under his feet again, and his right hand was struggling with his hip pocket. The girl's nickel-plated toy was coming back to aim. And behind him, the Saint knew that Morris Dolf was getting out another gun. Simon had only taken back the automatic he had lost a short while earlier. Morris Dolf still had his own gun. The Saint felt goose-pimples rising all over him.

'The lights, Hoppy!' he yelled. 'And scram out the front!'

He dived sideways as he spoke; and darkness engulfed the room mercifully as he did it. Cordite barked malignantly out of the blackness, licking hot orange tongues at him from two directions: he heard the hiss and smack of lead, but it did not touch him. And then his dive cannoned him into the man called Verdean.

It was Verdean that he had meant to reach. His instinct had mapped the campaign with a speed and sureness that deliberate logic still had to catch up with. But all the steps were there. The atmosphere of the moment showed no probability of simmering down into that mellow tranquillity in which heart-to-heart talks are exchanged. The Saint very much wanted a heart-to-heart talk with somebody, if only to satisfy a perfectly normal inquisitiveness concerning what all the commotion was about. But since Messrs Dolf and Kaskin had been asking the questions when he arrived, it appeared that Mr Verdean might know more of the answers than they did. Therefore Mr Verdean looked like the prize catch of the evening. Therefore Mr Verdean had to be transported to an atmosphere where heart-to-heart talking might take place. It was as simple as that.

The Saint gripped Verdean by the arm, and said: 'Let's go somewhere else, brother. Your friends are getting rough.'

Verdean took one step the way the Saint steered him, and then he turned into a convincing impersonation of a hysterical eel. He squirmed against the Saint's grasp with the strength of panic, and his free arm whirled frantically in the air. His knuckles hit the Saint's cheekbone near the eye, sending a shower of sparks across Simon's vision.

Simon might have stopped to reason with him, to persuasively point out the manifest arguments in favour of adjourning to a less hectic neighbourhood; but he had no time. No more shots had been fired, doubtless because it had been borne in upon the ungodly that they stood a two to one chance of doing more damage to each other than to him, but he could hear them blundering in search of him. The Saint raised his gun and brought the barrel down vigorously where he thought Verdean's head ought to be. Mr Verdean's head proved to be in the desired spot; and Simon ducked a shoulder under him and lifted him up as he collapsed.

The actual delay amounted to less than three seconds. The ungodly were still blinded by the dark, but Simon launched himself at the window with the accuracy of a homing pigeon.

He wasted no time fumbling with catches. He hit the centre of it with his shoulder – the shoulder over which Verdean was draped. Verdean, in turn, hit it with his hams; and the fastening was not equal to the combined load. It splintered away with a sharp crack, and the twin casements flew open crashingly. Verdean passed through them into the night, landing in soft earth with a soggy thud; and the Saint went on after him as if he were plunging into a pool. He struck ground with his hands, and rolled over in a fairly graceful somersault as a fourth shot banged out of the room he had just left.

A gorilla paw caught him under the arm and helped him up, and Mr Uniatz's voice croaked anxiously in his ear.

'Ya ain't stopped anyt'ing, boss?'

'No.' Simon grinned in the dark. 'They aren't that good. Grab hold of this bird and see if the car'll start. They probably left the keys in it.'

He had located Mr Verdean lying where he had fallen. Simon raised him by the slack of his coat and slung him into Hoppy's bearlike clutch, and turned back towards the window just as the lights of the living-room went on again behind the disordered curtains.

He crouched in the shadow of a bush with his gun raised, and said in a much more carrying voice: 'I bet I can shoot my initials on the face of the first guy who sticks his nose outside.'

The lights went out a second time; and there was a considerable silence. The house might have been empty of life.

Behind him, Simon heard an engine whine into life, drop back to a subdued purr as the starter disconnected. He backed towards the car, his eyes raking the house frontage relentlessly, until he could step on to the running-board.

'Okay, Hoppy,' he said.

The black sedan slid forward. Another shot whacked out behind as he opened the door and tumbled into the front seat, but it was yards wide of usefulness. The headlights sprang into brilliance as they lurched through an opening ahead and skidded round in the lane beyond. For the first time in several overcrowded minutes, the Saint had leisure to get out his cigarette case. The flame of his lighter painted jubilantly mephistophelian highlights on his face.

'Let's pick up our own car,' he said. 'Then we'll take our prize home and find out what we've won.'

He found out sooner than that. He only had to fish out Mr Verdean's wallet to find a half-dozen engraved cards that answered a whole tumult of questions with staggering simplicity. They said:

Mr Robert Verdean
Branch Manager
City & Continental Bank Ltd Staines

5

Patricia Holm put two lumps of sugar in her coffee and stirred it.

'Well, that's your story,' she said coldly. 'So I suppose you're sticking to it. But what were you doing there in the first place?'

'I told you,' said the Saint. 'We were looking for Hogsbotham.'

'Why should you be looking for him?'

'Because he annoyed me. You remember. And we had to do something to pass the evening.'

'You could have gone to a movie.'

'What, and seen a picture about gangsters? You know what a demoralizing influence these pictures have. It might have put ideas into my head.'

'Of course,' she said. 'You didn't have any ideas about Hogsbotham.'

'Nothing very definite,' he admitted. 'We might have just wedged his mouth open and poured him full of gin, and then pushed him in the stage door of a leg show, or something like that. Anyway, it didn't come to anything. We got into the wrong house, as you may have gathered. The bloke who told us the way said "the fourth house", but it was too dark to see houses. I was counting entrances; but I didn't discover until afterwards that Verdean's place has one of those U-shaped drives, with an in and out gate, so I counted him twice. Hogsbotham's sty must have been the next house on.

Verdean's house is called "The Shutters", but the paint was so bad that I easily took it for "The Snuggery". After I'd made the mistake and got in there, I was more or less a pawn on the chessboard of chance. There was obviously something about Verdean that wanted investigating, and the way things panned out it didn't look healthy to investigate him on the spot. So we just had to bring him away with us.'

'You didn't have to hit him so hard that he'd get concussion and lose his memory.'

Simon rubbed his chin.

'There's certainly something in that, darling. But it was all very difficult. It was too dark for me to see just what I was doing, and I was in rather a rush. However, it does turn out to be a bit of a snag.'

He had discovered the calamity the night before, after he had unloaded Verdean at his country house at Weybridge – he had chosen that secluded lair as a destination partly because it was only about five miles from Chertsey, partly because it had more elaborate facilities for concealing captives than his London apartment. The bank manager had taken an alarmingly long time to recover consciousness; and when he eventually came back to life it was only to vomit and moan unintelligibly. In between retchings his eyes wandered over his surroundings with a vacant stare into which even the use of his own name and the reminders of the plight from which he had been extracted could not bring a single flicker of response. Simon had dosed him with calomel and sedatives and put him to bed, hoping that he would be back to normal in the morning; but he had awakened in very little better condition, clutching his head painfully and mumbling nothing but listless uncomprehending replies to any question he was asked.

He was still in bed, giving no trouble but serving absolutely no useful purpose as a source of information; and the

Saint gazed out of the window at the morning sunlight lancing through the birch and pine glade outside and frowned ruefully over the consummate irony of the impasse.

'I might have known there'd be something like this waiting for me when you phoned me to come down for breakfast,' said Patricia stoically. 'How soon are you expecting Teal?'

The Saint chuckled.

'He'll probably be sizzling in much sooner than we want him – a tangle like this wouldn't be complete without good old Claud Eustace. But we'll worry about that when it happens. Meanwhile, we've got one consolation. Comrade Verdean seems to be one of those birds who stuff everything in their pockets until the stitches begin to burst. I've been going over his collection of junk again, and it tells quite a story when you put it together.'

Half of the breakfast table was taken up with the potpourri of relics which he had extracted from various parts of the bank manager's clothing, now sorted out into neat piles. Simon waved a spoon at them.

'Look them over for yourself, Pat. Nearest to you, you've got a couple of interesting souvenirs. Hotel bills. One of 'em is where Mr Robert Verdean stayed in a modest semi-boardinghouse at Eastbourne for the first ten days of July. The other one follows straight on for the next five days; only it's from a swank sin-palace at Brighton, and covers the sojourn of a Mr and Mrs Jones who seem to have consumed a large amount of champagne during their stay. If you had a low mind like mine, you might begin to jump to a few conclusions about Comrade Verdean's last vocation.'

'I could get ideas.'

'Then the feminine handkerchief – a pretty little sentimental souvenir, but rather compromising.'

Patricia picked it up and sniffed it.

'Night of Sin,' she said with a slight grimace.

'Is that what it's called? I wouldn't know. But I do know that it's the same smell that the blonde floozie brought in with her last night. Her name is Angela Lindsay; and she has quite a reputation in the trade for having made suckers out of a lot of guys who should have been smarter than Comrade Verdean.'

She nodded.

'What about the big stack of letters. Are they love-letters?'

'Not exactly. They're bookmaker's accounts. And the little book on top of them isn't a heart-throb diary – it's a betting diary. The name on all of 'em is Joseph Mackintyre. And you'll remember from an old adventure of ours that Comrade Mackintyre has what you might call an elastic conscience about his bookmaking. The story is all there, figured down to pennies. Verdean seems to have started on the sixth of July, and he went off with a bang. By the middle of the month he must have wondered why he ever bothered to work in a bank. I'm not surprised he had champagne every night at Brighton – it was all free. But the luck started to change after that. He had fewer and fewer winners, and he went on plunging more and more heavily. The last entry in the diary, a fortnight ago, left him nearly five thousand pounds in the red. Your first name doesn't have to be Sherlock to put all those notes together and make a tune.'

Patricia's sweet face was solemn with thought.

'Those two men,' she said. 'Dolf and Kaskin. You knew them. What's their racket?'

'Morrie was one of Snake Ganning's sparetime boys once. He's dangerous. Quite a sadist, in his nasty little way. You could hire him for anything up to murder, at a price; but he really enjoys his work. Kaskin has more brains, though. He's more versatile. Confidence work, the old badger game, living off women, protection rackets – he's had a dab at all of them. He's worked around racetracks quite a bit, too, doping horses and intimidating jockeys and bookmakers and so forth, which makes him an easy link with Mackintyre. His last stretch was for manslaughter. But bank robbery is quite a fancy flight even for him. He must have been getting ideas.'

Patricia's eyes turned slowly towards the morning paper in which the holdup at Staines still had a place in the headlines.

'You mean you think—'

'I think our guardian angel is still trying to take care of us,' said the Saint; and all the old impenitent mischief that she knew too well was shimmering at the edges of his smile. 'If only we knew a cure for amnesia, I think we could be fifteen thousand pounds richer before bedtime. Add it up for yourself while I take another look at the patient.'

He got up from the table and went through to the study which adjoined the dining-room. It was a rather small, comfortably untidy room, and the greater part of its walls were lined with built-in bookshelves. When he went in, one tier of shelving about two feet wide stood open like a door; beyond it, there appeared to be a narrow passage. The passage was actually a tiny cell, artificially lighted and windowless, but perfectly ventilated through a grating that connected with the air-conditioning system which served the rest of the house. The cell was no more than a broad gap between the solid walls of the room on either side of it, so ingeniously squeezed into the architecture of the house that it would have taken a clever surveyor many hours of work with a footrule to discover its existence. It had very little more than enough room for the cot, in which Verdean lay, and the table and chair at which Hoppy Uniatz was dawdling over his breakfast – if any meal which ended after noon, and was washed down with a bottle of Scotch whisky, could get by with that name.

Simon stood just inside the opening and glanced over the scene.

'Any luck yet?' he asked.

Mr Uniatz shook his head.

'De guy is cuckoo, boss. I even try to give him a drink, an'
he don't want it. He t'rows it up like it might be perzon.'

He mentioned this with the weighty reluctance of a psych-
iatrist adducing the ultimate evidence of dementia praecox.

Simon squeezed his way through and slipped a thermometer into the patient's mouth. He held Verdean's wrist with
sensitive fingers.

'Don't you want to get up, Mr Verdean?'

The bank manager gazed at him expressionlessly.

'You don't want to be late at the bank, do you?' said the
Saint. 'You might lose your job.'

'What bank?' Verdean asked.

'You know. The one that was robbed.'

'I don't know. Where am I?'

'You're safe now. Kaskin is looking for you, but he won't
find you.'

'Kaskin,' Verdean repeated. His face was blank, idiotic. 'Is
he someone I know?'

'You remember Angela, don't you?' said the Saint. 'She
wants to see you.'

Verdean rolled his head on the pillows.

'I don't know. Who are all these people? I don't want to see
anyone. My head's splitting. I want to go to sleep.'

His eyes closed under painfully wrinkled brows.

Simon let his wrist fall. He took out the thermometer, read
it, and sidled back to the door. Patricia was standing there.

'No change?' she said; and the Saint shrugged.

'His temperature's practically normal, but his pulse is high.
God alone knows how long it may take him to get his memory
back. He could stay like this for a week; or it might even be
years. You never can tell . . . I'm beginning to think I may
have been a bit too hasty with my rescuing-hero act. I ought

to have let Kaskin and Dolf work him over a bit longer, and heard what he had to tell them before I butted in.'

Patricia shook her head.

'You know you couldn't have done that.'

'I know.' The Saint made a wryly philosophic face. 'That's the worst of trying to be a buccaneer with a better nature. But it would have saved the hell of a lot of trouble, just the same. As it is, even if he does recover his memory, we're going to have to do something exciting ourselves to make him open up. Now, if we could only swat him on the head in the opposite direction and knock his memory back again—'

He broke off abruptly, his eyes fixed intently on a corner of the room; but Patricia knew that he was not seeing it. She looked at him with an involuntary tightening in her chest. Her ears had not been quick enough to catch the first swish of tyres on the gravel drive which had cut off what he was saying, but she was able to hear the car outside coming to a stop.

The Saint did not move. He seemed to be waiting, like a watchdog holding its bark while it tried to identify a stray sound that had pricked its ears. In another moment she knew what he had been waiting for.

The unmistakable limping steps of Orace, Simon Templar's oldest and most devoted retainer, came through the hall from the direction of the kitchen and paused outside the study.

'It's that there detective agyne, sir,' he said in a fierce whisper. 'I seen 'im fru the winder. Shall I chuck 'im aht?'

'No, let him in,' said the Saint quietly. 'But give me a couple of seconds first.'

He drew Patricia quickly out of the secret cell, and closed the study door. His lips were flirting with the wraith of a Saintly smile, and only Patricia would have seen the steel in his blue eyes.

'What a prophet you are, darling,' he said.

He swung the open strip of bookcase back into place. It closed silently, on delicately balanced hinges, filling the aperture in the wall without a visible crack. He moved one of the shelves to lock it. Then he closed a drawer of his desk which had been left open, and there was the faint click of another lock taking hold. Only then did he open the door to the hall – and left it open. And with that, a master lock, electrically operated, took control. Even with the knowledge of the other two operations, nothing short of pickaxes and dynamite could open the secret room when the study door was open; and one of the Saint's best bets was that no one who was searching the house would be likely to make a point of shutting it.

He emerged into the hall just as Chief Inspector Teal's official boots stomped wrathfully over the threshold. The detective saw him as soon as he appeared, and the heightened colour in his chubby face flared up with the perilous surge of his blood pressure. He took a lurching step forward with one quivering forefinger thrust out ahead of him like a spear.

'You, Saint!' he bellowed. 'I want you!'

The Saint smiled at him, carefree and incredibly debonair.

'Why, hullo, Claud, old gumboil,' he murmured genially. 'You seem to be excited about something. Come in and tell me all about it.'

6

Simon Templar had never actually been followed into his living-room by an irate mastodon; but if that remarkable experience was ever to befall him in the future, he would have had an excellent standard with which to compare it. The imitation, as rendered by Chief Inspector Claud Eustace Teal, was an impressive performance, but it seemed to leave the Saint singularly unconcerned. He waved towards one armchair and deposited himself in another, reaching for cigarette box and ashtray.

'Make yourself at home,' he invited affably. 'Things have been pretty dull lately, as I said last night. What can I do to help you?'

Mr Teal gritted his teeth over a lump of chewing gum with a barbarity which suggested that he found it an inferior substitute for the Saint's jugular vein. Why he should have followed the Saint at all in the first place was a belated question that was doing nothing to improve his temper. He could find no more satisfactory explanation than that the Saint had simply turned and calmly led the way, and he could hardly be expected to go on talking to an empty hall. But in the act of following, he felt that he had already lost a subtle point. It was one of those smoothly infuriating tricks of the Saint to put him at a disadvantage which never failed to lash Mr Teal's unstable temper to the point where he felt as if he were being garrotted with his own collar.

And on this occasion, out of all others, he must control

himself. He had no need to get angry. He held all the aces. He had everything that he had prayed for in the long sections of his career that had been consecrated to the heartbreaking task of trying to lay the Saint by the heels. He must not make any mistakes. He must not let himself be baited into any more of those unbelievable indiscretions that had wrecked such opportunities in the past, and that made him sweat all over as soon as he had escaped from the Saint's maddening presence. He told himself so, over and over again, clinging to all the tatters of his self restraint with the doggedness of a drowning man. He glared at the Saint with an effort of impassivity that made the muscles of his face ache.

'You can help me by taking a trip to the police station with me,' he said. 'Before you go any further, it's my duty to warn you that you're under arrest. And I've got all the evidence I need to keep you there!'

'Of course you have, Claud,' said the Saint soothingly. 'Haven't you had it every time you've arrested me? But now that you've got that off your chest, would it be frightfully tactless if I asked you what I'm supposed to have done?'

'Last night,' Teal said, grinding his words out under fearful compression, 'a Mr Robert Verdean, the manager of the City and Continental Bank's branch at Staines, was visited at his home in Chertsey by two men. They tied up his servant in the kitchen, and went on to find him in the living-room. The maid's description of them makes them sound like the two men who held up the same bank that morning. They went into the living-room and turned on the radio.'

'How very odd,' said the Saint. 'I suppose they were trying to console Comrade Verdean for having his bank robbed. But what has that got to do with me? Or do you think I was one of them?'

'Shortly afterwards,' Teal went on, ignoring the interruption, 'two other men entered the kitchen with handkerchiefs tied over their faces. One of them was about your height and build. The maid heard this one address the other one as "Hoppy".'

Simon nodded perfunctorily.

'Yes,' he said; and then his eyebrows rose. 'My God, Claud, that's funny! Of course, you're thinking—'

'That American gangster who follows you around is called Hoppy, isn't he?'

'If you're referring to Mr Uniatz,' said the Saint stiffly, 'he is sometimes called that. But he hasn't got any copyright in the name.'

The detective took a fresh nutcracker purchase on his gum.

'Perhaps he hasn't. But the tall one went into the living-room. The radio was switched off and on and off again, and then it stayed off. So the maid heard quite a bit of the conversation. She heard people talking about the Saint.'

'That's one of the penalties of fame,' said the Saint sadly. 'People are always talking about me, in the weirdest places. It's quite embarrassing sometimes. But do go on telling me about it.'

Mr Teal's larynx suffered a spasm which interfered momentarily with his power of speech.

'That's all I have to tell you!' he yelped, when he had partially cleared the obstruction. 'I mean that you and that Uniatz creature of yours were the second two men who arrived. After that, according to the maid, there was a lot of shooting, and presently some neighbours arrived and untied her. All the four men who had been there disappeared, and so did Mr Verdean. I want you on suspicion of kidnapping him; and if we don't find him soon there'll probably be a charge of murder as well!'

Simon Templar frowned. His manner was sympathetic rather than disturbed.

'I know how you feel, Claud,' he said commiseratingly. 'Naturally you want to do something about it; and I know you're quite a miracle worker when you get going. But I wish I could figure out how you're going to tie me up with it, when I wasn't anywhere near the place.'

The detective's glare reddened.

'You weren't anywhere near Chertsey, eh? So we've got to break down another of your famous alibis. All right, then. Where were you?'

'I was at home.'

'Whose home?'

'My own. This one.'

'Yeah? And who else knows about it?'

'Not a lot of people,' Simon confessed. 'We were being quiet. You know. One of these restful, old-fashioned, fire-side evenings. If it comes to that, I suppose there isn't an army of witnesses. You can't have a quiet restful evening with an army of witnesses cluttering up the place. It's a contradiction in terms. There was just Pat, and Hoppy, and of course good old Orace—'

'Pat and Hoppy and Orace,' jeered the detective. 'Just a quiet restful evening. And that's your alibi—'

'I wouldn't say it was entirely my alibi,' Simon mentioned diffidently. 'After all, there are several other houses in England. And I wouldn't mind betting that in at least half of them, various people were having quiet restful evenings last night. Why don't you go and ask some of them whether they can prove it? Because you know that being a lot less tolerant and forbearing than I am, they'd only tell you to go back to Scotland Yard and sit on a radiator until you'd thawed some of the clotted suet out of your brains. How the hell would you expect anyone to prove he'd spent a quiet evening at home? By bringing in a convocation of bishops for witnesses? In a case like this, it isn't the suspect's job to prove he was home. It's your job to prove he wasn't.'

Chief Inspector Teal should have been warned. The ghosts of so many other episodes like this should have risen up to give him caution. But they didn't. Instead, they egged him on. He leaned forward in a glow of vindictive exultation.

'That's just what I'm going to do,' he said, and his voice grew rich with the lusciousness of his own triumph. 'We aren't always so stupid as you think we are. We found fresh tyre tracks in the drive, and they didn't belong to Verdean's car. We searched every scrap of ground for half a mile to see if we could pick them up again. We found them turning into a field quite close to the end of Greenleaf Road. The car that made 'em was still in the field – it was reported stolen in Windsor early yesterday morning. But there were the tracks of another car in the field, overlapping and underlapping the tracks of the stolen car, so that we know the kidnappers changed to another car for their getaway. I've got casts of those tracks, and I'm going to show that they match the tyres on your car!'

The Saint blinked.

'It would certainly be rather awkward if they did,' he said uneasily. 'I didn't give anybody permission to borrow my car last night, but of course—'

'But of course somebody might have taken it away and brought it back without your knowing it,' Teal said with guttural sarcasm. 'Oh, yes.' His voice suddenly went into a squeak. 'Well, I'm going to be in court and watch the jury laugh themselves sick when you try to tell that story! I'm going to examine your car now, in front of police witnesses, and I'd like them to see your face when I do it!'

It was the detective's turn to march away and leave the Saint to follow. He had a moment of palpitation while he pondered whether the Saint would do it. But as he flung open the front door and crunched into the drive, he heard the Saint's footsteps behind him. The glow of triumph that was in him warmed like a Yule log on a Christmas hearth. The Saint's expression had reverted to blandness quickly enough, but not so quickly that Teal had missed the guilty start which had broken through its smooth surface. He knew, with a blind ecstasy, that at long last the Saint had tripped . . .

He waved imperiously to the two officers in the prowl car outside, and marched on towards the garage. The Saint's Hirondel stood there in its glory, an engineering symphony in cream and red trimmed with chromium, with the more sedate black Daimler in which Patricia had driven down standing beside it; but Teal had no aesthetic admiration for the sight. He stood by like a pink-faced figure of doom while his assistants reverently unwrapped the moulage impressions; and then, like a master chef taking charge at the vital moment in the preparation of a dish for which his underlings had laid the routine foundations, he took the casts in his own hands and proceeded to compare them with the tyres on the Hirondel.

He went all round the Hirondel twice.

He was breathing a trifle laboriously, and his face was redder than before – probably from stooping – when he turned his attention to the Daimler.

He went all round the Daimler twice, too.

Then he straightened up and came slowly back to the Saint. He came back until his face was only a few inches from the Saint's. His capillaries were congested to the point where his complexion had a dark purple hue. He seemed to be having more trouble with his larynx.

'What have you done to those tyres?' he got out in a hysterical blare.

The Saint's eyebrows drew perplexedly together.

'What have I done to them? I don't get you, Claud. Do you mean to say they don't match?'

'You know damn well they don't match! You knew it all the

time.' Realization of the way the Saint had deliberately lured him up to greater heights of optimism only to make his downfall more hideous when it came, brought something like a sob into the detective's gullet. 'You've changed the tyres!'

Simon looked aggrieved.

'How could I, Claud? You can see for yourself that these tyres are a long way from being new—'

'What have you done with the tyres you had on the car last night?' Teal almost screamed.

'But these are the only tyres I've had on the car for weeks,' Simon protested innocently. 'Why do you always suspect me of such horrible deceits? If my tyres don't match the tracks you found in that field, it just looks to me as if you may have made a mistake about my being there.'

Chief Inspector Teal did a terrible thing. He raised the casts in his hands and hurled them down on the concrete floor so that they shattered into a thousand fragments. He did not actually dance on them, but he looked as if only an effort of self-control that brought him to the brink of an apoplectic stroke stopped him from doing so.

'What have you done with Verdean?' he yelled.

'I haven't done anything with him. Why should I have? I've never even set eyes on the man.'

'I've got a search warrant—'

'Then why don't you search?' demanded the Saint snappily, as though his patience was coming to an end. 'You don't believe anything I tell you, anyhow, so why don't you look for yourself? Go ahead and use your warrant. Tear the house apart. I don't mind. I'll be waiting for you in the living-room when you're ready to eat some of your words.'

He turned on his heel and strolled back to the house.

He sat down in the living-room, lighted a cigarette, and calmly picked up a magazine. He heard the tramp of Teal and his minions entering the front door, without looking up. For an hour he listened to them moving about in various parts of the house, tapping walls and shifting furniture; but he seemed to have no interest beyond the story he was reading. Even when they invaded the living-room itself, he didn't even glance at them. He went on turning the pages as if they made no more difference to his idleness than a trio of inquisitive puppies.

Teal came to the living-room last. Simon knew from the pregnant stillness that presently supervened that the search had come to a stultifying end, but he continued serenely to finish his page before he looked up.

'Well,' he said at length, 'have you found him?'

'Where is he?' shouted Teal, with dreadful savagery.

Simon put down the magazine.

'Look here,' he said wearily. 'I've made a lot of allowances for you, but I give up. What's the use? I tell you I was at home last night, and you can't prove I wasn't; but just because you want me to have been out, I must be faking an alibi. You've got casts of the tyre tracks of a car that was mixed up in some dirty business last night, and they don't match the tracks of either of my cars; but just because you think they ought to match, I must have changed my tyres. I tell you I haven't kidnapped this fellow Verdean, and you can't find him anywhere in my house; but just because you think I ought to have kidnapped him, I must have hidden him somewhere else. Every shred of evidence is against you, and therefore all the evidence must be wrong. You couldn't possibly be wrong yourself, because you're the great Chief Inspector Claud Eustace Teal, who knows everything and always gets his man. All right. Every bit of proof there is shows that I'm innocent, but I must be guilty because your theories would be all wet if I wasn't. So why do we have to waste our time on silly little details like this? Let's just take me down to the police station and lock me up.'

'That's just what I'm going to do,' Teal raved blindly.

The Saint looked at him for a moment, and stood up.

'Good enough,' he said breezily. 'I'm ready when you are.'

He went to the door and called: 'Pat!' She answered him, and came down the stairs. He said: 'Darling, Claud Eustace has had an idea. He's going to lug me off and shove me in the cooler on a charge of being above suspicion. It's a new system they've introduced at Scotland Yard, and all the laws are being altered to suit it. So you'd better call one of our lawyers and see if he knows what to do about it. Oh, and you might ring up some of the newspapers while you're on the job – they'll probably want to interview Claud about his brainwave.'

'Yes, of course,' she said enthusiastically, and went towards the telephone in the study.

Something awful, something terrifying, something freezing and paralysing, damp, chilly, appalling, descended over Chief Inspector Teal like a glacial cascade. With the very edge of the precipice crumbling under his toes, his eyes were opened. The delirium of fury that had swept him along so far coagulated sickeningly within him. Cold, pitiless, inescapable facts hammered their bitter way through into the turmoil of his brain. He was too shocked at the moment even to feel the anguish of despair. His mind shuddered under the impact of a new kind of panic. He took a frantic step forward – a step that was, in its own way, the crossing of a harrowing Rubicon.

'Wait a minute,' he stammered hoarsely.

7

Fifteen minutes later, Simon Templar stood on the front steps and watched the police car crawl out of the drive with its cargo of incarnate woe. He felt Patricia's fingers slide into his hand, and turned to smile at her.

'So far, so good,' he said thoughtfully. 'But only so far.'

'I thought you were joking, at breakfast,' she said. 'How did he get here so soon?'

He shrugged.

'That wasn't difficult. I suppose he stayed down at Staines last night; and the Chertsey police would have phoned over about the Verdean business first thing this morning, knowing that he was the manager of the bank that had been held up. Claud must have shot off on the scent like a prize greyhound, and I'm afraid I can sympathize with the way he must have felt when he arrived here.'

'Well, we're still alive,' she said hopefully. 'You got rid of him again.'

'Only because his nerves are getting a bit shaky from all the times I've slipped through his fingers, and he's so scared of being made a fool of again that he daren't move now without a cast-iron case, and I was able to pick a few awkward holes in this one. But don't begin thinking we've got rid of him for keeps. He's just gone away now to see if he can stop up the holes again and put some more iron in the evidence, and he's sore enough to work overtime at it. He's going to be three times as dangerous from now on. Worse than that, he's not so dumb that he isn't going to put two and two together about all this commotion around Verdean coming right on top of the robbery. You can bet the Crown Jewels to a show-girl's virtue that he's already figured out that Verdean was mixed up in it in some way. While we're stuck with Verdean, and Verdean is stuck with amnesia.' The Saint closed the front door with sombre finality. 'Which is the hell of a layout from any angle,' he said. 'Tell Orace to bring me a large mug of beer, darling, because I think I am going to have a headache.'

His headache lasted through a lunch which Orace indignantly served even later than he had served breakfast, but it brought forth very little to justify itself. He had gone over the facts at his disposal until he was sick of them, and they fitted together with a complete and sharply focused deductive picture that Sherlock Holmes himself could not have improved on, without a hiatus or a loose end anywhere – only the picture merely showed a plump rabbit-faced man slinking off with fifteen thousand pounds in a bag, and neglected to show where he went with it. Which was the one detail in which Simon Templar was most urgently interested. He was always on the side of the angels, he told himself, but he had to remember that sanctity had its own overhead to meet.

Verdean showed no improvement in the afternoon. Towards five o'clock the Saint had a flash of inspiration, and put in a long-distance call to a friend in Wolverhampton.

'Dr Turner won't be back till tomorrow morning, and I'm afraid I don't know how to reach him,' said the voice at the other end of the wire; and the flash flickered and died out at the sound. 'But I can give you Dr Young's number—'

'I am not having a baby,' said the Saint coldly, and hung up.

He leaned back in his chair and said, quietly and intensely: 'God damn.'

'You should complain,' said Patricia. 'You Mormon.'

She had entered the study from the hall, and closed the door again behind her. The Saint looked up from under mildly interrogative brows.

'I knew you adored me,' he said, 'but you have an original line of endearing epithets. What's the origin of this one?'

'Blonde,' she said, 'and voluptuous in a careful way. Mushy lips and the-old-baloney eyes. I'll bet she wears black lace undies and cuddles like a kitten. She hasn't brought the baby with her, but she's probably got a picture of it.'

The Saint straightened.

'Not Angela?' he ventured breathlessly.

'I'm not so intimate with her,' said Patricia primly. 'But she gave the name of Miss Lindsay. You ought to recognize your own past when it catches up with you.'

Simon stood up slowly. He glanced at the closed section of the bookcase, beyond which was the secret room where Hoppy Uniatz was still keeping watch over Mr Verdean and a case of Vat 69; and his eyes were suddenly filled with an unholy peace.

'I do not recognize her, darling, now I think about it,' he said. 'This is the one who had the twins.' He gripped her arm, and his smile wavered over her in a flicker of ghostly excitement. 'I ought to have known that she'd catch up with me. And I think this is the break I've been waiting for all day . . .'

He went into the living-room with a new quickness in his step and a new exhilaration sliding along his nerves. Now that this new angle had developed, he was amazed that he had not been expecting it from the beginning. He had considered every other likely eventuality, but not this one; and yet this was the most obvious one of all. Kaskin and Dolf knew who he was, and some of his addresses were to be found in various directories that were at the disposal of anyone who could read: it was not seriously plausible that after the night before they would decide to give up their loot and go away and forget about it, and once they had made up their minds to attempt a comeback it could only have been a matter of time before they looked for him in Weybridge. The only thing he might not have anticipated was that they would send Angela Lindsay in to open the interview. That was a twist which showed a degree of circumspection that made Simon Templar greet her with more than ordinary watchfulness.

'Angela, darling!' he murmured with an air of pleased surprise. 'I never thought I should see you in these rural parts. When did you decide to study bird life in the suburbs?'

'It came over me suddenly, last night,' she said. 'I began to realize that I'd missed something.'

His eyes were quizzically sympathetic.

'You shouldn't be too discouraged. I don't think you missed it by more than a couple of inches.'

'Perhaps not. But a miss is—'

'I know. As good as in the bush.'

'Exactly.'

He smiled at her, and offered the cigarette box. She took one, and he gave her a light. His movements and his tone of voice were almost glisteningly smooth with exaggerated elegance. He was enjoying his act immensely.

'A drink?' he suggested; but she shook her head.

'It mightn't be very good for me, so I won't risk it. Besides, I want to try and make a good impression.'

He was studying her more critically than he had been able to the night before, and it seemed to him that Patricia's description of her was a little less than absolutely fair. She had one of those modern streamlined figures that look boyish until they are examined closely, when they prove to have the same fundamental curves that grandma used to have. Her mouth and eyes were effective enough, even if the effect was deplorable from a moral standpoint. And although it was true that even a comparatively unworldly observer would scarcely have hesitated for a moment over placing her in her correct category, it was also very definitely true that if all the other members of that category had looked like her, Mr Ebenezer Hogsbotham would have found himself burning a very solitary candle in a jubilantly naughty world.

The Saint went on looking at her with amiable amusement at the imaginative vistas opened up by the train of thought. He said: 'You must have made quite an impression on Comrade Verdean. And you drank champagne with him at Brighton.'

She put her cigarette to her lips and drew lightly at it while she gazed at him for a second or two in silence. Her face was perfectly composed, but her eyes were fractionally narrowed.

'I'll give you that one,' she said at length. 'We've been wondering just how much you really knew. Would you care to tell me the rest, or would that be asking too much?'

'Why, of course,' said the Saint obligingly. 'If you're interested. It isn't as if I'd be telling you anything you don't know already.'

He sat down and stretched out his long legs. He looked at the ceiling. He was bluffing, but he felt sure enough of his ground.

'Kaskin and Dolf picked up Verdean on his holiday at Eastbourne,' he said. 'Kaskin can make himself easy to like when he wants to – it's his stock in trade. They threw you in for an added attraction. Verdean fell for it all. He was having a swell time with a bunch of good fellows. And you were fairly swooning into his manly arms. It made him feel grand, and a little bit dizzy. He had to live up to it. Kaskin was a sporty gent, and Verdean was ready to show that he was a sporty gent too. They got him to backing horses, and he always backed winners. Money poured into his lap. He felt even grander. It went to his head – where it was meant to go.

He left his boardinghouse, and pranced off to Brighton with you on a wild and gorgeous jag.'

Simon reached for a cigarette.

'Then, the setback,' he went on. 'You had expensive tastes, and you expected him to go on being a good fellow and a sporty gent. But that looked easy. There was always money in the geegees, with Kaskin's expert assistance. So he thought. Only something went haywire. The certainties didn't win. But the next one would always get it back. Verdean began to plunge. He got wilder and wilder as he lost more and more. And he couldn't stop. He was infatuated with you, scared stiff of losing you. He lost more money than he had of his own. He started embezzling a little, maybe. Anyway, he was in the cart. He owed more money than he could hope to pay. Then Kaskin and Dolf started to get tough. They told him how he could pay off his debt, and make a profit as well. There was plenty of money in the bank every week, and it would be very easy to stage a holdup and get away with it if he was co-operating. Kaskin and Dolf would do the job and take all the risk, and all he had to do was to give them the layout and make everything easy for them. He'd never be suspected himself, and he'd get his cut afterwards. But if he didn't string along – well, someone might have to tell the head office about him. Verdean knew well enough what happens to bank managers who get into debt, particularly over gambling. He could either play ball or go down the drain. So he said he'd play ball. Am I right?'

'So far. But I hope you aren't going to stop before the important part.'

'All right. Verdean thought some more – by himself. He was sunk, anyhow. He had to rob the bank if he was going to save his own skin. So why shouldn't he keep all the boodle for himself? . . . That's just what he decided to do. The branch is a small one, and nobody would have thought of questioning anything he did. It was easy for him to pack a load of dough into a small valise and take it out with him when he went home to lunch – just before the holdup was timed to take place. Nobody would have thought of asking him what he had in his bag; and as for the money, well, of course the holdup men would be blamed for getting away with it. But he didn't want Judd and Morrie on his tail, so he tipped off the police anonymously, meaning for them to be caught, and feeling pretty sure that nobody would believe any accusations they made about him – or at least not until he had plenty of time to hide it . . . There were still a few holes in the idea, but he was too desperate to worry about them. His real tragedy was when Kaskin and Dolf didn't get caught after all, and came after him to ask questions. And naturally that's when we all started to get together.'

'And then?'

The Saint raised his head and looked at her again.

'Maybe I'm very dense,' he said apologetically, 'but isn't that enough?'

'It's almost uncanny. But there's still the most important thing.'

'What would that be?'

'Did you find out what happened to the money?'

The Saint was silent for a moment. He elongated his legs still farther, so that they stretched out over the carpet like a pier; his recumbent body looked as if it were composing itself for sleep. But the eyes that he bent on her were bright and amused and very cheerfully awake.

She said: 'What are you grinning about?'

'I'd just been wondering when it was coming, darling,' he murmured. 'I know that my dazzling beauty brings admiring sightseers from all quarters like moths to a candle, but they usually want something else as well. And it's been very nice to see you and have this little chat, but I was always afraid you were hoping to get something out of it. So this is what it is. Morrie and Judd sent you along to get an answer to that question, so they'd know whether it was safe to bump me off or not. If Verdean is still keeping his mouth shut, they can go ahead and fix me a funeral; but if I've found out where it is I may have even moved it somewhere else by now, and it would be awkward to have me buried before I could tell them where I'd moved it to. Is that all that's worrying you?'

'Not altogether,' she said, without hesitation. 'They didn't have to send me for that. I talked them into letting me come because I told them you'd probably talk to me for longer than you'd talk to them, and anyhow you wouldn't be so likely to punch me on the nose. But I really did it because I wanted to see you myself.'

The flicker that passed over Simon's face was almost imperceptible.

'I hope it's been worth it,' he said flippantly; but he was watching her with a coolly reserved alertness.

'That's what you've got to tell me,' she said. She looked away from him for a moment, stubbed out her cigarette nervously, looked back at him again with difficult frankness. Her hands moved uncertainly. She went on in a rush: 'You see, I know Judd doesn't mean to give me my share. I could trust you. Whatever happens, they're going to give you trouble. I know you can take care of yourself, but I don't suppose you'd mind having it made easier for you. I could be on your side, without them knowing, and I wouldn't want much.'

The Saint blew two smoke rings with leisured care, placing them side by side like the lenses of a pair of horn-rimmed spectacles. They drifted towards the ceiling, enlarging languidly.

His face was inscrutable, but behind that pleasantly non-committal mask he was thinking as quickly as he could.

He might have come to any decision. But before he could say anything there was an interruption.

The door was flung open, and Hoppy Uniatz crashed in.

Mr Uniatz's face was not at all inscrutable. It was as elementarily easy to read as an infant's primer. The ecstatic protrusion of his eyes, the lavish enthusiasm of his breathing, the broad beam that divided his physiognomy into two approximately equal halves, and the roseate glow which suffused his homely countenance, were all reminiscent of the symptoms of bliss that must have illuminated the features of Archimedes at the epochal moment of his life. He looked like a man who had just made the inspirational discovery of the century in his bath.

'It woiked, boss,' he yawped exultantly, 'it woiked! De dough is in Hogsbotham's bedroom!'

8

Simon Templar kept still. It cost him a heroic effort but he did it. He felt as if he were balanced on top of a thin glass flagpole in the middle of an earthquake, but he managed to keep the surface of his nonchalance intact. He kept Angela Lindsay's hands always within the radius of his field of vision, and said rather faintly: 'What woiked?'

Mr Uniatz seemed slightly taken aback.

'Why, de idea you give me dis afternoon, boss,' he explained, as though he saw little need for such childish elucidations. 'You remember, you are saying why can't we sock dis guy de udder way an' knock his memory back. Well, I am t'inkin' about dat, an' it seems okay to me, an' I ain't got nut'n else to do on account of de door is locked an' I finished all de Scotch; so I haul off an' whop him on de toinip wit' de end of my Betsy. Well, he is out for a long time, an' when he comes round he still don't seem to know what it's all about, but he is talkin' about how dis guy Hogsbotham gives him a key to look after de house when he goes away, so he goes in an' parks de lettuce in Hogsbotham's bedroom. It is a swell idea, boss, an' it woiks,' said Mr Uniatz, still marvelling at the genius which had conceived it.

The Saint felt a clutching contraction under his ribs which was not quite like the gastric hollowness of dismay and defensive tension which might reasonably have been there. It was a second or two before he could get a perspective on it; and when he did so, the realization of what it was made him feel slightly insane.

It was simply a wild desire to collapse into helpless laughter. The whole supernal essence of the situation was so immortally ludicrous that he was temporarily incapable of worrying about the fact that Angela Lindsay was a member of the audience. If she had taken a gun out of her bag and announced that she was going to lock them up while she went back to tell Kaskin and Dolf the glad news, which would have been the most obviously logical thing for her to do, he would probably have been too weak to lift a finger to prevent it.

Perhaps the very fact that she made no move to do so did more than anything else to restore him to sobriety. The ache in his chest died away, and his brain forced itself to start work again. He knew that she had a gun in her bag – he had looked for it and distinguished the outline of it when he first came into the room to meet her, and that was why he had never let himself completely lose sight of her hands. But her hands only moved to take another cigarette. She smiled at him as if she was sharing the joke, and struck a match.

'Well,' he said dryly, 'it looks like you've got your answer.'

'To one question,' she said. 'You haven't answered the other. What shall I tell Judd?'

Simon studied her for the space of a couple of pulse-beats. In that time, he thought with a swiftness and clarity that was almost clairvoyant. He saw every angle and every prospect and every possible surprise.

He also saw Patricia standing aghast in the doorway behind the gorilla shoulders of Mr Uniatz, and grinned impudently at her.

He stood up, and put out his hand to Angela Lindsay.

'Go back and tell Morrie and Judd that we found out where the dough was last night,' he said. 'Verdean had buried it in a flowerbed. A couple of pals of mine dug it out in the small hours of this morning and took it to London. They're sitting over it with a pair of machine-guns in my apartment at Cornwall House now, and I dare anybody to take it away. That ought to hold 'em . . . Then you shake them off as soon as you can, and meet me at the Stag and Hounds opposite Weybridge Common in two hours from now. We'll take you along with us and show you Hogsbotham's nightshirts!'

She faced him steadily, but with a suppressed eagerness that played disturbing tricks with her moist lips.

'You mean that? You'll take me in with you?'

'Just as far as you want to be taken in, kid,' said the Saint.

He escorted her to the front door. There was no car outside, but doubtless Messrs Kaskin and Dolf were waiting for her a little way up the road. He watched her start down the drive, and then he closed the door and turned back.

'You'd look better without the lipstick,' said Patricia judicially.

He thumbed his nose at her and employed his handkerchief.

'Excuse me if I seem slightly scatterbrained,' he remarked. 'But all this is rather sudden. Too many things have happened in the last few minutes. What would you like to do with the change from fifteen thousand quid? There ought to be a few bob left after I've paid for my last lot of shirts and bought a new distillery for Hoppy.'

'Have you fallen right off the edge,' she asked interestedly, 'or what is it?'

'At a rough guess, I should say it was probably "What".' The Saint's happy lunacy was too extravagant to cope with. 'But who cares? Why should a little thing like this cause so much commotion? Have you no faith in human nature? The girl's better nature was revived. My pure and holy personality has done its work on her. It never fails. My shining example has made her soul pant for higher things. From now on, she is going to be on the side of the Saints. And she is going to take care of Judd and Morrie. She is going to lead them for us, by the nose, into the soup. Meanwhile, Professor Uniatz has shaken the scientific world to its foundations with his new and startling treatment for cases of concussion. He has whopped Comrade Verdean on the turnip with the end of his Betsy and banged his memory back, and we are going to lay our hands on fifteen thousand smackers before we go to bed tonight. And we are going to find all this boodle in the bedroom of Ebenezer Hogsbotham, of all the superlative places in the world. I ask you, can life hold any more?'

He exploded out of the hall into the study, and went on into the secret room, leaving her staring after him a trifle dazedly.

He was bubbling with blissful idiocy, but his mind was cool. He had already diagnosed the effects of the Uniatz treatment so completely that his visit was really only intended to reassure himself that it had actually worked. He studied Verdean coldbloodedly. The bank manager's eyes were vacant and unrecognizing: he rolled his head monotonously from side to side and kept up a delirious mumble from which the main points of the summary that Hoppy Uniatz had made were absurdly easy to pick out. Over and over again he reiterated the story – how Mr Hogsbotham had asked him as a neighbour to keep an eye on the house during some of his absences, how he had been entrusted with a key which he had never remembered to return, and how when he was wondering what to do with the stolen money he had remembered the key and used it to find what should have been an unsuspectable hiding place for his booty. He went on talking about it . . .

'He is like dis ever since he wakes up,' Hoppy explained, edging proudly in behind him.

The Saint nodded. He did not feel any pity. Robert Verdean was just another man who had strayed unsuccessfully into the paths of common crime; and even though he had been deliberately led astray, the mess that he was in now was directly traceable to nothing but his own weakness and cupidity. In such matters, Simon Templar saved his sympathy for more promising cases.

'Put his clothes back on him,' he said. 'We'll take him along too. Your operation was miraculous, Hoppy, but the patient is somewhat liable to die; and we don't want to be stuck with his body.'

Patricia was sitting on the study desk when he emerged again, and she looked at him with sober consideration.

'I don't want to bore you with the subject,' she said, 'but are you still sure you haven't gone off your rocker?'

'Perfectly sure,' he said. 'I was never rocking so smoothly in my life.'

'Well, do you happen to remember anyone by the name of Teal?'

He took her arm and chuckled.

'No, I haven't fogotten. But I don't think he'll be ready for this. He may have ideas about keeping an eye on me, but he won't be watching for Verdean. Not here, anyway. Hell, he's just searched the house from top to bottom and convinced himself that we haven't got Verdean here, however much he may be wondering what else we've done with him. And it's getting dark already. By the time we're ready to go, it'll be easy. There may be a patrol car or a motor cycle cop waiting down the road to get on our tail if we go out, but that'll be all. We'll drive around the country a bit first and lose them. And then we will go into this matter of our old age pensions.'

She might have been going to say some more. But she didn't. Her mouth closed again, and a little hopeless grimace that was almost a smile at the same time passed over her lips. Her blue eyes summed up a story that it has already taken all the volumes of the Saint Saga to tell in words. And she kissed him.

'All right, skipper,' she said quietly. 'I must be as crazy as you are, or I shouldn't be here. We'll do that.'

He shook his head, holding her.

'So we shall. But not you.'

'But—'

'I'm sorry, darling. I was talking about two other guys. You're going to stay out of it, because we're going to need you on the outside. Now, in a few minutes I'm going to call Peter, and then I'm going to try and locate Claud Eustace; and if I can get hold of both of them in time the campaign will proceed as follows . . .'

He told it in quick cleancut detail, so easily and lucidly that it seemed to be put together with no more effort than it took to understand and remember it. But that was only one of the tricks that sometimes made the Saint's triumphs seem deceptively facile. Behind that apparently random improvisation there was the instant decision and almost supernatural fore-sightedness of a strategic genius which in another age might have conquered empires as debonairly as in this twentieth century it had conquered its own amazing empire among thieves. And Patricia Holm was a listener to whom very few explanations had to be made more than once.

Hoppy Uniatz was a less gifted audience. The primitive machinery of conditioned reflexes which served him for some of the simpler functions of a brain had never been designed for one-shot lubrication. Simon had to go over the same ground with him at least three times before the scowl of agony smoothed itself out of Mr Uniatz's rough-hewn façade, indicating that the torture of concentration was over and the idea had finally taken root inside his skull, where at least it could be relied upon to remain with the solidity of an amal-gam filling in a well-excavated molar.

The evening papers arrived before they left, after the hectic preliminaries of organization were completed, when the Saint was relaxing briefly over a parting glass of sherry, and Mr Uniatz was placidly sluicing his arid tonsils with a fresh bottle of Scotch. Patricia glanced through the *Evening Standard* and giggled.

'Your friend Hogsbotham is still in the news,' she said. 'He's leading a deputation from the National Society for the Preservation of Public Morals to demonstrate outside the London Casino this evening before the dinnertime show. So it looks as if the coast will be clear for you at Chertsey.'

'Probably he heard that Simon was thinking of paying him another call, and hustled himself out of the way like a sensible peace loving citizen,' said Peter Quentin, who had arrived shortly before that. 'If I'd known what I was going to be dragged into before I answered the telephone, I'd have gone off and led a demonstration somewhere myself.'

The Saint grinned.

'We must really do something about Hogsbotham, one of these days,' he said.

It was curious that that adventure had begun with Mr Hogsbotham, and had just led back to Mr Hogsbotham; and yet he still did not dream how importantly Mr Hogsbotham was still to be concerned.

9

The Hirondel's headlights played briefly over the swinging sign of the Three Horseshoes, in Laleham, and swung off to the left on a road that turned towards the river. In a few seconds they were lighting up the smooth grey water and striking dull reflections from a few cars parked close to the bank; and then they blinked out as Simon pulled the car close to the grass verge and set the handbrake.

'Get him out, darling,' he said over his shoulder.

He stepped briskly out from behind the wheel; and Hoppy Uniatz, who had been sitting beside him, slid into his place. The Saint waited a moment to assure himself that Angela Lindsay was having no trouble with the fourth member of the party; and then he leaned over the side and spoke close to Hoppy's ear.

'Well,' he said, 'do you remember it all?'

'Sure, I remember it,' said Mr Uniatz confidently. He paused to refresh himself from the bottle he was still carrying, and replaced the cork with an air of reluctance. 'It's in de bag,' he said, with the pride of knowing what he was talking about.

'Mind you don't miss the turning, like we did last night. and for God's sake try not to have any kind of noise. You'll have to manage without headlights, too – someone might notice them . . . Once you've got the Beef Trust there, Pat'll take care of keeping them busy. I don't want you to pay any attention to anything except watching for the ungodly and passing the tip to her.'

'Okay, boss.'

The Saint looked round again. Verdean was out of the car.

'On your way, then.'

He stepped back. The gears meshed, and the Hirondel swung round in a tight semicircle and streaked away towards the main road.

Angela Lindsay stared after it, and caught the Saint's sleeve with sudden uncertainty. Her eyes were wide in the gloom.

'What's that for? Where is he going?'

'To look after our alibi,' Simon answered truthfully. 'Anything may happen here tonight, and you don't know Teal's nasty suspicious mind as well as I do. I'm pretty sure we shook off our shadows in Walton, but there's no need to take any chances.'

She was looking about her uneasily.

'But this isn't Chertsey—'

'This is Laleham, on the opposite side of the river. We came this way to make it more confusing, and also because it'll make it a lot harder for our shadows if they're still anywhere behind. Unless my calculations are all wrong, Hogsbotham's sty ought to be right over there.' His arm pointed diagonally over the stream. 'Let's find out.'

His hand took Verdean's arm close up under the shoulder. The girl walked on the bank manager's other side. Verdean was easy to lead. He seemed to have no more will of his own. His head kept rolling idiotically from side to side, and his voice went on unceasingly with an incoherent and practically unintelligible mumbling. His legs tried to fold intermittently at the joints, as if they had turned into putty; but the Saint's powerful grip held him up.

They crossed a short stretch of grass to the water's edge. The Saint also went on talking, loudly and irrelevantly, punctuating himself with squeals of laughter at his own wit. If any of the necking parties in the parked cars had spared them any attention at all, the darkness would have hidden any details, and the sound effects would infallibly have combined to stamp them as nothing but a party of noisy drunks. It must have been successful, for the trip was completed without a hitch. They came down to the river margin in uneventful co-ordination; and any spectators who may have been there continued to sublimate their biological urges unconcerned.

There was an empty punt moored to the bank at exactly the point where they reached the water. Why it should have been there so fortunately was something that the girl had no time to stop and ask; but the Saint showed no surprise about it. He seemed to have been expecting it. He steered Verdean on board and lowered him on to the cushions, and cast off the mooring chain and settled himself in the stern as she followed.

His paddle dug into the water with long deep strokes, driving the punt out into the dark. The bank which they had just left fell away into blackness behind. For a short while there was nothing near them but the running stream bounded by nebulous masses of deep shadow on either side. Verdean's monotonous muttering went on, but it had become no more obtrusive than the murmur of traffic heard from a closed room in a city building.

She said, after a time: 'I wonder why this all seems so different?'

He asked: 'Why?'

She was practically invisible from where he sat. Her voice came out of a blurred emptiness.

'I've done all sorts of things before – with Judd,' she said. 'But doing this with you . . . You make it an adventure. I always wanted it to be an adventure, and yet it never was.'

'Adventure is the way you look at it,' he said, and did not feel that the reply was trite when he was making it.

For the second time since he had picked her up at the Stag and Hounds he was wondering whether a surprise might still be in store for him that night. All his planning was cut and dried, as far as any of it was under his control; but there could still be surprises. In all his life nothing had ever gone mechanically and unswervingly according to a rigid and inviolable schedule: adventure would soon have become boring if it had. And tonight he had a feeling of fine-drawn liveness and that was the reverse of boredom.

The feeling stayed with him the rest of the way across the water, and through the disembarkation on the other side. It stayed with him on the short walk up Greenleaf Road from the towpath to the gates of Mr Hogsbotham's house. It was keener and more intense as they went up the drive, with Verdean keeping pace in his grasp with docile witlessness. It brought up all the undertones of the night in sharp relief – the stillness everywhere around, the silence of the garden, the whisper of leaves, the sensation of having stepped out of the inhabited world into a shrouded wilderness. Some of that could have been due to the trees that shut them in, isolating them in a tenebrous closeness in which there was no sight or sound of other life, so that even Verdean's own house next door did not intrude on their awareness by so much as a glimmer of light or the silhouette of a roof, and the Saint could not tell whether a light would have been visible in it if there had been a light to see. Some of the feeling was still left unaccounted for even after that. The Saint stood on the porch and wondered if he was misunderstanding his own intuition, while Verdean fumbled with keys at the door, muttering fussily about his stolen fortune. And his mind was still divided when they went into the hall, where a single dim light was burning, and he saw the bank manager stagger drunkenly away and throw himself shakily up the stairs.

He felt the girl's fingers cling to his arm. And in spite of all he knew about her, her physical nearness was something that his senses could not ignore.

'He's going to get it,' she breathed.

The Saint nodded. That psychic electricity was still coursing through his nerves, only now he began to find its meaning. From force of habit, his right hand slid under the cuff of his left sleeve and touched the hilt of the razor-edged throwing knife in its sheath strapped to his forearm, the only weapon he had thought it worth while to bring with him, making sure that it would slip easily out if he needed it; but the action was purely automatic. His thoughts were a thousand miles away from such things as his instinct associated with that deadly slender blade. He smiled suddenly.

'We ought to be there to give him a cheer,' he said.

He took her up the stairs with him. From the upper landing he saw an open door and a lighted room from which came confused scurrying noises combined with Verdean's imbecile grunting and chattering. Simon went to the door. The room was unquestionably Mr Ebenezer Hogsbotham's bedroom. He would have known it even without being told. Nobody but an Ebenezer Hogsbotham could ever have slept voluntarily in such a dismally austere and mortifying chamber. And he saw Robert Verdean in the centre of the room. The bank manager had lugged a shabby suitcase out of some hiding place, and had it open on the bed; he was pawing and crooning crazily over the contents – ruffling the edges of packets of pound notes, crunching the bags of silver. Simon stood for a moment and watched him, and it was like looking at a scene from a play that he had seen before.

Then he stepped quietly in and laid his hand on Verdean's shoulder.

'Shall I help you take care of it?' he said gently. He had not thought much about how Verdean would be likely to respond to the interruption, but had certainly not quite expected the response he got.

For the first time since Hoppy had applied his remarkable treatment, the bank manager seemed to become aware of outside personalities in a flash of distorted recognition. He squinted upwards and sidelong at the Saint, and his face twisted.

'I won't give it to you!' he screamed. 'I'll kill you first!'

He flung himself at the Saint's throat, his fingers clawing, his eyes red and maniacal.

Simon had very little choice. He felt highly uncertain about the possible results of a third concussion on Verdean's already inflamed cerebral tissue, following so closely upon the two previous whacks which it had suffered in the last twenty-four hours; but on the other hand he felt that in Mr Verdean's present apparent state of mind, to be tied up and gagged and left to struggle impotently while he watched his loot being taken away from him would be hardly less likely to cause a fatal hemorrhage. He therefore adopted the less troublesome course, and put his trust in any guardian angels that Mr Verdean might have on his overburdened payroll. His fist travelled up about eight explosive inches, and Mr Verdean travelled down . . .

Simon picked him up and laid him on the bed.

'You know,' he remarked regretfully, 'if this goes on much longer, there is going to come a time when Comrade Verdean is going to wonder whether fifteen thousand quid is really worth it.'

Angela Lindsay did not answer.

He looked at her. She stood close by the bed, gazing without expression at Verdean's unconscious body and the suitcase full of money at his feet. Her face was tired.

Still without saying anything, she went to the window and stood there with her back to him.

She said, after a long silence: 'Well, you got what you wanted, as usual.'

'I do that sometimes,' he said.

'And what happens next?'

'You'll get the share you asked for,' he answered carefully. 'You can take it now, if you like.'

'And that's all.'

'Did we agree to anything else?'

She turned round; and he found that he did not want to look at her eyes.

'Are you sure you're never going to need any more help?' she said.

He did not need to hear any more. He had known more than she could have told him, before that. He understood all the presentiment that had troubled him on the way there. For that moment he was without any common vanity, and very calm.

'I may often need it,' he said, and there was nothing but compassion in his voice. 'But I must take it where I'm lucky enough to find it . . . I know what you mean. But I never tried to make you fall in love with me. I wouldn't wish that kind of trouble on anyone.'

'I knew that,' she said, just as quietly. 'But I couldn't help wishing it.'

She came towards him, and he stood up to meet her. He knew that she was going to kiss him, and he did not try to stop her.

Her mouth was hot and hungry against his. His own lips could not be cold. That would have been hypocrisy. Perhaps because his understanding went so much deeper than the superficial smartness that any other man might have been feeling at that time, he was moved in a way that would only have been cheapened if he had tried to put word to it. He felt her lithe softness pressed against him, her arms encircling him, her hands moving over him, and did not try to hold her away.

Presently she drew back from him. Her hands were under his coat, under his arms, holding him. The expression in her eyes was curiously hopeless.

'You haven't got any gun,' she said.

He smiled faintly. He knew that her hands had been learning that even while she kissed him; and yet it made no difference.

'I didn't think I should need one,' he said.

It seemed as if she wanted to speak, and could not.

'That was your mistake,' said the harsh voice of Judd Kaskin. 'Get your hands up.'

The Saint turned, without haste. Kaskin stood just inside the door, with a heavy automatic in his hand. His florid face was savagely triumphant. Morris Dolf sidled into the room after him.

They were tying the Saint to a massive fake-antique wooden chair placed close to the bed. His ankles were corded to the legs, and Kaskin was knotting his wrists behind the back of it. Dolf kept him covered while it was being done. The gun in his thin hand was steady and impersonal: his weasel face and bright beady eyes held a cold-blooded sneer which made it plain that he would have welcomed an opportunity to demonstrate that he was not holding his finger off the trigger because he was afraid of the bang.

But the Saint was not watching him very intently. He was looking most of the time at Angela Lindsay. To either of the other two men his face would have seemed utterly impassive, his brow serene and amazingly unperturbed, the infinitesimal smile that lingered on his lips only adding to the enigma of his self-control. But that same inscrutable face talked to the girl as clearly as if it had used spoken words.

Her eyes stared at him in a blind stunned way that said: 'I know. I know. You think I'm a heel. But what could I do? I didn't have long enough to think . . .'

And his own cool steady eyes, and that faintly lingering smile, all of his face so strangely free from hatred or contempt, answered in the same silent language: 'I know, kid. I understand. You couldn't help it. What the hell?'

She looked at him with an incredulity that ached to believe.

Kaskin tightened his last knot and came round from behind the chair.

'Well, smart guy,' he said gloatingly. 'You weren't so smart, after all.'

The Saint had no time to waste. Even with his wrists tied behind him, he could still reach the hilt of his knife with his fingertips. They hadn't thought of searching for a weapon like that, under his sleeve. He eased it out of its sheath until his fingers could close on the handle.

'You certainly did surprise me, Judd,' he admitted mildly.

'Thought you were making a big hit with the little lady, didn't you?' Kaskin sneered. 'Well, that's what you were meant to think. I never knew a smart guy yet that wasn't a sucker for a jane. We had it all figured out. She tipped us off as soon as she left your house this afternoon. We could have hunted out the dough and got away with it then, but that would have still left you running around. It was worth waiting a bit to get you as well. We knew you'd be here. We just watched the house until you got here, and came in after you. Then we only had to wait until Angela got close enough to you to grab your gun. Directly we heard her say you hadn't got one, we walked in.' His arm slid round the girl's waist. 'Cute little actress, ain't she, Saint? I'll bet you thought you were in line for a big party.'

Simon had his knife in his hand. He had twisted the blade back to saw it across the cords on his wrists, and it was keen enough to lance through them like butter. He could feel them loosening strand by strand, and stopped cutting just before they would have fallen away altogether; but one strong jerk of his arms would have been enough to set him free.

'So what?' he inquired coolly.

'So you get what's coming to you,' Kaskin said.

He dug into a bulging coat pocket.

The Saint tensed himself momentarily. Death was still very near. His hands might be practically free, but his legs were still tied to the chair. And even though he could throw his knife faster than most men could pull a trigger, it could only be thrown once. But he had taken that risk from the beginning, with his eyes open. He could only die once, too; and all his life had been a gamble with death.

He saw Kaskin's hand come out. But it didn't come out with a gun. It came out with something that looked like an ordinary tin can with a length of smooth cord wound round it. Kaskin unwrapped the cord, and laid the can on the edge of the bed, where it was only a few inches both from the Saint's elbow and Verdean's middle. He stretched out the cord, which terminated at one end in a hole in the top of the can, struck a match, and put it to the loose end. The end began to sizzle slowly.

'It's a slow fuse,' he explained, with vindictive satisfaction. 'It'll take about fifteen minutes to burn. Time enough for us to get a long way off before it goes off, and time enough for you to do plenty of thinking before you go skyhigh with Verdean. I'm going to enjoy thinking about you thinking.'

Only the Saint's extraordinarily sensitive ears would have caught the tiny mouselike sound that came from somewhere in the depths of the house. And any other ears that had heard it might still have dismissed it as the creak of a dry board.

'The only thing that puzzles me,' he said equably, 'is what you think you're going to think with.'

Kaskin stepped up and hit him unemotionally in the face.

'That's for last night,' he said hoarsely, and turned to the others. 'Let's get started.'

Morris Dolf pocketed his automatic and went out, with a last cold stare over the scene.

Kaskin went to the bed, closed the bulging valise, and picked it up. He put his arm round the girl again and drew her to the door.

'Have a good time,' he said.

The Saint looked out on to an empty landing. But what he

saw was the last desperate glance that the girl flung at him as Kaskin led her out.

He tensed his arms for an instant, and his wrists separated. The scraps of cord scuffed on the floor behind him. He took a better grip on his knife. But he still made no other movement. He sat where he was, watching the slowly smouldering fuse, waiting and listening for two sounds that all his immobility was tuned for. One of them he knew he would hear, unless some disastrous accident had happened to cheat his calculations; the other he was only hoping for, and yet it was the one that his ears were most wishfully strained to catch.

Then he saw Angela Lindsay's bag lying on a corner of the dresser, and all his doubts were supremely set at rest.

He heard her voice, down on the stairs, only a second after his eyes had told him that he must hear it.

And he heard Kaskin's growling answer.

'Well, hurry up, you fool . . . The car's out in front of the house opposite.'

The Saint felt queerly content.

Angela Lindsay stood in the doorway again, looking at him.

She did not speak. She picked up her bag and tucked it under her arm. Then she went quickly over to the bed and took hold of the trailing length of fuse. She wound it round her hand and tore it loose from the bomb, and threw it still smouldering into a far corner.

Then she bent over the Saint and kissed him, very swiftly.

He did not move for a moment. And then, even more swiftly, his free hands came from behind him and caught her wrists.

She tried to snatch herself back in sudden panic, but his grip was too strong. And he smiled at her.

'Don't go for a minute,' he said softly.

She stood frozen.

Down on the ground floor, all at once, there were many

sounds. The sounds of heavy feet, deep voices that were neither Dolf's nor Kaskin's, quick violent movements . . . Her eyes grew wide, afraid, uncomprehending, questioning. But those were the sounds that he had been sure of hearing. His face was unlined and unstartled. He still smiled. His head moved fractionally in answer to the question she had not found voice to ask.

'Yes,' he said evenly. 'It is the police. Do you still want to go?'

Her mouth moved.

'You knew they'd be here.'

'Of course,' he said. 'I arranged for it. I wanted them to catch Morrie and Judd with the goods on them. I knew you meant to double-cross me, all the time. So I pulled a double doublecross. That was before you kissed me – so you could find out where I kept my gun . . . Then I was only hoping you'd make some excuse to come back and do what you just did. You see, everything had to be in your own hands.'

Down below, a gun barked. The sound came up the stairs dulled and thickened. Other guns answered it. A man screamed shrilly, and was suddenly silent. The brief fusillade rattled back into throbbing stillness. Gradually the muffled voices droned in again.

The fear and bewilderment died out of the girl's face, and left a shadowy kind of peace.

'It's too late now,' she said. 'But I'm still glad I did it.'

'Like hell it's too late,' said the Saint.

He let go of her and put away his knife, and bent to untie his legs. His fingers worked like lightning. He did not need to give any more time to thought. Perhaps in those few seconds after his hands were free and the others had left the room, when he had sat without moving and only listened, wondering whether the girl would come back, his subconscious mind had raced on and worked out what his adaptation would be if she did come back. However it had come to him, the answer was clear in his mind now – as clearly as if he had known that it would be needed when he planned for the other events which had just come to pass.

And the aspect of it that was doing its best to dissolve his seriousness into a spasm of ecstatic daftness was that it would also do something towards taking care of Mr Ebenezer Hogsbotham. He had, he realized, been almost criminally neglectful about Mr Hogsbotham, having used him as an excuse to start the adventure, having just borrowed his house to bring it to a dénouement, and yet having allowed himself to be so led away by the intrusion of mere sordid mercenary objectives that he had had no spare time to devote towards consummating the lofty and purely idealistic mission that had taken him to Chertsey in the first place. Now he could see an atonement for his remissness that would invest the conclusion of that story with a rich completeness which would be something to remember.

'Listen,' he said, and the rapture of supreme inspiration was blazing in his eyes.

In the hall below, Chief Inspector Claud Eustace Teal straightened up from his businesslike examination of the two still figures sprawled close together on the floor. A knot of uniformed local men, one of whom was twisting a handkerchief round a bleeding wrist, made way for him as he stepped back.

'All right,' Teal said grimly. 'One of you phone for an ambulance to take them away. Neither of them is going to need a doctor.'

He moved to the suitcase which had fallen from Judd Kaskin's hand when three bullets hit him, and opened it. He turned over some of the contents, and closed it again.

A broad-shouldered young officer with a sergeant's stripes on his sleeve shifted up from behind him and said: 'Shall I look after it, sir?'

Teal surrendered the bag.

'Put it in the safe at the station for tonight,' he said. 'I'll get somebody from the bank to check it over in the morning. It looks as if it was all there.'

'Yes, sir.'

The sergeant stepped back towards the door.

Chief Inspector Teal fumbled in an inner pocket, and drew out a small oblong package. From the package he extracted a thinner oblong of pink paper. From the paper he unwrapped a fresh crisp slice of spearmint. He slid the slice of spearmint into his mouth and champed purposefully on it. His salivary glands reacted exquisitely to succulent stimulus. He began to feel some of the deep spiritual contentment of a cow with a new cud.

Mr Teal, as we know, had had a trying day. But for once he seemed to have earned as satisfactory a reward for his tribulations as any reasonable man had a right to expect. It was true that he had been through one disastrously futile battle with the Saint. But to offset that, he had cleared up the case to which he had been assigned, with the criminals caught red-handed while still in possession of their booty and justifiably shot down after they had tried to shoot their way out, which would eliminate most of the tedious legal rigmaroles which so often formed a wearisome anticlimax to such dramatic victories; and he had recovered the booty itself apparently intact. All in all, he felt that this was one occasion when even his tyrannical superiors at Scotland Yard would be unable to withhold the commendation which was his due. There was something almost like human tolerance in his sleepy eyes as they glanced around and located Hoppy Uniatz leaning against the wall in the background.

'That was quick work,' he said, making the advance with some difficulty. 'We might have had a lot more trouble if you hadn't been with us.'

Mr Uniatz had a jack-knife of fearsome dimensions in one

hand. He appeared to be carving some kind of marks on the butt of his gun. He waved the knife without looking up from his work.

'Aw, nuts,' he said modestly. 'All youse guys need is a little practice.'

Mr Teal swallowed.

Patricia Holm squeezed through between two burly constables and smiled at him.

'Well,' she said sweetly, 'don't you owe us all some thanks? I won't say anything about an apology.'

'I suppose I do,' Teal said grudgingly. It wasn't easy for him to say it, or even to convince himself that he meant it. The sadly acquired suspiciousness that had become an integral part of his souring nature had driven its roots too deep for him to feel really comfortable in any situation where there was even a hint of the involvement of any member of the Saint's entourage. But for once he was trying nobly to be just. He grumbled halfheartedly: 'But you had us in the wrong house, all the same. If Uniatz hadn't happened to notice them coming in here—'

'But he did, didn't he?'

'It was a risk that none of you had any right to take,' Teal said starchily. 'Why didn't the Saint tell me what he knew this morning?'

'I've told you,' she said. 'He felt pretty hurt about the way you were trying to pin something on to him. Of course, since he knew he'd never been to Verdean's house, he figured out that the second two men the maid saw were just a couple of other crooks trying to hijack the job. He guessed that Kaskin and Dolf had scared them off and taken Verdean away to go on working him over in their own time—'

That hypersensitive congenital suspicion stabbed Mr Teal again like a needle prodded into a tender boil.

'You never told me he knew their names!' he barked. 'How did he know that?'

'Didn't I?' she said ingenuously. 'Well, of course he knew. Or at any rate he had a pretty good idea. He'd heard a rumour weeks ago that Kaskin and Dolf were planning a bank holdup with an inside stooge. You know how these rumours get around; only I suppose Scotland Yard doesn't hear them. So naturally he thought of them. He knew their favourite hide-outs, so it wasn't hard to find them. And as soon as he knew they'd broken Verdean down, he had me get hold of you while he went on following them. He sent Hoppy to fetch us directly he knew they were coming here. Naturally he thought they'd be going to Verdean's house, but of course Verdean might always have hidden the money somewhere else close by, so that's why I had Hoppy watching outside. Simon just wanted to get even with you by handing you the whole thing on a platter; and you can't really blame him. After all, he was on the side of the law all the time. And it all worked out. Now, why don't you admit that he got the best of you and did you a good turn at the same time?'

Chief Inspector Teal scowled at the toes of his official boots. He had heard it all before, but it was hard for him to believe. And yet it indisputably fitted with the facts as he knew them . . . He hitched his gum stolidly across to the other side of his mouth.

'Well, I'll be glad to thank him,' he growled; and then a twinge of surprising alarm came suddenly into his face. 'Hey, where is he? If they caught him following them—'

'I was wondering when you'd begin to worry about me,' said the Saint's injured voice.

Mr Teal looked up.

Simon Templar was coming down the stairs, lighting a cigarette, mocking and immaculate and quite obviously unharmed.

But it was not the sight of the Saint that petrified Mr Teal into tottering stillness and bulged his china-blue eyes half out of their sockets, exactly as the eyes of all the other men in the hall were also bulged as they looked upwards with him. It was the sight of the girl who was coming down the stairs after the Saint.

It was Angela Lindsay.

The reader has already been made jerry to the fact that the clinging costumes which she ordinarily affected suggested that underneath them she possessed an assortment of curves and contours of exceptionally enticing pulchritude. This suggestion was now elevated to the realms of scientifically observable fact. There was no further doubt about it, for practically all of them were open to inspection. The sheer and diaphanous underwear which was now their only covering left nothing worth mentioning to the imagination. And she seemed completely unconcerned about the exposure, as if she knew that she had a right to expect a good deal of admiration for what she had to display.

Mr Teal blinked groggily.

'Sorry to be so long,' Simon was saying casually, 'but our pals left a bomb upstairs, and I thought I'd better put it out of action. They left Verdean lying on top of it. But I'm afraid he didn't really need it. Somebody hit him once too often, and it looks as if he has kind of passed away . . . What's the matter, Claud? You look slightly boiled. The old tum-tum isn't going back on you again, is it?'

The detective found his voice.

'Who is that you've got with you?' he asked in a hushed and quivering voice.

Simon glanced behind him.

'Oh, Miss Lindsay,' he said airily. 'She was tied up with the bomb, too. You see, it appears that Verdean used to look after this house when the owner was away – it belongs to a guy named Hogsbotham – so he had a key, and when he was looking for a place to cache the boodle, he thought this would be as safe as anywhere. Well, Miss Lindsay was in the bedroom when the boys got here, so they tied her up along with Verdean. I just cut her loose—'

'You found 'er in '*Ogsbotham's* bedroom?' repeated one of the local men hoarsely, with his traditional phlegm battered to limpness by the appalling thought.

The Saint raised his eyebrows.

'Why not?' he said innocently. 'I should call her an ornament to anyone's bedroom.'

'I should say so,' flared the girl stridently. 'I never had any complaints yet.'

The silence was numbing to the ears.

Simon looked over the upturned faces, the open mouths, the protruding eyeballs, and read there everything that he wanted to read. One of the constables finally gave it voice. Gazing upwards with the stalk-eyed stare of a man hypnotized by the sight of a miracle beyond human expectation, he distilled the inarticulate emotions of his comrades into one reverent and pregnant ejaculation.

'Gor-blimy!' he said.

The Saint filled his lungs with a breath of inenarrable peace. Such moments of immortal bliss, so ripe, so full, so perfect, so superb, so flawless and unalloyed and exquisite, were beyond the range of any feeble words. They flooded every corner of the soul and every fibre of the body, so that the heart was filled to overflowing with a nectar of cosmic content. The very tone in which that one word had been spoken was a benediction. It gave indubitable promise that within a few hours the eyewitness evidence of Ebenezer Hogsbotham's depravity would have spread all over Chertsey, within a few hours more it would have reached London, before the next sunset it would have circulated over all England; and all the denials and protestations that Hogsbotham might make would never restore his self-made pedestal again.

11

Simon Templar braked the Hirondel to a stop in the pool of blackness under an overhanging tree less than a hundred yards beyond the end of Greenleaf Road. He blinked his lights three times, and lighted a cigarette while he waited. Patricia Holm held his arm tightly. From the back of the car came gurgling sucking sounds of Hoppy Uniatz renewing his acquaintance with the bottle of Vat 69 which he had been forced by circumstances to neglect for what Mr Uniatz regarded as an indecent length of time.

A shadow loomed out of the darkness beside the road, whistling very softly. The shadow carried a shabby valise in one hand. It climbed into the back seat beside Hoppy.

Simon Templar moved the gear lever, let in the clutch; and the Hirondel rolled decorously and almost noiselessly on its way.

At close quarters, the shadow which had been added to the passenger list could have been observed to be wearing a policeman's uniform with a sergeant's stripes on the sleeve, and a solid black moustache which obscured the shape of its mouth as much as the brim of its police helmet obscured the exact appearance of its eyes. As the car got under way, it was hastily stripping off these deceptive scenic effects and changing into a suit of ordinary clothes piled on the seat.

Simon spoke over his shoulder as the Hirondel gathered speed through the village of Chertsey.

'You really ought to have been a policeman, Peter,' he murmured. 'You look the part better than anyone I ever saw.'

Peter Quentin snorted.

'Why don't you try somebody else in the part?' he inquired acidly. 'My nerves won't stand it many more times. I still don't know how I got away with it this time.'

The Saint grinned in the dark, his eyes following the road.

'That was just your imagination,' he said complacently. 'There wasn't really much danger. I knew that Claud wouldn't have been allowed to bring his own team down from Scotland Yard. He was just assigned to take charge of the case. He might have brought an assistant of his own, but he had to use the local cops for the mob work. In the excitement, nobody was going to pay much attention to you. The local men just thought you came down from Scotland Yard with Teal, and Teal just took it for granted that you were one of the local men. It was in the bag – literally and figuratively.'

'Of course it was,' Peter said sceptically. 'And just what do you think is going to happen when Teal discovers that he hasn't got the bag?'

'Why, what on earth could happen?' Simon retorted blandly. 'We did our stuff. We produced the criminals, and Hoppy blew them off, and Teal got the boodle. He opened the bag and looked it over right here in the house. And Pat and Hoppy and I were in more or less full view all the time. If he goes and loses it again after we've done all that for him, can he blame us?'

Peter Quentin shrugged himself into a tweed sports jacket, and sighed helplessly. He felt sure that there was a flaw in the Saint's logic somewhere, but he knew that it was no use to argue. The Saint's conspiracies always seemed to work out, in defiance of reasonable argument. And this episode had not yet shown any signs of turning into an exception. It would probably work out just like all the rest. And there was un-arguably a suitcase containing about fifteen thousand pounds in small change lying on the floor of the car at his feet to lend weight to the probability. The thought made Peter Quentin reach out for Mr Uniatz's bottle with a reckless feeling that he might as well make the best of the crazy life into which his association with the Saint had led him.

Patricia told him what had happened at the house after he faded away unnoticed with the bag.

'And you left her there?' he said, with a trace of wistfulness.

'One of the local cops offered to take her back to town,' Simon explained. 'I let him do it, because it'll give her a chance to build up the story . . . I don't think we shall hear a lot more about Hogsbotham from now on.'

'So while I was sweating blood and risking about five hundred years in penal servitude,' Peter said bitterly, 'you were having a grand time helping her take her clothes off.'

'You have an unusually evil mind,' said the Saint, and drove on, one part of his brain working efficiently over the alibi that Peter was still going to need before morning, and all the rest of him singing.

Watch for the sign of the Saint!

If you have enjoyed this Saintly adventure, look out for the other Simon Templar novels by Leslie Charteris – all available in print and ebook from Mulholland Books

You've turned the last page.

But it doesn't have to end there . . .

If you're looking for more first-class, action-packed, nail-biting suspense, join us at **Facebook.com/ MulhollandUncovered** for news, competitions, and behind-the-scenes access to Mulholland Books.

For regular updates about our books and authors as well as what's going on in the world of crime and thrillers, follow us on **Twitter@MulhollandUK**.

There are many more twists to come.

MULHOLLAND:
You never know what's coming around the curve.

HODDER